CW01500645

This book series was originally published in September 2023 on Kindle Vella.

Edited by Studio ENP

Copyediting and Proofreading: The Fiction Fix

Paperback Formatting by Prince Finnick James @princefinnickreads

Cover design by Steamy Designs http://steamydesigns.net

Dear Puck Bunnies,

Thank you for reading Triple Power Play 2.

This series is a wild ride. Please check the trigger warnings. If you've read the first book, you're aware that Jax struggles with mental health issues and addiction. Book one ended with Jackson's relapse. Book two dives further into his past traumas and mental state. This may be difficult for some readers.

I can't promise book two will answer all your questions from book one, but hopefully, most. There's always book three and maybe a few novellas coming up. Please follow my social media for bonus chapters in between.

I love creating these characters, and I hope you'll enjoy reading them just as much.

Thank you,

Jessica :)

First and foremost, your mental health is important.
This book series is a dark romance.
It contains themes related to mental illness and addiction, including intrusive thoughts and ideations, flashbacks and hallucinations, past trauma/abuse, PTSD, obsession, manipulation, and substance use.
Please understand that everyone's journey and experience with mental illness, trauma, addiction, and pregnancy are different.
Visit authorjessicalyn.com for a full list of content and trigger warnings.
This is a work of fiction. The characters in this series are imperfect but no less deserving of love.
"Fixing" them is not within the plot.
This book series was originally published in September 2023 on Kindle Vella. Current events and other similarities are purely coincidental.

For those who dream of a villain to chase away their nightmares,
I give you Ethan Blackwood.

1

JACKSON

No phone. No Uber. Just a slow, mindless walk back to the hotel with a throbbing headache. Reporters swarm me with their never-ending questions. One blocks the door, and I shove him aside. He falls to the ground, dropping his camera, and I don't give the slightest fuck.

Things aren't adding up. I can't remember returning last night—I woke this afternoon in my bed, fully dressed and feeling like death.

The Hard Rock isn't within a reasonable walking distance. Maybe I took a taxi, but how'd I find my hotel room blackout drunk?

I want to throw myself in bed and sleep off this hangover, but my paranoia mounts when I find my phone and an envelope on my bed. I know my phone wasn't there earlier; I practically tore this room apart looking for it. A glance around shows my clothes still strewn across the floor. No maid found it while cleaning and placed it there.

And the envelope... I doubt it's a receipt for my hotel stay.

When I pick up my phone, I'm not blasted with notifications—someone has already cleared them. There's only a text message from Kyle.

I can make this all go away.

Kyle protects my image solely because it reflects on him, but it always comes at a cost.

Ignoring him, I check for anything from Aurora.

Nothing.

Despite knowing what I'm in for, I attempt to call her. No answer, no voicemail. She's blocked me, as expected. I honestly don't blame her, but it doesn't hurt any less.

In the envelope, I discover what Kyle threatened me with last night, how he got me to the Hard Rock: pictures of Ethan and Aurora kissing at a diner.

I drop my ass on the floor, rest against the bed, and toss my head back. Sharp pain lances through my stomach, nausea hitting me all over again.

I wanted to talk to Aurora before I crashed. Withdrawals can be brutal, depending on what and how much I ingested. My body is already going through familiar symptoms: fatigue, agitation, cravings.

Then, there's the mental turmoil, and she doesn't need that psychotic trainwreck.

At least I can check on her even if she won't speak to me.

Is Aurora okay?

RICKY

Fuck off. I no longer work for you.

Fucking great. Now I have no access to her. I could argue with him, but what good will that do?

I review my other messages, expecting drunk me to have sent a bunch of shit, but there's only a string of sappy texts to Aurora. That's it.

My mind is cloudy, and this headache gets worse by the minute. Exhausted, I close my eyes and let my thoughts wander.

How can I fix this?

My chest tightens, each inhale shallow, and I struggle to pull air into my lungs. My throat constricts, and tears burn my eyes.

I've lost not only the love of my life but my very existence. Without her, I'm nothing but regret and loneliness. There's no fucking point.

This is worse than last time. This time, we shared hope and a future. Why would I risk that?

Why *did* I risk that? Why did I allow myself to be manipulated by Kyle's threats?

I'd give anything to turn back time. I can pay TMZ to remove the pictures, but I'll never erase the images from her memory.

And what happened after those photos? Not even I know.

My mind races, searching for answers, something to prove I didn't cheat on her. I grab my phone and force myself to scrutinize every damning image.

Thank fuck, there are no pictures of me touching these girls intimately. I can deal with the pics of me doing lines and drinking, but if I'd touched someone else, slept with someone else... I'd find the tallest building in Vegas and end this.

Odd to consider right now, but I'm reasonably certain I'm demisexual or some shit. My dick isn't attracted to anyone else, especially someone random. I have trust issues.

I'm scrolling through the pictures again when it hits me, the dots connecting in my lagging brain. I'm dumb as fuck. Each image features me alone, photographed from a single perspective, nothing in the background. There are no photos of Kyle or anyone else—only me.

This has never happened before because Kyle carefully covers all his bases. He's in the public eye, and evidence of his vices would lead to his political downfall, if not an indictment.

How does he assure fidelity besides an ironclad NDA? Blackmail.

One person took and sold last night's photos. *Kyle*. I'm fucking sure of it. He has done it to others—senators, cops, celebrities, friends, women...in compromising positions.

But to his own son?

Why am I even questioning it?

He revels in his ability to control me, using my vulnerabilities as a weapon to maintain his twisted hold. My mother, my mental health, Aurora—they're all pawns in his sick game.

I've lost everything, all so he can keep me on a tight leash, support his perverse lifestyle, and prove that without him, I'm fucked.

Desperation turns to fury, and I clench my fists until my nails dig into my palms.

He set me up. He destroyed my relationship—not only with Aurora, but with Ethan too.

And he finally pushed me over the edge.

Before I can think it through, I pick up the phone and call his number.

"Jack—"

"What the fuck do you want? You want my trust fund? You can have it."

In the background, a crowd of voices babble, and I realize he's at the game.

"Why aren't you on the ice?"

"Are you that fucking stupid? You think Ethan would play me after last night?"

A moment of quiet follows, and the noise dissipates before I receive his usual entitled response. "He can't do that. Without a drug test, he can't prove anything. I'm calling the GM."

"Don't bother. I've already left. You've outdone yourself this time. You've fucked us both." This splitting headache is the only reason I'm not laughing at how spectacularly his plan failed. "Did you think I'd try to save myself and my career? Did you think I'd come crawling back, begging you to fix my reputation, to fix my inevitable drug test, forgetting all about Aurora?"

"*Boy*," he snarls, a warning that, as a child, would accompany his fist.

"You can't hurt me. The only thing I want is Aurora, and since you obliterated that, I'll spend all my time in New York groveling. Forget my trust fund. Forget hockey. I quit. Have fun explaining that to your entourage."

"Don't be dramatic. Get your ass on the ice."

"You won't see me on the ice until I have Aurora. I'll do everything in my power to get her back, and I'll make sure it's as public as possible. I'll rent billboards in Times Square if I have to. Fuck, I'll move to New York."

"Jackson. Don't you fucking dare! I told you last night, I'll destroy her!"

His intimidation tactics are meaningless. The damage is done.

"They'll find you dead before I allow you to take another person from me. You're fucked. When I'm through, you'll have the same as me: nothing."

I don't bother listening to his sputtering. I end the call and dial my lawyer, then my agent. Then, to drive my point home, I get arena security to have him and his posse removed from *my* suite.

2

AURORA

There's this blissful moment between asleep and awake when the sounds of the city seeps into my consciousness, and for a brief second, I don't remember.

I'm suspended in time, neither happy nor sad.

Then, reality sets in, and my heart shatters all over again. It pounds frantically against my sternum, and I lie there just listening to it.

I didn't at first—the first time, I gasped for air and ugly cried.

Now, I focus on the steady rhythm and wonder why it beats so fervently for someone impossible to love.

Next is guilt. I shouldn't have left. He begged me to stay, and I didn't listen. I should've stayed. I want to scream it into the abyss until it becomes reality.

I should've stayed.

Why didn't I stay?

Then comes fear—the fear he'll harm himself.

But I can't bring myself to reach out to him, to offer him hope. I don't want to speak to him, and I don't want him back.

I'm angry, so fucking angry.

A hot tear slips down my cheek, landing on my nose, and I don't bother brushing it away. I gaze out at the dreary gray sky over New York City, staring into nothingness until there's a soft knock at my door.

There's only one person it could be: Ricky.

Taking a deep breath, I gather every ounce of strength to sit up in bed. I've never felt so exhausted.

"I'm awake," I call out.

He peeks his head in. "Hey, come eat." He scans my face, and his tone softens. "Breakfast is ready."

I swallow the lump in my throat and do what's necessary. "I can't afford to keep you." My lips quiver, and I struggle to remain strong.

He clenches his jaw, the muscle bunching, and enters the room. "Do you want me to leave?"

"No, but..."

"Jackson already paid me."

I wince, pain lancing through my chest at his name. "You work for him."

He shakes his head. "You're my client, regardless of my employer. Anyhow, I ended it."

"I can't afford you, though." The words barely escape, my throat tight with emotion. I don't want to let him go, but I need to save every penny for the baby.

"He paid me for this trip. If he demands I reimburse him, which I doubt he will, we'll talk. Now, come eat."

In cotton pajama pants and a camisole, I remove the blanket and stand. I catch a wave of dizziness and nausea and return my ass to the bed. I'm shaking, and I briefly question whether I should call the doctor, but I know it's only stress.

Ricky's long stride eats up the distance. "You went to bed at seven last night. It's been over twelve hours since you ate or drank anything."

I lie down on the mattress. "I just need a minute."

"You're not going back to sleep, Aurora. I'll carry you out of here." His tone is low and gruff. "Let's go."

He extends his hand, and I take it, allowing him to guide me into the kitchen, where he has everything laid out on the breakfast table. He made scrambled eggs covered in mozzarella, along with toast and a bowl of strawberries. Beside my plate sits a steaming mug of coffee and my favorite vanilla creamer. He went through all this trouble for me, and a sharp pang of shame fills my chest.

We eat in silence while the rain pelts the terrace windows. I sense his irritation and try to remain as quiet as possible, my body trembling. I'm in that dark place again, and no matter how much I tell myself I'm resilient and safe, I can't pull myself out of it.

It's as if Jackson set me back right along with him.

My stomach churns, and I lightly place my fork down to sip my coffee. "You don't have to stay here, you know. If you want to do something, I'll be fine."

I have no desire to burden anyone else with my misery; I feel foolish enough as it is. I brought Ricky here, and he probably feels obligated to care for me. He probably thinks I'm too weak to care for myself.

He responds with a curt nod, his gaze fixed on his food. "Eat a little more, or your prenatal pill will make you sick. Drink some orange juice."

He's typically patient and polite, and maybe it's all in my head—or maybe the shred of self-confidence I earned over the last few months has been obliterated—but I'm certain he's annoyed with me.

"You're very bossy today." I shoot for humor, but my attempt to lighten the mood falls flat.

"I spent all night worried about you," he says, jaw tight.

That bit of courage I gathered crumbles. My shoulders droop, and I cast my gaze downward. "I'm fine."

"What'd I tell you about saying that?" he barks. "You're not fine."

I push my chair back, readying to escape. Sleep is the only place I find solace. "What do you want from me?" My raised voice shakes. "I'll never be fine." It comes out with a sob, and I hate feeling this pathetic. "I'm horrible! I should've stayed!" The regret is gut-wrenching, and I fear the pain will never go away.

Elbows on the table, his hands shoot out, and I flinch at the sudden movement. He pauses, and his eyes, the color of the ocean beneath the dark moon, bore into mine. When I don't retreat, he slowly cups my face in his warm palms.

"Stop," he says in a firm yet gentle tone. "This is not your fault. Nothing is your fault."

His thumb traces my cheekbone, and a shuddering breath escapes my lips, the tension in my coiled muscles releasing.

"He. Is. Not. Worth it." He emphasizes each word, his intense gaze unwavering. "Pick your chin up, put one foot in front of the other, and move the fuck on." The weight of his words hangs heavy in the air. "You deserve better than this. Act like it."

So I do.

Or, at least, I try.

3

AURORA

THE ACHE NEVER CEASES, NO MATTER HOW DEEPLY I TRY TO bury it.

I communicate only with those who are necessary. I fight the urge to check the constant stream of texts, calls, and notifications, anticipating something from Jackson, even though I've blocked him.

My stupid, stupid heart refuses to accept that it's over.

I tell Ethan I'm fine. It's a lie, and we both know it. I'm shattered.

I place ice over my eyes, attempting to erase the puffiness from crying the last few days, and I repeat to myself over and over that Jackson isn't my problem and this baby isn't his.

He doesn't matter.

This mindset lasts about three minutes until another snapshot of him with someone else invades my peace. Then, I use all my willpower to push that image away and pray never to see it again.

I don't allow myself to feel. I can't afford to feel. I'm able to look pretty. That's something I can control.

I adorn cat eyes as sharp as the knife I'd like to plunge into Jackson's heart, plus seductive, matte red lipstick. I wear my long hair in my signature beach waves, a reminder of who I was before I got comfortable.

Scouring the designer clothes, I select an outfit that demands the most attention—a stunning, slinky silver minidress. The fabric is almost sheer and clings gracefully to my curves. Delicate spaghetti straps and a plunging neckline add a tempting allure. Completing the sex appeal is a pair of four-inch heels I long ago became an expert at walking in.

The attire may not be ideal for the New York fall weather, but it conveys the message. It hides my pregnancy and proves I'll have no trouble gracing the runway.

It also screams—*fuck Jackson O'Reilly*.

I eat when Ricky puts food in front of me every four hours like clockwork, along with a prenatal pill in the morning, and I soak up all his affection and motivating words.

Wherever he leads, I follow.

We exit the car to meet Felicity and the designer, and I don't evade the cameras. My heels hit the sidewalk, and Ricky takes my hand so delicately, that for a fleeting moment, I can pretend I'm appreciated, cared for, and loved, even if it's just an illusion born out of desperation.

I wear a playful smile, masking the storm of emotions that rage within me.

When the paparazzi mention Jackson, I arch a brow and ask, "Who?" with feigned indifference.

They laugh and snap their photos until the elevator doors close, and I sag against my bodyguard.

He gives my fingers an encouraging squeeze. "Deep breaths. Nail this contract, and you can go home to a bubble bath. I'll even order you some books."

I gaze up at him in awe, wondering how he knows I enjoy reading. Before I can verbalize my thoughts, the bell dings, signaling our destination, and he breaks contact, dropping my hand.

Once we step off the elevator, Felicity waves me into her office and shuts the door.

She wraps her arms around me. "I'm so sorry, babe."

"Don't be. Everyone warned me. I didn't listen." I pull out of her embrace, afraid if someone holds me for too long, I'll break down. I won't let Jackson's betrayal overshadow a day that's all mine.

"What are you going to do?"

"Never talk to him again." What else is there?

"And the baby?"

I had forgotten about our lie, the façade of him being the baby's father, and the curiosity in her voice turns my stomach sour. It's no one's business.

"We'll be fine. Let's move on." I gesture with my hand, a dismissive wave. I refuse to satisfy anyone's need for gossip.

"Certainly." She holds me at arm's length and scans me from head to toe. "Stunning! Paulo is already in love with you. You're going to *kill* this."

She draws me in for another embrace, and I exhale in relief, releasing the tension in my stiff shoulders.

The designer, Paulo, kisses my cheeks, his ruddy face lit with enthusiasm despite my predicament.

Our meeting is straightforward. He only has two requests: I walk the runway and work in New York through Fashion Week.

Winter Fashion Week is seven weeks away, and surprisingly, being in New York for such an extended period is a weight off my chest. It's the first overwhelmingly positive emotion since seeing my boyfriend snorting cocaine with a pair of puck bunnies.

I glance at Felicity for confirmation. Her urgent nod reminds me of all the commitments we've canceled to appease my ex.

Since I'd love nothing more than to avoid LA, staying in New York is a fan-freaking-tastic idea. Ethan will either understand or not care, considering his busy schedule.

Besides, I'm still determining the direction of our relationship.

A selfish side of me needs him to be here, and his absence adds to my sense of abandonment. But a rational—or critical—part of my mind tells me I'm ridiculous for even thinking that.

Why would he neglect his responsibilities to console me over a breakup, for fuck's sake?

Felicity widens her eyes, and I realize Paulo is talking to me while I agonize over men like an idiot.

"Fashion Week is more about exposure, and you, my dear, bring the paparazzi wherever you go. There's a huge buildup to the main event, so plan on being available to attend an assortment of fittings and photo shoots."

On the outside, I muster a bright smile. On the inside, I grimace. *Yay me, social events.* "Fabulous. Where do I sign?"

My mask is convincing enough to secure the contract and hopefully open doors to a desperately needed future.

Paulo and I exchange numbers before other commitments whisk him away. Then, Felicity and I review the financial details, my attention shifting to practicalities. I'm back in the game, focusing on providing stability for myself and my child.

"The pay is standard. Fifty-five hundred per day, all expenses covered. You'll get a guaranteed four hundred grand for walking the runway during Fashion Week. There's also the possibility of extending your contract or securing another designer."

I calculate everything in my head. The earnings are enough for a nice down payment on a place. Plus, I still receive royalties from my magazine covers. Hope flutters, mingling with the weight of responsibility. Life in both LA and New York is costly. I'll need to cover Ricky's expenses, even though he tells me not to worry about it, plus my grandmother's nursing home, which is an absolute necessity.

"What's wrong? We can negotiate," Felicity interrupts my anxious thoughts.

I recline in her plush office chair, crossing and uncrossing my legs. "I'm not disappointed with the pay. That's not the issue. I need to maintain it, and I'm willing to move from LA if necessary."

The more I consider it, the more excited I am to leave my past behind. I can fly to visit Grams. It wasn't what I wanted, but fuck, neither is this heartache.

On the West Coast, Jackson O'Reilly will haunt me.

"Don't make any hasty decisions while you're hurt and

emotional. We'll talk more about future projects as they become available. What's the next step with your infamous ex?"

"What are my choices? It's over."

"We can issue a public statement asking everyone to respect your privacy, blah, blah, blah. *Or...*" She emphasizes the word with a raise of her perfectly manicured brows. "You can take proactive measures to manage the situation, appearing together—"

"That's not happening." I immediately reject the idea, shaking my head emphatically. "I never want to see Jackson again."

"Then we ignore it and move on." Felicity shrugs, hands up in a gesture of nonchalance.

As if moving on is a quick fix.

As if Jackson didn't just shred my heart and stomp on it for the world to witness.

Burying the pain, I adopt her attitude. "It's not worth the effort of making a statement. I'm focused on my career right now, and that's all."

I don't care how much it hurts. I'll paint on a fake smile until everyone believes I've moved on from Jackson O'Reilly.

Including me.

4

ETHAN

From my office window, I watch the Zamboni smooth the ice after practice, my mind restless and my concentration absolute shit. Spinning a pen between my fingers, I contemplate the last few days. The guys played their hearts out in a brutal game, only losing to Vegas by one.

For the millionth time, I question whether benching Jackson was the correct decision. Even hungover, he would've scored and we would've won, putting us closer to playoffs.

My commitment to win wars with my emotions toward Jax.

I toss the pen onto the desk, rest my head against the leather chair, and close my eyes. I refuse to enable Jackson. The previous staff pumped him full of drugs to get him through the game, only for him to repeat the cycle by getting shitfaced after.

I can put an end to his abuse. It's what I came here for, and it's the right thing to do.

Regret creeps in, and I drop my face into my hands. I promised Aurora I would care for Jax. I failed her, and I failed him. If only I had realized he was on a quick path to self-destruction. I just never believed he'd relapse, never thought he'd jeopardize Aurora.

I grind my palms into my eyes, the images of Jackson's drunken night replaying on repeat—images that have torn our trio apart.

He didn't just relapse; he destroyed everything.

Aurora is drifting away, her voice distant. She built a wall, unwilling to open up to me. Perhaps she's resentful I wasn't looking after Jackson, or because I'm not there for her.

With every beat, the ache in my heart intensifies, a constant reminder of my need to fix this.

I thought I'd revel in the moment Jax fucked up and Aurora was all mine, but my stomach is in knots, my gut telling me this isn't how it's supposed to be.

We're meant to be together, the three of us.

My office door creaks open and snaps me out of my worries. Grant pops his head in, dark circles under his bloodshot eyes, appearing as sleep-deprived as I am.

I massage my temples, trying to ward off the looming headache. "Hey, man. What's up?"

He collapses into the leather chair in front of my desk. "Do you know where O'Reilly is? He's not returning my calls or texts."

Mine neither, but I won't allow myself to consider the worst. There's only one place he'd go. *Aurora*. "I have a strong hunch."

I have mixed feelings about him rushing to New York, but I can't control him.

Jax running to Aurora means he still has hope, but his showing up in New York and forcing his presence on her will cause her more distress.

Grant's knee bounces, and he pushes his fingers through his dark hair. "Are you going?"

I've been asking myself that very question since waking up to this shitstorm. I'd give anything to be in New York, Aurora wrapped in my arms, but I doubt Grant and I are on the same page. "After Jackson?"

"Or to Aurora," he says matter-of-fact.

I tilt my head and furrow my brows in confusion. Maybe I was wrong.

"I'm not stupid; I only play dumb. Your connection with Jax has been obvious since you started here. He's my best friend, and nothing gets him more worked up than Aurora. You went to dinner with her, you left with her, and he didn't kill you. He *listens* to you."

Grant stares at me, waiting for me to challenge him, but I remain silent. Aurora talked to several players the night we met. Anyone could've seen us.

"No one will hold it against you for being there for her or Jackson. Someone needs to step up."

I sit back and fold my arms over my chest, swallowing the lump in my throat. While I appreciate Grant's honesty, he's crossing boundaries into personal territory, and I'd like to keep my job.

"Thanks, but out of respect for everyone's privacy, I'm choosing not to respond. Just know I've been trying to do what's best for the team."

He leans in, placing his elbows on my desk. "Out of respect for you and the team, it's not working. Yes, we're playing better than ever, but we've lost our captain, and you'll eventually burn out. The baby is yours, right?" My mouth opens in shock, but he stops me with a raised hand. "I can count the months between now and the dinner."

My heart races. How did I think we could hide this?

"If it wasn't for the team, what would you be doing right now?" he asks.

Doesn't that sum up my life in one straightforward question? I'd be with Aurora. She and the baby would be my proudest achievement.

The dream swells in my chest, and my lips stretch into a soft smile.

He returns my smile. "Exactly. That's what you need to do. Go to Aurora. Help Jackson. His father is relentless. Few people know about Kyle's shit, and I'm not at liberty to say anything more, but I know he's behind this. He's threatened them in the past."

Before I can mull over the implications of Grant's words, my cell rings with a call from Ricky. "Sorry, I gotta take this. Talk later?"

He nods, and I answer as he exits. "Ricky, everything okay?"

"I'm returning your call."

"Oh, right. Sorry, it's been a long fucking day." I take a deep breath and exhale slowly. "I wanted to talk to you about taking over your contract. I'd prefer you didn't communicate with Jackson until he gets his shit together."

"No need. I ended my contract after he ruined his chances with my client. Conflict of interest and all."

The bitterness in his tone toward Jax only amplifies my agitation.

"I have one stipulation. Keep your hands off my girl."

He scoffs. "What?"

"You've become affectionate with Aurora. Don't touch unless it's necessary for her safety."

There's a long pause. "You have no worries. I, ah, don't swing your way—I mean, I do, if you get my drift."

I don't. "I'm not one for riddles, Ricky. Speak plainly."

"I'm in a committed relationship with a man," he spits out, almost too fast for me to comprehend. "I'm friendly with Aurora because she deserves it, and I like her. She's kind, sweet, and resilient. She took over my contract after landing a huge project today, and tomorrow, I'm taking her to look at apartments because she's sick of dealing with two men who, together, can't manage the bare minimum."

Dumbfounded, especially since Aurora hasn't mentioned staying in New York, I only muster, "Say that again?"

"She accepted an extended contract in New York. There's a good chance she'll continue to work here. She deserves better, and I'm glad she's finally figured that out. Anything else?"

"Nope."

Well, fuck me and fuck that. No way am I losing Aurora and my child.

5

AURORA

I WAKE WITH RENEWED ENERGY, FRESH COFFEE, AND PASTRIES, ALL thanks to my teddy bear of a bodyguard, who's quickly becoming one of my favorite people. Over breakfast, we discuss apartments, and I don't feel as though I'm being stabbed in the chest with an ice pick. A flicker of hope and faith lights my spirit.

I put on my sexiest outfit and flirtiest smile for the paparazzi.

Then, I go to work.

My first day back on set.

I try to brush off the lingering stares and obvious whispers, but my confidence shakes even with Ricky's comforting presence. I can't pretend they're not talking about me, because they are. Not only am I returning pregnant and alone—no boyfriend and no assistant—I'm returning after being publicly humiliated by my so-called baby daddy.

Cheated on by a man every woman desires, by a man I considered mine.

No matter how much I tell myself I don't care, my social anxiety cares a whole fucking lot. My skin burns with raw vulnerability, my chest erupts with hives, and my fingers tremble.

Before, modeling empowered me. Fashion is art, and I was proud to show off something unique and beautiful.

Now, as I strip naked backstage with my changing body while people snicker and talk behind my back, I'm terrified.

For what? Because they want me to feel ashamed?

I glance down at my tiny baby bump. Torn and afflicted with guilt, I wrap my arms around my swollen stomach in a tight embrace.

Why should I be ashamed of my baby? I'm not.

I may have lost Jackson and Emily, but I have this child, and he's my everything.

Our designated stations are separated by racks of appointed outfits, and I grab the first one—a delicate, pink, silk-and-lace slip. The fabric feels luxurious on my bare skin, and the matching dainty heels make my toned legs appear a mile long.

Heading out to the runway to experience the full effect under the lights, I catch a glimpse of myself in the mirror. The soft shade contrasts flawlessly with my tanned complexion, and my courage soars.

My smile grows when my gaze meets ocean-blue eyes brimming with pride. Ricky winks from his seat, and I stand a little taller, my head held high.

For the rest of the workday, I focus on my appearance and technique. I ignore all else, and by the time I'm strutting my last piece, my legs are cramping, and it's evident in my stiff gait. I drank a bottle of water between sets, but that could've been hours ago.

At the end of the catwalk, Ricky stands and crosses his arms over his chest, a stern expression on his handsome face. He nods to the exit, and I don't argue.

When we leave the building, my cheerful demeanor toward the paps is no longer phony. My muscles may be sore, but my energy is high.

～

NOT EVERYTHING CAN BE PERFECT, however, and finding an apartment in the city is more difficult than I expected. I've never searched for a rental, and once again, I'm reminded of my inexperience.

We tour a complex in the Fashion District reminiscent of Gram's old nursing home—white-painted cement walls, stained Berber carpet that trigger terrible memories.

After seeing my revulsion and being less than pleased with the flimsy locks on the doors, Ricky insists on taking a much-needed break.

"I didn't realize Central Park was this big." I link my arm with his. "It's beautiful."

When I glance up, his gaze is already on me.

"It is," he agrees. "You should sit. You've been on your feet all day."

I refuse to answer, knowing he's right but wanting to enjoy the park.

He flashes me a playful glare. "Don't you dare say *I'm fine*." He mimics my girlish voice, and I burst into laughter.

A few heads turn our way, and my anxiety kicks up a notch. We're an odd pairing, and I'm likely being paranoid. He's massive. He garners attention in all black, including combat boots, whereas I'm in leggings, an oversized New York Stars hoodie, and matching red Converse.

I found this hoodie hanging in my dressing station; I may have smirked slightly when I put on the replica jersey of the competing hockey team.

Fuck it—a feral grin split my face, mirroring the reckless fury burning inside me.

Ricky leads us to an open stone bench, and we get comfortable, his arm behind me and my head on his shoulder. We watch the falling orange leaves and chat about his time in the military. Having someone else's past to focus on is a welcome distraction.

A photographer kneels and lifts a camera. I have no reason to be awkward or anxious, but my heart rate spikes, and I scan our surroundings for more.

In the distance, I spot a familiar face and gasp.

No way.

No *freaking* way.

"Are they bothering you?" Ricky asks, misreading my panic.

My body tenses. "Did you do this?"

I know I'm not imagining him. I would recognize that tall figure and assertive stride anywhere.

Ricky offers a sly smile. "Maybe he reads the society pages."

I slap his bicep. "It's a five-hour flight!"

His smile turns into a deep chuckle.

I steal a glance over my shoulder, and heat rushes through my veins. Ethan's stormy gray eyes lock on me, and a shiver runs down my spine. The weight of his stare feels tangible, a touch that caresses my skin and electrifies every nerve ending.

Ricky jumps up from the bench. "And this is when I make my exit."

Ethan gets closer, and my mind scrambles. Do I throw myself into his arms? I want to, but if I do, tears will follow, and it may go viral. Or do I play it cool, as if this is a random encounter with the coach of my ex's team?

With each step, the tension grows. When he's in front of me, time stands still. I'm frozen, staring up at him, caught between wanting him and not wanting to harm his reputation.

Before I can react, he fists my hoodie and draws me to him. "Hey, baby girl."

I've listened to his voice over the phone, but nothing compares to hearing that deep, husky tone in person.

I surrender, needing to feel his body pressed against mine. I bury my face in his chest and wrap my arms around his waist. His scent is pure masculinity, wholly Ethan, and I close my eyes as I breathe him in. His embrace feels more like home than any property or city ever could, and tears well in my eyes.

A camera snaps, capturing our moment, and I couldn't care less. All that matters is the connection between us, the unspoken promise that hangs in the air by a delicate thread.

Because he's here, with me, for all to witness, and that has to mean something.

I cling to him, and the agony of the past week diminishes.

He grasps my chin and directs my gaze to his. "I missed you." He cups my face and kisses me, hard and claiming. It's languid yet passionate, fueled by pent-up emotions. He's demanding. His fingers tangle in my hair, gripping the strands, and I whimper, yearning for his possessive touch.

Our tongues intertwine, and a low groan rumbles from his chest.

God, I love that sound.

I trace the contours of his strong jawline, savoring the rough texture of his stubble, and I can't help but smile. "I missed you, too."

My words are breathless, and our chests rise and fall in unison. Ethan brushes my tears away with his knuckles, and the bubble pops.

Filled with dread, I frown, and my brows knit together. "We're in public. There are cameras."

"I know." He kisses my forehead, lips lingering, as if he can't bear to separate.

I glance at the two photographers just off the trail. "Are you sure?"

My only concern is the potential backlash he'll face. My career thrives off publicity. The repercussions for me are insignificant compared to what he might endure from the team.

"Too late, baby girl. But yes, I'm more than sure." He pulls away and interlaces our fingers. "Now, what's this I hear about you looking at apartments?" His eyes darken beneath his lowered brows. "You trying to escape me?"

"I toured a place today. Is that what this is about?" My stomach churns. Is he here for me or because he thinks he's losing me? Does it matter?

His jaw clenches. "If this is an ultimatum, it's unnecessary."

"And why's that?"

"Because you're mine." His tone is firm, his gaze unwavering. "Can we go somewhere and talk?"

"Only if there's food involved. Your son is being demanding." I can't resist the cheeky jab. "Much like his father."

His face breaks into an unrestrained smile that crinkles his eyes and shows off those dimples. "Mind walking? I know a great place with all-day breakfast."

"Sounds perfect."

Before we part, he fists my hoodie once more, his bicep bulging in his pullover as he peers down at me. "Wearing another man's jersey is a cardinal sin. Do it again, and you'll be wearing my handprint on your ass. Understood?"

My retort is a salacious smile, my panties wet. If he thinks that's a punishment, he's greatly mistaken.

6

ETHAN

"YOU HAVE YOUR OWN TABLE?" AWE COLORS AURORA'S TONE, confirming my suspicion she put on the New York hoodie without knowing which team I played for or where I came from.

It also tells me Jackson isn't here, because he'd tear it off her.

"I do. Just wait."

I ignore the blatant stares and interlace our fingers, leading her to a secluded booth in the back. Once there, I guide her into the seat before sliding in next to her, eager to be close.

Her gaze moves to the photos on the wall, and recognition dawns on her face. She radiates excitement, a sight that tugs at my heartstrings.

Aurora may pretend to be strong, but she's not fake, and her genuine interest in my life surpasses all comprehension. How is it possible this girl adores me? It's both flattering and petrifying.

I'm thankful we're having a kid together, so she can't ghost me as she has Jax. If I lost this, I'd probably go mad too.

"Hold on—you grew up here?" Whiskey eyes flicker between me and a faded photo of my younger self working in the kitchen.

"Yup. I lived in that apartment above the barbershop. Right

there." I point out the window to the building across the street. "My first job was washing dishes. Shorty, the owner, paid me with food. Cheap bastard."

I joke, but honestly, food was exactly what I needed, and I later learned his reasoning was to stop my mother from using the money on drugs.

Her eyes soften, fixated on the old photograph. "When was that?"

"When I was ten, maybe eleven."

She turns to me with that mischievous grin. "So before I was born? Were there child labor laws back then?"

Even when she's busting my balls, she ignites a thrill in me, and I can't resist touching her. It's a welcome problem to have.

It's the best problem I've ever had.

"Wow. Thanks for that." I lean in and place a kiss under her ear. "Forget breakfast. Maybe that smart mouth of yours needs something else." Her seductive scent envelops me, a sweet hint of vanilla that shatters my self-restraint.

"Oh no, you're feeding me, Blackwood."

The intensity between us grows, and everything fades away.

"I'll feed you, all right. You just won't be able to talk back." I brush my thumb across her lower lip, and I envision exactly what I'd like her mouth to do.

"Stop giving me those smoldering eyes. That's how we ended up in this mess."

She bites my thumb, and my cock twitches. "I highly doubt my eyes had anything to do with it. In fact, I vividly remember you sliding my hand up your skirt."

I'm glad we're in a private area, because she has me dying to make out like horny teenagers.

"You didn't put up much of a fight. But then again, you're getting old. Memory might be slipping..."

Her caress trails up my thigh, and my jeans become uncomfortable.

"My memory is impeccable. I remember every detail of that night, and unless you want to miss brunch to reenact it, you better stop teasing me." I break from her gaze to glance over the menu, a feeble attempt to steady my thickening erection.

It's no use. She traces her fingers over the outline of my traitorous hard-on, and I lose all focus.

Hoping to prevent a wet spot in my jeans, I shove her hand away. "Baby girl," I growl, my eyes forward, though I'm not reading a single word in front of me. "You're asking for it."

"Fine, I'll stop." The frustration in her voice is unmistakable.

She scoots toward the wall and picks up her menu. Her face hardens with dejection, and I hate it. I can ignore her sulking but never her insecurity, especially if it's caused by me.

I clasp the back of her neck and draw her to me. "Let's get one thing straight—I don't ever want you to stop." I desire her clinginess. There's no greater fulfillment than her needing me.

Her reply is barely audible, her eyes lowered. "I don't want to smother you."

"Look at me." I nudge her chin. "Smother me, love. Do your worst."

She hesitates, and I slip her hand under my shirt against my bare stomach. It's a soothing gesture she does often, and her resistance crumbles. She rests her head on my shoulder, her fingers tracing an arousing path along the top of my jeans.

I realize how much she needs the assurance of our subtle touches, and I wonder how she's managing alone. She's not. I saw her in the park snuggled with Ricky, his arm around her.

The thought of someone else experiencing this connection triggers an unwelcome pang of jealousy, prompting me to blurt, "Ricky has a boyfriend."

With pinched brows, she glances up at me. "What?"

Did he not tell her? "He has a boyfriend."

A range of emotions dance in her eyes. Confusion. Shock. *Disappointment.* "Oh."

I can't help it. I need to know. "Do you like him?"

She nibbles on her bottom lip and gives a half-assed shrug. "As friends. Why?"

Unease swirls in my gut. I twist a lock of her silky hair

around my finger as I gather my thoughts. "Just taking mental stock of how many men I have to contend with."

She cocks her head to the side and scoffs. "You're joking, right? Do we need to discuss your ex-wife?"

That's laughable. "You have nothing to worry about, I promise you."

"Well, neither do you."

Her tone is cutting, laced with self-deprecation, and I question once again whether she'll ever be truly whole without Jax.

7

ETHAN

Despite her denials, Aurora has been teasing me all day, so I'm not surprised when I find her straddling my lap on the couch, not thirty seconds after we get our shoes off at her Tribeca apartment.

Her red lips are deliciously swollen from our kiss, and my mind flashes to her on her knees, those lips wrapped around my cock. She works her mouth along my jaw and down my throat, a sure way to turn my thoughts into reality if I don't slow this down.

"Baby girl, we're supposed to be talking."

Her teeth sink into my skin, and my words come out somewhere between a groan of regret and one of pleasure.

Sitting up, she pulls her hoodie over her head. "Not a single time have we been able to resist each other long enough to talk."

Like a magnet, my hands are irresistibly drawn to her tits, palming them over her shirt. "More reason for us to have a rare conversation."

"Well, if you weren't so fuckable."

She grinds against my relentless hard-on, and I lose all restraint. I grip her waist and flex my hips. "I'm glad you think so, baby. It'll make convincing you to come home and move in with me much easier."

Her head pops up, brows furrowed. "Come home with you?"

"Yes. I meant what I said."

"What do you mean exactly?"

It's obvious to me, but I spell it out for her so there's no confusion. "You and I together. Now. Return to LA. Be mine."

The playful atmosphere vanishes faster than Ricky when I arrived. Aurora averts her gaze and shifts in my lap, a torturous silence falling between us.

I clench my jaw and urge my temper to remain in check. "At least give me a chance."

She glances up, tears in her eyes. "I can't."

My mood plummets, the tips of my ears burning. The absolute last thing I want is my world on the other side of the country. "Why? You plan to stay in New York?"

"I can't just abandon my job, and I can't live with you without..." *Becoming attached.* She doesn't have to say it; it's in the way she clings to me, the way she surrenders to me. "I'm not your ex, and I'm not playing house until someone of her caliber comes along."

My heart beats an angry, violent rhythm. Does she think I'd toss her aside? Leave her and my child? Even if I previously said I didn't want a relationship.

I try to hold back—I really do—but I shoot my hand out and wrap my fingers around her delicate throat. "Why do you think so fucking terrible of me?"

"I don't. Don't you get that? I think terrible of *me*." Her tears fall, and she takes a shuddering breath. "Jackson waited, what? Four whole hours before he was with someone else? Why wouldn't you do the same? I'm nothing—"

I tighten my fist, silencing her. "Stop. Don't say another fucking word." My voice has never been this vicious toward her, and I hope she understands it comes from a place of concern, not malice. "I don't want to be with anyone else. Get that through your pretty little head. Why would I?"

I loosen my grip, but she doesn't respond.

"That's the second time you've mentioned my ex today. Start talking."

I'm a demanding asshole, but fuck, she trips every bit of my self-control.

She lowers her sheepish gaze, and I growl, "Look at me."

Her eyes meet mine—after rolling—and I swear, I'm bending her over my knee next.

"My grandmother and I Googled you. She wanted to see pictures of you."

She was gossiping about me, and despite being frustrated and pissed, a satisfied smirk tugs at my lips.

We have so much to learn about each other. She doesn't fully comprehend my need for dominance. She desires it, but she has no idea what it involves. If she did, she wouldn't be setting me off constantly.

Unless she likes my reaction, which may very well be the case, at least partly, I can't say I don't enjoy her taunting me.

I have yet to meet her grandmother, and we don't take pictures together as she did with Jackson. I add it to my list of things that'll change, along with her putting herself down, but I need her to trust me first.

My anger fades, and my tone softens. "And what? You saw photos of me with my ex and thought...?"

"Do we have to do this?" she whines, trying to scramble off my lap.

Unfortunately for her, I'm quicker. I twist my torso and toss her onto the couch, pinning her with my body. "Yes, it affects how you think of us." I raise her shirt and kiss her slightly rounded stomach. I splay my hand over our baby possessively. This is mine. *She's* mine. "Tell me, Aurora. I can't fix what I don't know."

She answers in a flurry of words. "Your ex is successful and wealthy, and maybe you wouldn't have left if she hadn't been unfaithful."

I trail kisses over her belly. "I wasn't happy. Catching her with someone else was my wake-up call, my escape. You make me happy, happier than I can remember."

Her retort is immediate. "You deserve better. I'm a mess."

"You are." I lean back and strip off her leggings or yoga pants or whatever the fuck these things are that highlight her fine ass. "But I'd have you no other way." Grabbing her by the thighs, I yank her to me, working her shirt over her head. "So stop putting yourself down. You're testing my patience tonight."

Finally, she gives me that flirty smile and those adoring eyes. "That's too bad. I like you all growly and rough."

I bite her nipple through her bra. "Do you? I'll have to come up with better punishments."

She tangles her fingers in my hair. "Please don't. I love you exactly as you are."

And there it is, what I've been attempting to avoid since finding out we were irrevocably connected—attachment and the dreaded '*I love you.*'

I don't know when I stopped pushing away the idea of something permanent and let my desires take a front seat in my brain, but now, it's everything I want.

Alone with her, there's no panic over our relationship interfering with coaching, no fear of being exposed publicly and dealing with my ex, whose endearments were never real.

I remove my shirt, and her soft hands glide over the contours of my stomach, leaving an inferno in their wake. She unbuttons my jeans and palms my length over my boxer briefs.

My breath hitches. "You keep doing that, and we won't reach the bedroom."

Raw lust gleams in her devilish eyes. "Screw the bedroom. You can fuck me on every surface here."

"That's my dirty girl."

I'm hard and leaking. I've had a merciless erection since kissing her in Central Park. Her touch has me aching, and when she gets my boxers down and her lips wrap around the head of my cock, her tongue flicking the sensitive underside, desire becomes desperation.

"Fuck, baby. Lie back and strip. I need to fill that pretty pussy."

She does precisely that, gracefully revealing every erotic,

stunning inch of her while I nearly fall off the couch, struggling to get my jeans and boxers off in a hurry.

"At some point, I swear, I'm taking my time with you in a bed."

I push inside her glistening cunt, and her sweet giggle turns into a seductive groan.

"Always so wet for me." I spread my fingers over her ass and raise her hips to mine as I sink in to the hilt. "God, you fit me like a glove."

She wraps her legs around my waist. "Finally. Now—"

A hard thrust has her crying out, her nails digging into my wrists.

"Open that smart mouth other than to scream for me, and you won't walk straight tomorrow." I slam into her to empha-size my point because, honestly, if she's talking, I'm not doing my job right.

"Who's in control here, Aurora?" I continue my relentless pace, bottoming out with each slap of my hips.

"You."

That one word unleashes something feral within me. "Good girl." *Thrust.* "Always me." *Thrust.* "Remember that after you come on my cock."

City lights shine through the terrace windows, highlighting her smooth, tanned skin and the bounce of her perfectly round breasts with every stroke.

"Fuck..." Her lips part in a silent moan, and she arches her back, deepening the angle. "Ethan."

She whimpers my name, and my veins alight with ecstasy. I move her legs to my shoulders and pound into her. "Don't think about leaving me, Aurora," I say roughly. "It'll never happen."

My wild words and our heavy breaths become nothing but primal sounds of pleasure. My gaze alternates between her tits and watching our bodies come together so beautifully. I'm close from her edging me all day, and the sight of her bare pussy stretched around me, taking me so fucking well, has my balls hugging my shaft.

I find her clit, circling my thumb in sync with my thrusts, and her walls tighten.

I suck air through my teeth, hissing, "Damn, baby. You're going to make me come."

Her lilting moans turn high-pitched, and her cunt grips me. My knees grow weak, and I collapse over her, careful of her stomach. I fist her hair and bite into her shoulder until she's coming harder, convulsing around me a second time, soaking my cock.

"Oh God, Ethan," she cries, her legs trembling around my waist.

"Jesus, fuck, Aurora…" I tuck my face into her neck and grit my teeth. A wave of emotions crash over me with each electrifying jolt. "So fucking good… Holy fucking shit."

8

AURORA

WE DESCEND FROM OUR POST-SEX HIGH, CATCHING OUR BREATHS. Sudden raindrops batter the windows, the pitter-patter growing louder, obscuring the sounds of the city below.

The downpour blurs the outdoor lights, transforming them into fragmented glimmers that dance across the room. The storm brings a sense of tranquility, and the security of being in Ethan's arms allows me to relax, fatigue taking hold.

Tomorrow, I have another long day, and I'm pregnant, which leaves me perpetually tired. Add sex with Ethan, and yeah, I'm exhausted.

Yet, my brain won't shut off, constantly preparing for the next impending fallout, betrayal, or heartbreak. My anxiety and trauma are raising alarm bells, all because the man beside me is quiet.

He's lying on his back, my head on his chest, his fingers in my hair, a blanket thrown over us. His broody demeanor suggests something is plaguing his mind.

"Are you staying?" I ask. "Tonight?"

He has a team to coach. I know he won't be here long, but I fear he's pulling away because we're getting too close. Or maybe it's because I refuse to leave with him.

I've lost Jackson and might lose Ethan because I can't bear to be near Jackson—the irony.

Ethan clears his throat. "Just tonight. I have to fly back tomorrow evening."

I yearn to run my fingers through his hair and kiss his neck, but I don't.

I'm affectionate—or clingy, whatever. It's part of my personality and everything I need to be happy. But right now, I'm not up for the disappointment of Ethan's rejection.

When I remain silent, he asks, "Are you staying in New York?"

If leaving is *his* ultimatum, our relationship will be over before it starts.

My muscles tense, readying for a fight. "I signed a contract for seven weeks."

His fingers pause while combing through my hair. "That puts you at six months pregnant. I need you home, taking care of yourself and the baby."

Raw vulnerability resonates in his voice, and I nearly cave.

I want him. I want this. But the three of us are so intertwined, it's impossible to separate him and Jackson. I can't go back to LA and risk seeing my ex and falling apart. I need space and time to figure myself out.

Ethan kisses my forehead, breaking me from the uncertainties wreaking havoc inside my mind. I glance up, and his thunderous gray eyes capture me, their intensity matching the storm raging outside.

His brows furrow in that distinctive scowl. "Come home with me. I can give you everything you need."

In my heart of hearts, I would love nothing more than to surrender fully to Ethan, but I've already done that with another man, and look where that got me.

"Don't you think the next step should be dating before we move in together?"

"I think we've skipped a few steps." He glances at my stomach. "I also think this isn't about me."

His stern gaze penetrates through me, dissecting my insecurities with surgical precision.

As usual, he's right, and, at an impasse, we stare at each other.

His expression softens, and before I'm able to brace myself, he slips past the walls I've painstakingly erected.

"You can talk to me about Jax."

I wince. That shortened name, a term of endearment, is a sharp knife piercing my soul. I realize Ethan will continue to call him *Jax*—will continue his close relationship with my ex.

Where does that leave me? On the outside? Or constantly being confronted with the greatest loss of my life?

No thanks.

I push away, opening my mouth to end this, when his arms tighten around me.

"What did I tell you? Don't try it, Aurora. It's pointless."

"This won't work." I swallow the painful lump in my throat. "I'm not returning to LA."

He clenches his jaw, and his nostrils flare. "You are, even if I have to drag you back. Jackson relapsed—it's part of addiction. He didn't mean it."

Tears of anger sting my eyes, and I laugh incredulously. How many times did I tell myself the same thing? *He didn't mean it.*

Fuck that.

I hurl all my hurt and frustration at Ethan in a single word. "Don't."

He ignores my plea. "I was there. I saw the devastation on his face when he found out what he did. He'd *never* cheat on you."

"But he did, and where is he?"

Ethan's cheeks flush, and I know I've got him.

"I thought he'd be here with you."

"So that's why you're here: searching for him." I shove at his chest in vain. "Let me go!"

"No," he grits through his teeth. "I came here for you. I don't want to lose you. You can't run from this. You can't run from *him*. He may not be here now, but he will be."

"How do you know that? Have you talked to him?"

Why am I asking? Why do I even care?

His deep flush spreads, and his ears redden. "I've tried."

I don't have the energy or strength to worry about where Jackson is; in the end, I'll only blame myself.

Giving in to the fatigue, I rest my head on Ethan's shoulder and squeeze my eyes shut, failing to prevent the dread his words provoke.

He brushes away the tears I can't stop from escaping. When he speaks, his voice is strained. "I'll find him. I'll send him to rehab. He loves you—"

"I. Don't. Want. Him. Back," I say with conviction.

Then, guilt and fear take hold, that boyish smile flashes through my mind, and I crumble.

I sob into Ethan's chest, reliving the nightmare.

He envelops me in his firm embrace and tucks my head under his chin, his touch and gentle tone easing my grief.

"I'm here, baby. You don't have to bear this pain alone. Let me fix this. I'll do whatever it takes."

9

JACKSON

"Stop." I push at his chest. My hands are small, too small, and panic floods my system. My feet flail, striking a solid wall that descends over me. "Don't touch me."

   "No one's here to save you, pretty boy."

   A cruel laugh echoes, bouncing around in my skull until it morphs into a child's sobs. I press my palms to my ears, but the cries only become louder.

   I attempt to scream, to call for help, but it's trapped in my chest and only emerges as a faint whisper. "It's not real."

   It's not real.

   It's not real.

   Drenched in sweat and trembling, I gasp for air, my unfocused gaze fixed straight ahead, my mind locked in darkness.

   My least favorite demons have come out to play. I must have done a shit ton of coke, drinking, and whatever else, because these withdrawals are kicking my ass—*hard.*

   Detox is the fucking worst.

   Cravings, nausea, mood swings, feeling utterly miserable, migraines, and, this time around, terrifying nightmares. I've had them in the past, which contributed to my addiction. I'd get blackout drunk to avoid them, avoid seeing the monster in my head. The vivid, warped memories intensify during withdrawals, making the vicious cycle nearly impossible to escape.

The only thing standing between me and a bottle of vodka and oxy is Aurora.

But I can't go to her. If I do and she refuses me, which she most likely will, it'll be my undoing.

I'm in a dark place, and she doesn't deserve to deal with my addiction on top of everything else. I won't do that to her again.

After days of nonstop vomiting, severe headaches, and nightmares, life feels unbearable. If I don't reach out for help, I might succumb, and then I'll have no chance of recovery.

Despite our confrontation, my gut tells me Ethan is the person to call, and I won't lie: I wish he were here. He'd set me straight, or at least put me out of my misery.

He picks up on the first ring. "Give me a minute." A rustling of clothes, and then his gruff rumble softens to that gentle tone all men use with their girlfriends. "I'll be right back."

They're together. My stomach knots, and tears sting my eyes.

"Is everything okay?" *Aurora.*

Her sweet voice steals my breath, and knowing it's not directed at me is a dagger plunged into my heart.

"I'll take care of it. Sleep, love. You have an early morning."

Love? Really? Just fucking kill me now. I suppress a sob and ask, "Can I talk to her?"

His response is quiet but firm. "No." Two doors shut before he speaks again. "Where are you?"

I don't answer. My mind is focused on one thing. "You're in New York."

If he's with Aurora, he left the team, and that's alarming.

"Yes, and it's three a.m." His rough tone gives nothing away. He could be jet-lagged, pissed, or his crotchety self.

"Is she alright?"

"No, she's exhausted and devastated."

What did I expect? Sunshine and rainbows? No, but I'd prefer anger over pain. Still, I can't believe he would leave the team unless...

"Is the baby okay?"

With one hundred percent certainty, I'd jump out the window if my fuck-up harmed her pregnancy.

"As far as we know." There's a brief pause. "Where are you, Jax?"

"Home." Humbling myself—which isn't much—I spell it out. "I need help. I was hoping you—" My voice breaks, and I swallow to wet my dry throat. "Can you send the trainer or doctor? They only listen to you."

"Detox, or for some STD?"

"Fuck off. I should have known calling you was a mistake." I'm tempted to hang up, but I have no one left.

"I'm asking as your coach. You think I enjoy being put in this position? Where I have to choose between my captain and..."

He trails off, giving me a glimmer of hope, since he can't clearly define their relationship.

"... the woman I want to be with? You think I enjoy watching you break her and destroy what little trust she had in *either* of us? You've ruined everything. Grow up and answer the question so I know what I'm dealing with."

"I. Didn't. Fuck. Anyone." Even though the words are uttered through clenched teeth, it's hard to embody outrage when your heart is shattered and your body is weak.

"So, detox? Withdrawals?"

"Yes, fucking awful. I couldn't drag myself out of bed if I wanted to. And believe me, I want to."

"You need to go to rehab."

People assume rehab is some quick fix. You go, they wave a magic wand, and poof! Addiction disappears. I went. I was agitated and paranoid at being locked up, and when I returned to the real world, my problems had multiplied.

"I don't need rehab. I've tried it. I need *her*... I need *you*."

He falls silent. I can picture him clenching his jaw and giving me that death glare. "I'm notifying the doctor. Have you taken a drug test?"

"No, but I'll enroll in the league's substance use program and accept whatever suspension they impose."

Ethan releases a frustrated growl, likely because I'm fucking up his dream season. "Why would you do this, Jackson? You've lost everything. You could've reached out to anyone on the team for help. Why would you party before a big game? It makes no sense, not even for you."

Isn't that the million-dollar question? Could I have handled Kyle without meeting him at the Hard Rock? What made me grab that first drink?

I'm on the brink of lying. It's much easier to pretend to be rich, spoiled, and not give a fuck than to admit I'm...broken? Lost? Ashamed?

Besides, I learned a long time ago that no one cares.

"What did he do or say to get you there?" Ethan asks.

I'm so shaken by his skill at connecting the dots, the truth tumbles out. "He has pictures of you and Aurora together. He threatened to publicize our relationship, have you fired, and ruin Aurora's reputation."

I scoffed when Kyle said he'd *expose my character*. Never did I think that meant setting me up to lose Aurora. My addiction, the slew of mental health disorders I've been diagnosed with, being in a situationship with another man—any of that, I was prepared for and okay with.

If I had known *cheating* was what he was aiming for, I would've never left my hotel room.

"You should have told me. I'm not your fucking rival!" Ethan shouts. "You walked right into his trap, gave him precisely what he wanted. If I hadn't been ready for the consequences, would I have stood with you and Aurora at the arena?"

I squeeze my eyes shut to ward off the impending migraine.

My voice is hoarse from throwing up, my tone flat from sleep deprivation. "For her, yeah. You'd endure anything for her, but it doesn't matter. The damage is done, and you two are fine..." My words trail off, this headache slamming into me.

"We are not fine! Aurora is not fine!"

I don't know why he's so angry, but he's not helping this piercing pain.

"Jax!"

I jolt at Ethan calling my name.

"Jax!"

"Hm?"

"I'm texting Doc. Are you at your place downtown?"

"Yup," I mumble.

"Okay, he's on his way. Can you let him in?"

"The doorman will. The elevator opens into my penthouse."

There's silence, and I concentrate on breathing through the pulsing behind my eyes.

"You know," he says, releasing a defeated sigh, "part of me wishes I could sit back and smile while you fuck it all up. But this hurts Aurora, and I can't do that. She extended her contract in New York and started looking at apartments. If she stays here, I swear, I'll kill you myself. You need to get your shit together and fix this."

I rise too fast, and the glaring headache pummels me, knocking me down. "Don't fuck with me. What are you implying?"

He can't want me with her. Not with my problems. Not with a baby.

"She'll forgive you for relapsing if you stay sober. If you can do that, I'll support you. I'll talk to her."

"Are you serious?" My heart races, tears threaten my eyes, and my throat constricts with emotion. "I was sober for months. I can't explain why I picked up that first drink, but I'll never do it again. I'll never put myself in that situation. I'll do anything." Those last three words are strained, the biggest plea of my life.

"I know you will. Be honest with her. She believes you rushed out to get laid as soon as she left. She thinks she's not good enough. It's messing with her head."

That uncomfortable lump in my throat throbs painfully. "I wouldn't sleep with anyone else. I *can't* sleep with anyone else. I didn't."

"You embarrassed her. Emily was the one who told her. I eased that sting a bit. You can thank me later."

Smug bastard.

And Emily? Does the universe hate me?

"Are you always an asshole? What did you do?"

"Surprised her in Central Park. Made out like two teenagers."

Given Ethan's paranoia toward anything public, that's a massive step, but there's no way in hell I'm wasting this opportunity to bust his balls.

"Funny, old man, considering she's not much older than a teenager. Did you buy her cotton candy and take her on the Ferris wheel too?" Despite my cracked lips, I can't help but grin.

"Wow." He drags out the word. "Thanks for reminding me why I hate you."

"Don't worry, the feeling is mutual."

10

ETHAN

MY PHONE RINGS JUST AS THE SUN'S SOFT GLOW SPILLS INTO THE bedroom. Worried it might be Doc or Jackson, I check it. It's a familiar Boston number, and I mentally curse.

I send it to voicemail repeatedly, but my toxic ex lingers worse than the stench of a locker room after a weekend tournament. She'll undoubtedly give me hell, especially if news of my relationship has made its way through her social circles.

Of course, it has. Why else would she care?

I have zero to be ashamed of. My divorce is final, and Aurora is mine. Nothing matters except for the girl snuggling my chest, gazing up at me, probably wondering why my phone keeps waking her.

"Sorry." I refuse the call again and set the phone on the nightstand.

I tangle my fingers in her messy hair and lower my mouth to her lips just as the damn device vibrates on the table. I close my eyes, drop my forehead to hers, and release a frustrated sigh.

When I pull away, her brows are pinched in confusion, and as much as I wish to keep this from her, I know I can't, not if I want her to trust me.

"This will not be a pretty conversation. I can go outside or have it here, but my ex won't stop until she bitches me out."

Aurora scoffs and reaches for my phone. I attempt to snatch it to prevent the impending nightmare, but before I'm able, she's answering.

"Hello."

"This must be the *swimsuit model*." Every word drips indignation. "Screening his calls already?"

My brat rolls her eyes. "That would be me. And you are?"

"His *wife*, or at least I was, until you started riding his dick."

"Were you? That's too bad."

Aurora's dry sarcasm trumps my ex's taunting. This is not at all how I thought this would go.

"So, how's my husband's cock?"

God, I hate that voice. The tone is obnoxious, as if she were sitting down with her snobby friends and asking about someone's kid. *So, how's little Michael?*

Whiskey eyes fix on mine, and she breaks into a satisfied smile. "Very well, thank you. Ten out of ten. Will definitely come again. In fact, I have. Many, *many* times."

My cheeks heat. I can't believe this girl has me blushing.

She bites her bottom lip to hold in her fit of naughty giggles, and I throw my arm over my face to keep from laughing too.

I think my ex is stunned speechless. I doubt anyone has dared speak to her this way.

"Well, good talk. Don't call again." Aurora ends the pointless conversation and reaches over me to set the phone on the nightstand.

I pull her on top of me but can't kiss her because I'm cheesing too hard. "Ten out of ten, huh?"

She straddles me, wearing only my T-shirt, and my dick takes notice. "I may have been exaggerating." She playfully shrugs.

"Oh, yeah? Get on your knees, and I'll remind you."

When she doesn't, I slap her ass, and those eyes twinkle with mischief.

She smiles—fucking smiles—and drags her shirt over her head.

The best set of tits I've ever seen momentarily distract me. Although I'm fond of staring at them, she's being defiant.

"You trying to work me up?" I pinch her nipples. "Get. On. Your. Knees."

She whimpers and grinds against my erection. "I wanna taste you."

As much as I'd love her mouth wrapped around me, that's not what I said, and I'm not allowing her to defy me.

"I'm going to fuck you into next week for ignoring me. Is that what you want?"

The teasing brat grins and scrambles onto her knees, face in the mattress.

I remove my boxers and position myself behind her, taking a minute to appreciate what's mine.

That arch. Those butt dimples. That bare, pink pussy.

"Fucking perfect."

I sink my teeth into her ass cheek, resulting in a breathy gasp, then a whiny moan when I lick from clit to hole. I'm drooling over her sweet, tangy taste, my dick throbbing at the thought of my cum still inside her.

In the bedroom, I have no shame. I enjoy everything about sex, the nastier, the better, especially with Aurora. She lets me do whatever I want and is always so responsive.

I continue my exploration, paying close attention to her swollen clit and pink pucker. I run my thumb around her tight hole. "Anyone ever fuck your ass, baby girl?"

I drip precum when she replies with a nervous "No."

"We'll have to work up to that."

My voice is breathless. I'll be dreaming about taking her ass. She has no idea what she's unleashed. I want to ruin her in the best of ways, have her on her knees for me, begging.

I clasp the back of her neck, pressing her into the mattress as I alternate between rubbing her clit and finger-fucking her.

Not until she's pleading, "Ethan, please," do I give her what she wants, pounding into her with punishing thrusts.

Gruff words flow from my lips with no restraint. "This needy pussy loves taking my cock, doesn't it?"

She releases a whimpering moan and fists the sheets.

I slap her ass with enough force to leave a handprint. "Tell me."

"Oh God, Ethan, yes. Don't stop."

She's so close, she's gripping me, and I'm not far behind.

I move my hand from her nape to fist her hair, bringing my other arm around her chest to lift her onto my lap. Aurora doesn't hesitate. She rides me like a porn star, her head falling to my shoulder, her fingers teasing her nipples as her ass bounces on my thighs.

Fuck, I love it. All of it.

I clasp her throat, working her clit with my other hand. "Come for me." My voice is gravelly, a growl in her ear. "Squeeze that tight cunt around me. Milk my fucking cock."

A few more strokes, and she's screaming my name.

Her intense orgasm triggers mine, and I can't hold back.

"Fuck, baby. I'm addicted to this pussy." My stomach clenches, and my heart races so fast, I can barely breathe. "I never want this to end."

I'm losing it, caught up in the high. I have no control when I'm buried deep inside this girl.

We collapse to the mattress, my forehead on her shoulder, both of us gasping. It takes all my energy to roll off her and draw her to me.

11

JACKSON

A MEDIC SENT BY THE TEAM DOCTOR IS THE FIRST TO ARRIVE. SHE sets out medical supplies and asks a billion questions. *What did you take? How much did you take? When did you stop drinking? What do you remember? List your symptoms from most distressing to least, but leave nothing out.*

When I mention the loss of memory, her fingers freeze while preparing an IV. "Any tremors?"

"Just normal shakes and shivers." As if there's anything *normal* about detox.

When Doc joins the assessment, they exchange information while giving each other knowing glances I can't decipher.

"You're sure you only used for one night?" Doc asks.

"Yes," I say, defensive. "I was sick before, but I wasn't using. My girlfriend was leaving for New York, and I was physically ill."

Again, they silently communicate. For whatever reason, they don't believe me. Why would I lie? I'm already in deep shit.

I run my fingers through my sweat-soaked hair and decide to tell them what they probably assume. "I was diagnosed with a mood disorder. During the game, I had racing thoughts, agitation, pressured speech... I was having an episode, but I wasn't using."

Doc nods in understanding. "These episodes don't just go away, Jackson. They can worsen and lead to impulsive behaviors, especially when paired with emotional distress."

My muscles tense. I will fight my way out of here if he even thinks about committing me. "Believe me, I know, but I'm not manic. I'm not suicidal. I'm not on a bender. I relapsed, and I have no intention of doing it again."

He pats my arm and gives me a kind smile. "No worries. I'm glad you reached out for help."

After pissing in a cup, giving blood, receiving two IVs, taking some pills, and grabbing a long, hot shower, I realize it's five in the morning. They've left, and I'm feeling semi-human.

It's eight o'clock on the East Coast, which is all I care about. My conversation with Ethan has renewed my confidence, and as soon as I'm not burdening Aurora with these withdrawals, I'll be flying to New York.

More stable, I check my phone notifications for the first time since migraines made it impossible to stare at the screen. There are texts and calls from Grant I've neglected. He's a ride-or-die best friend, and honestly, I don't deserve the loyalty after my behavior in the locker room.

I swallow my pride and text back.

> Thanks, G-Man. I'm sorry I fucked up. I'm getting my shit together. Tell everyone I'll see 'em soon.

Then, there are manipulative messages from Kyle and pictures of us hugging in the tunnel, which I ignore. One line, however, piques my interest.

KYLE

> I spoke with the trust attorney. Let's negotiate. We can get past this.

He must have found out I hired another law firm, or maybe it's because I've restricted his access to every facet of my life: box seats, bank accounts, credit cards, properties, clubs, suites —if he had access to it, I've canceled it.

I should've done it years ago, but I hoped to appease him, thinking he'd leave Aurora alone. It's a mistake I won't repeat.

> I'll negotiate once I have my girlfriend back.

I sound like a petulant child, but I don't give a fuck. It's Aurora or nothing.

Despite the early hour, Kyle responds with pictures of Aurora and Ethan in Central Park.

KYLE

Your girlfriend? You're delusional. It's over.
Move on.

> I'm not moving on. You set me up to lose everything. You got exactly what you wanted. Now, get out of my life.

KYLE

Who's the father? You or him?

> Why do you give a fuck?

KYLE

Because you're not responsible enough for a child.

> As if you care.

KYLE

Your child support will be horrendous.

Ah, there it is. *Money*.

> I'll give her more than any court demands.

KYLE

That's the problem! You're not smart.

I'm not smart?

> You manipulated me into meeting with you, knowing I'd relapse. Threw some drugs and half-naked women at me and took pictures to fuck my career and relationship, all to avoid me paying child support? Now I'll definitely have to pay. And what if I got one of those girls pregnant? Who's not smart?

I won't have to pay child support, but he doesn't need to know that.

KYLE

> Like I'd allow that. I had your ass dragged out of there once you were piss drunk.

Well, that's a relief. At least I have confirmation I didn't fuck anyone.

> You mean after you arranged the photos?

He doesn't answer, and while I contemplate his motives, I torment myself by scanning through the pictures of Ethan and Aurora.

Seeing them all lovey-dovey has me conflicted, regretful, and missing her. I miss her so fucking much, it hurts. Even with his body pressed against hers and their lips locked, I'm not jealous—quite the opposite. The only thing I envy is that I'm not there.

It's strange, but *we* work.

I appreciate him stepping up and caring for Aurora after I hurt her. In one picture, he's wiping tears from her face, sending that wrecking ball through my chest again. She believes she's not good enough when I'm the one who has failed.

Kyle is right; I'm not smart. Not because I'd give Aurora anything, but because I didn't protect her. I thought I could handle him. He played me, and it destroyed the person I love most. Again.

The next picture is taken from behind. All it shows is Ethan kissing her forehead— Wait. What the fuck? Is that a Stars hoodie? It's partly obscured, the hood covering the name, but it looks an awful lot like a jersey.

My fingers fly over the screen.

> You let her wear a fucking Stars jersey? Whose number is that?

COACH

😂😂😂

COACH

Carmichael. I already warned her.

> Burn it.

Carmichael is a defensive beast. I'm fast. I don't carry the bulk this guy does. When he hits, it's comparable to being smashed into a brick wall by a Mack truck.

Touché, baby. Tou-fucking-ché.

COACH

This is what she's wearing to work today. I may need you to bail me out of jail.

Following is a picture of Aurora bent over the bathroom counter as she applies her makeup in the mirror. She stands on her tippy toes, her legs a mile long. Her plaid skirt rides up, ending just below her luscious ass, and since it sits high on her waist, it's difficult to tell she's pregnant.

For a shirt, she's wearing a cropped band tee, and from this angle, you can see a peek of under-boob. No bra.

Goddamn.

She's stunning. Beautiful. Sexy. Every man's wet dream. And I hate myself for fucking it up.

> How about we trade?

COACH

Not a chance in hell.

I save every photo, even those of Aurora with Ethan, before conducting an obsessive internet search for more. I find an IG page for a photographer who has taken an interest in Aurora. He has a handful of new pictures and videos of her.

Of course, she's gorgeous in each picture, but the one in which she's wearing a tiny, transparent silver dress is out of this world. I can see her rosy nipples and the outline of her incredible tits. It reminds me of when we were separated and she was posing naked on beaches, strutting seductively in lingerie.

It hits me—we *are* separated. I'm instantly irritated, especially by the comments stating how hot Aurora is and ripping me to shreds for cheating on her.

I'm typing so fast, I can't control myself. **Look at her. Do you think I'd cheat on that? Fuck no.**

My mouth twists into a smirk. Under a picture of her and Ethan, I write: **Thanks for taking care of our girl.**

I scroll through the outlandish comments and find one that asks: **Ménage?** and heart the reply. Let people assume what they want—they already think I'm unhinged, so why not have some fun?

12

JACKSON

DOC RETURNS IN THE LATE AFTERNOON TO EVALUATE MY condition. I've progressed from the bed to the couch—a vast improvement over my earlier inability to lift my head without vomiting. I'm exhausted, but my mind isn't racing. I'm not bouncing between panic and agitation.

Unfortunately, I'm still having flashbacks and nightmares.

Doc completes his assessment and settles into a chair across from me. He's in his sixties, with salt-and-pepper hair and glasses. He carries himself with a quiet demeanor that puts me at ease.

He leans forward, his voice earnest. "Did you know Ethan hired me because I have a background in addiction? He wanted to ensure you weren't being enabled and received the help you needed. And it's not just you. We have others on the team who struggle with substance use, but I believe you were the main reason."

Is he trying to make me feel guilty? I already know I'm indebted to Ethan. He's my coach, but he also loves Aurora. He wants to win, but any other man would've taken advantage of my situation and snatched up my girl.

"The trainer mentioned something during my last game when I asked for a med, but besides that, I just figured he was a control freak." *Because he is.*

A tiny smirk tugs at his lips. "As true as that may be, he still cares about you. He finds it difficult to believe you'd relapse, even if you were experiencing an episode beforehand." He clears his throat and pushes his glasses up his nose. "He's emotionally invested, but I can't treat you unless I know the truth. Were you using PEDs? Be honest with me."

His intense gaze makes me shift uncomfortably, irritation flitting in my chest. "I've never taken a performance-enhancing drug. Ever. I played sports my entire life and went to a boarding school in Canada. I had nothing better to do than play hockey."

His nod is slow and deliberate, as if he's mulling over my words, not dismissing them as lies. "When did you start feeling off or sick?"

"It's hard to say. Maybe the night before Aurora left. My thoughts have been chaotic, which isn't abnormal, but usually, I can reel myself in. My memory is spotty after arriving in Vegas."

Doc glances at the ceiling, silently pondering and tapping his pen on his knee.

Impatience gets the better of me, and I demand, "What? What is it?"

"You tested positive for GHB and cocaine, along with opiates. I ran multiple tests, because your symptoms don't align with one night of cocaine and alcohol. Some bodybuilders mix GHB and cocaine in their workout formula to enhance performance and offset the crash."

A wave of nausea washes over me, and my stomach knots. My heartbeat thumps loudly in my ears. Fear slithers through my veins, and I brace myself for the inevitable truth.

Trying to keep my voice steady, I ask, "What's GHB?"

Doc's empathetic gaze confirms my worst fears. "It's a designer drug, a sedative if used in larger quantities. Some refer to it as..."

Please don't say it. Please don't let me be right about this.

"...the date rape drug."

The room tilts, and I squeeze my eyes closed, allowing the floor beneath me to crumble. It's Kyle's favorite party drug, and

I can't help but wonder if this is some twisted karma for harboring the knowledge of his transgressions.

I've kept my mouth shut. Why would he go this far?

So I'd be caught and have to lean on him to skirt the test results. Okay, I get that. It has happened in the past.

So I'd lose Aurora and control of my trust fund...which becomes available in about six months...

Aurora's due date and my twenty-sixth birthday are only two months apart. Right now, I have no access to my trust, and if Kyle proves I'm still incompetent, that'll continue.

It's possible that, in his eyes, my child support would only be based on my income from hockey, not the hundreds of millions my mother left me.

Aurora is unaware of my trust, nor would she care, but Kyle does—a lot. He's a greedy bastard. He thinks this baby is mine and wants to prevent Aurora from taking the money *he* controls and uses.

If I lost hockey, she'd get even less. PEDs would do it. My achievements on the ice would be a farce, and I'd lose my endorsements. If things went south, I'd be forced to turn to him to keep my properties and live comfortably, or I'd have to beg him to help me get my career back.

Either way, I'm dependent on him. I'd have to meet his demands. It's happened...

Then, something more frightening occurs to me.

He could've done this before.

I use a workout formula or protein mix multiple times a day, and not long ago, he had access to the locker room, training facility, and my downtown penthouse, maybe even my cars.

My mind floods with childhood memories, and that dark place threatens to swallow me whole. I shake my head—I can't think about it. If I do, I might wrap my fingers around Kyle's throat and squeeze the life right out of him.

I should do it. He deserves nothing less than a slow death, and I'd enjoy watching the light leave his eyes.

Doc's gentle tone breaks through my morbid thoughts. "Some people become violently ill in response to GHB. Some have erratic behavior. Walk me through everything so we can figure this out."

13

ETHAN

"We don't have to turn it in. I ran private tests, and GHB won't show in a urinalysis after this long."

I'm surrounded by walls devoid of color, their monotonous presence suffocating. My office is cold and unyielding, mocking my desire to be elsewhere. Sure, black, white, and blue are the team's colors, and a few months ago, every part of this place excited me, but now, I can't focus on anything other than checking my phone.

My text to Aurora this morning has yet to be returned. I hate being ignored and worry about her being alone—with her bodyguard.

I'm counting down the days until we're reunited. Before I left New York, I insisted she take time off and keep the baby's appointments in LA. She was reluctant until I promised not to kidnap her. The thought is tempting, though.

Eight days.

Eight days remain until I see her again.

Late last night, my plane landed in LA. I slept a few hours then met with the biggest pain in my ass. Before Doc joined us, Jax explained the financial situation with his father. The entire ordeal is mind-blowing. I can't imagine anyone being so greedy, they'd harm their own child to maintain their wealth.

I scan the lab results and toss the paper onto my desk. I

suspected Kyle was involved in Jackson's relapse, but to drug him is some *Dateline*-level shit. "Run a second test, turn it in, and accept the required four-game penalty. The organization will expect nothing less, given the picture evidence. Might as well face the consequences head-on."

My captain reclines in the chair, dark circles under his eyes with zero emotion regarding a suspension. His sole motivation is getting to Aurora, and I can't say I blame him.

Doc nods and claps Jax on the shoulder. "Meet me in the training room when you're finished." He offers a soft smile and exits.

An awkward silence envelops us. I'm not skilled at comforting others, particularly men, and there's no chapter in the coach's handbook on guiding your player through being drugged and set up by his father.

"Kyle thinks the child is yours or believes it's a possibility. Have you told him otherwise?"

He averts his gaze, and his knee bounces. "No. It was our plan for me to claim the pregnancy. I doubt he'll believe me if I deny it now."

I clench my jaw. Me and my brilliant ideas. It was my scheme for Jax and Aurora to fake date, for him to act as the father. "What's he want with the Santa Monica house?"

His shoulder lifts in a half-ass shrug. "To hold it over my head."

"Is it in your name?"

"I completed all the paperwork, and the lawyer processed the closing. As far as I know, everything was finalized. I was in a rush, and it was my only option."

"Yeah, in a rush to fuck me over."

"No," he says in a drawn-out, sarcastic tone. "I was solidi-fying my position. You have the baby, and I have the house."

"That wasn't the agreement. Now, Kyle has the house. Can you sell it to me?"

His brows snap together. "So you can swoop in and play the hero? Not happening."

"You are one stubborn motherfucker. Sell it to me, or I'm

calling Aurora and telling her you walked into my office with a blonde on your arm with a double-D rack."

His face goes blank, and a laugh bursts out of me.

"I won't hesitate to come across this desk. You better be fucking joking."

"I'd never do that to her. She's hurt enough."

He narrows his eyes, catching on to my guilt trip. "It cost thirteen million."

"I'm well aware. This might shock you, but I know how to use the internet."

"That is a shock, old man. Are you sure your retirement can handle it?"

Despite his obnoxious behavior, I can't help but smile. "Unlike you, I don't blow my money. I have investments. I can manage it just fine."

"Spending money on others is my love language. Don't knock it."

"I'll sell it back to you once you're of age, if that's what you need." Then, another thought occurs to me. "Are you able to ask the court for a different trustee or conservator or whatever? Anyone but Kyle."

"I hired a law firm to explore my options. They're awaiting the trust documents."

We stare at each other, the light and playful mood giving way to the inevitable.

"What are you gonna do?"

He wrings his hands. "Head to New York as soon as I get out of here."

My gut clenches, and I take a deep breath to ease the anxiety of Aurora's reaction. "Be prepared. She's not taking this well. I've tried talking to her, but she's... Be careful. Please don't end up hurting her more. I mean it, Jax."

"I'm not leaving without her. I'll move there if I have to."

Great. "No, you won't. I'll drag both of you back here. You're contracted to me, don't forget that."

14

AURORA

I BOLT OUT OF BED, MAKE A BEELINE FOR THE TOILET, AND DROP to my knees. My stomach turns and empties the small amount of food I managed to ingest in the past twenty-four hours.

Ethan left, and no matter how hard I tried, I couldn't sleep. I couldn't eat. Emptiness and regret slammed into me once I was alone with my thoughts.

Unable to hold my head up, I lay my cheek on my forearm to avoid directly touching the toilet seat with my face.

Pregnancy: glamorous, it's not.

Another round of nausea strikes, and I clutch the porcelain. The wave finally recedes, leaving me weak and trembling, and I collapse on the tile. I need a strong coffee and to crawl back under the covers.

Too bad I have to work.

I shut my eyes, thinking *I'll just lie here for a moment.*

The door creaks open, and a shadow looms over me. A rough palm brushes my sweaty hair from my forehead.

"Damn," Ricky curses. "You're burning up...and pale."

I emit a sound of agreement, and my teeth chatter.

"Okay, I'm taking you to bed." He lifts me into his brawny arms with ease and carefully sets me on the mattress, pulling the blanket to my chin.

I snuggle into the sheets, the cool pillow a relief to my

heated skin. "You smell like leather and winter," I mumble, a bit delirious. "It's nice."

"Oh, yeah?" he chuckles. "That's because I went for a walk to find you breakfast, and it's nasty out."

"Sorry." I sigh remorsefully. "I'll get up and eat in a minute."

His knuckles press against my temple and cheek. "No, you won't. I'll bring it to you."

"Your hands feel amazing. Keep doing that." It comes out more provocative than intended, and I rush to clarify, "They're icy."

"Because you're on fire," he says in a low tone. "Let me get a cold compress."

"It's just morning sickness. It'll pass soon. Plus, I'm due on set at nine."

"You won't make it," he calls out over the running water. "It's after eight-thirty, and traffic is a bitch in this weather."

"Shit!" How long was I asleep on the floor? Adrenaline pumps through my veins, my eyelids pop open, and I toss the covers to the side. "I can't be late! I have a photo shoot."

My feet hit the hardwood, and I race into the bathroom, throwing on the shower. I remove my shorts, kicking them away, and yank my camisole over my head. A choking noise snags my attention, and wide blue eyes meet mine in the mirror.

I thrust my hand in a dismissive gesture. Too late now. "What? You have a boyfriend." I break his stare and step into the glass shower.

"What if I'm bisexual?" he yells. "And I can still see you! Perfectly."

"Then leave, weirdo."

Bisexual or not, he was bound to catch me undressing at some point. Modeling isn't for the modest, and he's seen me practically nude plenty of times.

"Tell your boyfriend I said sorry."

The adrenaline fades while I'm rinsing, and doubt creeps in. Forget the city traffic. My thick hair has to dry, and that takes at least an hour with a professional stylist.

I have to get dressed and in full makeup, without my talented assistant. I'll never be ready. I'll miss the photo shoot, and they'll believe I'm incapable of meeting the requirements of my contract. I *can't* fuck this up.

My chest tightens, and my stomach churns.

Not again.

With a hand clamped over to my mouth, I dash out of the shower, nearly slipping on my ass. Ricky awaits with an open towel, pursed lips, and an "I told you so" expression.

Wrapped tightly, I fall to my knees and repeat the same process as earlier, and even though I elbow him, my bodyguard insists on holding my wet hair back.

"Will you leave me alone? This is embarrassing enough."

"Shut up. I'm a medic—*was* a medic," he corrects. "I've witnessed much worse...like you naked. Disgusting."

"I miss when you were quiet."

It's not true, and he knows it. Whether by forced proximity or divine intervention, we've become close, and I'd be lost without him.

When there's nothing left in my system, my abdomen cramps, and anxiety turns to fear.

I place a hand on my belly. "The baby? Should I—"

My phone rings in the bedroom, and, overwhelmed, I release a sob, tears burning my eyes.

I attempt to rise, but my head spins, and I wobble.

Once again, I'm in Ricky's arms.

"I'm calling Ethan," he says, his voice strained and clears his throat. "I know you'll listen to him."

Jackson

BEFORE I LEAVE Ethan's office, his phone rings and his demeanor brightens. The sight of happiness on his typically serious mug is strange, taboo, as if we share a secret.

We share *something* more than a professional relationship.

A situationship—if I miraculously get Aurora back.

Even during moments of success on the ice, he wears a mask of irritation. I score a goal. He wants another. We win a game. He's prepping for the next one. The only person who brings a huge smile to his face is Aurora, and my heart surges with hope.

Then, his gaze fixates on the caller ID, and the scowl returns, deepening the furrow between his brows. He signals for me to keep my mouth shut, sets the phone on his desk, and puts the call on speaker.

"Ricky," he says, as curt as ever.

Now I understand Ethan's abrupt mood shift and my need to stay quiet. Aurora's bodyguard is one more person who hates me.

"You busy?"

Ricky's urgent tone grabs my attention, and I lean closer.

"No." Ethan adjusts the knot of his tie, loosening it from around his neck. "Everything okay?"

"She's sick and in a panic about not being at work."

Ethan's sharp gaze meets mine. "Sick how?"

"Throwing up and running a fever. I found her passed out on the bathroom floor."

My shoulders stiffen, and my heart thumps wildly. "I'll go," I insist on a whisper.

If she's not well, one of us needs to be there. She loved me through my addiction, withdrawals, and countless hangovers. It's time I step up and care for her.

"Make sure she stays in bed." Ethan puts his finger to his lips to silence me. "Put her on the phone."

Ragged breaths fill the line, and I rake my fingers through my hair, tugging on the strands. She's having a panic attack.

"Baby, you need me to come get you?"

A shaky exhale, and, "No."

My throat constricts. Fuck, I'd give anything to be there, to wrap her in my arms.

"What's the matter, love?"

"A...bad day."

Her voice cracks, and it takes everything in me not to grab the phone. Only the fear of her hanging up holds me back.

"Just breathe for me." A few inhales and some sniffles. "Good girl. Tell me what's going on."

Her reply comes out in a burst of sobs. "I'm sick and missing a photo shoot. I can't—"

"Yes, you can," he soothes in a low rumble. "And if you're sick and not resting, I'm a five-hour flight from bringing you home."

"My contract—"

"Don't care." He shakes his head, although she can't see him. "Nothing is more important than you and the baby."

I nod in agreement. At least we're on the same page there.

His voice softens. "How about I send you someone?"

There's a long pause, and I suspect she knows he means me. "Who? Emily?" Bitterness and sarcasm lace her tone, but there's also a tinge of interest.

Ethan must pick up on it too. "Will that help?"

"A lot more than who you're thinking."

Ouch.

The asshole finds her resentment toward me amusing and smirks. "Get Felicity to extend her an offer. It's just business. She doesn't have to live with you."

"Good," Aurora says with a yawn. "I don't want her to."

"Stay in bed. Do I need to find you a doctor?"

"No, I'm sure it's morning sickness, but I'll call mine."

Ricky grumbles in the background. Wherever she is, he is, and dark jealousy curls in my stomach. I tell myself it's his responsibility, what he was hired for, but I hate it. It should be me.

It *will* be me.

Ethan and Aurora say their goodbyes, our girl promising to rest and keep him updated, and I leave to track down a certain blonde who'll do anything for money.

15

RICKY

"YOU GONNA BE ALRIGHT?" CHARLIE, MY PARTNER, ASKS FROM the driver's seat.

I shoot him a side-eye. "Do I have a choice?"

He scrunches his nose and shakes his head. "Not exactly."

I return my focus to the dismal alley, specifically the car three spaces ahead. "Then why ask?"

Drenched in rain, Jackson leans on the hood of a rental and stares up at the second-story terrace windows.

My gaze follows his to Aurora, who's sitting up in bed, bathed in the orange glow of the fireplace, lost in a monster romance novel—a gift I bought her to celebrate her modeling contract.

Her lips curve into a soft smile as she reads, and warmth blossoms in my chest.

She's finally keeping food down, and she's healthy enough for me to leave.

Just in time for her progress to be shattered by her ex.

"I'm your boyfriend. Your mental health is important to me."

I scoff. "Speaking of which, Aurora wanted me to apologize to you."

His brows furrow. "For what?"

I press my lips together to stifle my shit-eating grin. "For me seeing her naked."

Aquamarine eyes widen, and his mouth pops open on a gasp. "You bastard."

"She stripped in front of me. It was totally not my fault."

"Fuck you. I hate you."

"Blasphemy."

Jackson rises to his full height and strides toward the building, drawing us back to the task at hand.

"He's quite the stalker, isn't he? I'm surprised he hasn't figured you out."

A wave of dread washes over me, erasing my cheerful mood, the happiness in my heart replaced by a lead weight.

Charlie glances over, then quickly away. "You need to shut that shit down. *Now*. It can't happen, and you know it."

16

JACKSON

New York is fucking cold and miserable. I've never liked it here.

I pull down my baseball cap to conceal my face and gaze at Aurora through her bedroom window. If anyone notices me, I'm bound to be arrested for being a creepy stalker.

She's cozy in bed reading, a cute smile on her face, adorable and peaceful, and I'm about to blow it all to hell.

Seeing her has me fucked up, questioning if pursuing her is the right thing.

All the controlling shit I did to keep her—buying the house in Santa Monica, canceling her gigs, pissing off Emily—only hurt her.

And I'd do it again.

I'd spend every dime I had on her. She doesn't need to work, and she doesn't need to be around that vile influence. The only thing I did right was hire Ricky, and I regret it simply because I'm jealous.

This is who I am. It's inside me; it won't disappear when I walk through that apartment door.

Paralyzed with uncertainty, I stare at the daylight to my darkness, a thousand thoughts racing through my mind. My endgame is her, and I'll do whatever it takes. If that makes me selfish, so be it, but I *only* want Aurora.

And maybe Ethan.

For most of my life, I didn't think I was capable of love, but I undoubtedly love her and the baby.

Still, I'm toxic. Even sober, there's Kyle. He's a danger, but I can't walk away. It's too late.

When my mother died, I was old enough to understand Kyle's cruelty but too young to save her. They never married, but he used his position of authority to trap her. He'd threaten to take full custody of me if she ever left—or worse, kill us both.

She tried to protect me to the best of her ability. She put herself in front of me or pushed his buttons to redirect his focus.

Nothing compares to the helplessness of watching my mother get beaten—not even my own abuse. Alone with Kyle or his sick fucking friends, I learned to disassociate, but with her, I never could.

Around twelve, something within me snapped. All that fear and powerlessness turned to rage, and I refused to cower like the little bitch he thought I was.

I couldn't physically defeat him, but it didn't prevent me from trying.

When physical force failed, I made his life hell. I became his worst nightmare.

I rebelled at every prestigious private school he sent me to, engaging in drugs and violence. He received nonstop calls, and I received repeated suspensions and expulsions. I vandalized property and committed other crimes, getting arrested and making him the laughingstock of the police force. I stole his alcohol and pills, depleted his stash, got wasted. Eventually, addiction became my escape.

By fourteen, I needed to be locked in some facility, but my actions kept Kyle's attention on me and my mother relatively safe.

Everything changed one brutal night, when Kyle thought he'd teach me a lesson by sending me to jail, but it backfired. I showed up to juvie with cracked ribs, a split lip, a broken nose, and a gash in my brow, courtesy of my father, and people started asking questions.

A social worker was called to complete an assessment, and, feeling safe, I talked. Whatever transpired after scared Kyle enough to send me to boarding school in Canada.

Far away from my mother.

She ended her life during my first semester, before I could get back to her. Whether it was truly intentional doesn't matter. I'll never forgive myself. If I had kept my mouth shut, she might still be alive. I left her helpless against a monster, and I won't do that a second time.

I stand at Aurora's door, awash in déjà vu and Kyle's taunting words.

"I'll take her away, and you'll never see her again."

"I'll bury her. Is that what you want?"

"I'll kill her, and there's nothing you can do about it."

Words once aimed at my mother now threaten the only person besides her to ever love me.

The only other person I've ever loved.

With a deep breath, I gather my courage and knock on the plain white door.

No doorbell, no cameras, no security. Only a keypad.

The main entrance wasn't even locked.

I don't like it at all. The hallway and stairwell are too dark, the terrace easily accessible, and I could see Aurora's bedroom from the street, for fuck's sake.

So, when she opens without hesitation, I ask, "Did you check who it was?"

Her smile falls, and her eyes widen. "I should have."

She goes to shut the door in my face, but I wedge my boot in the opening and shoulder my way in. I slam it behind me, and she spins around, startled.

In leggings and a hoodie—*my hoodie*—she takes my breath away.

I urge myself to remain calm, but all rational thought vanishes with her in front of me. The pull to her is unlike anything I've ever felt. She's my other half, ripped from me, and my skin is torn raw without her.

She stands rigid, her eyes filled with fear. "Get out."

"I have something to tell you." My voice shakes, and my teeth rattle with nerves.

She crosses her arms over her chest and scoffs. "Spare me the details. I know enough."

I swallow hard, my throat thick with emotion. "It's not about the pictures."

Her expression changes to one of horror, a hand flying to her mouth while the other drops to her stomach. "Oh my God. Please don't tell me you have some STD."

I throw my hands in the air. "Jesus fucking Christ! For the millionth time, I did not cheat on you!" My temper skyrockets, and I find myself in her face. "I. Did. Not. Fuck. Anyone!"

Her chin quivers. She stares up at me, tears clinging to her eyelashes, and I see myself in her reflection, furious and towering over her.

A monster.

I drop to my knees and beg. "I'm sorry. I know I fucked up. I won't scream at you again."

Her jaw tightens, her words barely above a whisper. "Get out."

"Please." My eyes well with tears that blur my vision. "I swear to you, nothing happened."

"Get out, Jackson."

I blink the tears away. "Let me explain."

"GET! OUT!"

She has never yelled at me, and her agonizing cry slices through me, destroying what's left of my sanity.

"I'm. Not. Leaving." I rise to my feet but don't crowd her. "I didn't do it! Be mad. Yell at me. Hit me. I fucked up! But I did absolutely *nothing* with those girls."

"Hmm. Where have I heard that before?" She has lost all trust in me, but I can earn it back. I've done it once. I'll do it again. "Just leave, Jackson."

But that, I can't do. "Tell me what to do. I'll do anything." I dare to take a step closer. "I love you."

"You don't know what love is." Her voice is strained, and she struggles to speak more than a few words.

"That's not true." I place a hand on my aching chest. "I know I love you because it hurts so fucking much. I love you unconditionally—"

"Stop."

"You're taking a job in New York? I guess we're living in New York. You want to be with Ethan? Fine. I'll get a bigger house. You're having a baby? *We're* having a baby. You refuse to talk to me? I'll be here waiting, caring for you. The only thing I won't do is be without you."

With each word, I inch closer.

"Last time, you hurt me." She sucks in a shaky inhale. "But I saw it coming. This time, you blew my whole fucking world apart, ripped my heart right out of my chest. I can't even look at you without seeing those pictures, seeing what likely happened after."

Tears stream down her beautiful face, and it hurts to breathe, my heart shattering along with hers.

"Nothing happened. I can prove it to you." I reach out, in need of our connection.

She pulls away, hugging her arms tight to her body. "Don't touch me!"

"Let me hold you. Let me make this up to you, *please*. I'll do anything to fix this." I'd take her pain if I wasn't consumed with it already.

"No," she grits through her teeth. "You lost the right to touch me when you touched someone else. You'll never touch me again."

I shake my head. The idea of never being with her is a death sentence. "Don't say that."

"You'll never touch me again," she repeats with conviction.

I tug at my hair, my thoughts a jumble of madness. I can't stand how she glares at me, as if it's over, as if she's already made her mind up.

"You'll kill me, Aurora. Is that what you want? Because that's exactly what will happen."

17

RICKY

I'VE HEARD ENOUGH. RED CLOUDS MY VISION, AND I SNAP.

That immature, manipulative shit. How dare Jackson threaten Aurora with his life?

It'll work, too. She'll cave for fear he'll harm himself, and he might. He has in the past, and he's desperate, at the end of his rope.

Doesn't matter. I'll wring his fucking neck.

I whip off my headphones and throw them onto the dash while reaching for the handle.

"No. No. No. You can't—"

I slam the door on Charlie's words, and he follows me out of the vehicle, cursing. He catches up to my long strides as I approach the sidewalk across the alley.

He grabs the back of my shirt, breaking me from my murderous thoughts.

"Don't do it. Don't go barging in there. It's not worth it."

I spin around, shooting him a piercing glare. "Not worth it? When did we stop protecting people? This entire case was built on protecting women."

He drops his hands to his sides. "For that very reason, we need him. We can't take down Kyle without Jackson."

A contemptuous sound escapes my throat, and I shake my head in frustration.

"You know it's true. Think about it. If Jackson leaves, you don't have justification to be here. We're watching *him*, not her."

Fucking hell, I hate that he's right. Still… "He can stay, but he doesn't get to abuse her."

I resume my path through the building and up the stairs, taking them two at a time, Charlie grumbling in my wake.

At the door, he shuffles his feet and lowers his voice. "What are you going to do?"

He prefers to remain in the background, listening to surveillance, reviewing footage, tinkering with high-tech gadgets, and consuming copious amounts of caffeine. He's not someone who seeks the spotlight. Plus, he rambles when he's anxious.

"Introduce you and say I forgot something. Just stay quiet. Can you do that?"

Unfortunately for Charlie, he became my cover when Ethan grew suspicious of my affections for Aurora. It's a terrible lie, but when I was put on the spot, being gay stumbled out of my mouth.

Ethan is possessive. He doesn't mess around when it comes to what's *his*. He tries to hide it, but his emotions burst out of him when his temper flares, and I couldn't let his jealousy get me removed from Aurora.

Err, from the case. Whatever.

I was "hired" as Jackson's bodyguard during public events. I'd hoped the position would lead to more private functions involving his father, but Jackson seldom acknowledged my presence, and the opportunity never arose.

When he asked me to provide security for his pregnant girlfriend, I eagerly accepted, despite knowing nothing about protecting a supermodel. It was my chance to gain his trust and collect evidence.

Along the way, Aurora crawled under my skin. I never expected her to tick all my proverbial boxes, ones I hadn't even realized I had, such as caring for her. Who knew bringing food to someone you adored was so damn fulfilling? Not me, that's for fucking sure.

I remained dedicated to my responsibilities as a special agent until the moment I allowed Kyle into Jackson's penthouse. I anticipated overhearing their conversations or getting into Kyle's good graces—anything that strengthened our case.

But when he harmed Aurora, something in me broke, and my loyalties shifted.

Don't get me wrong, I'm fiercely devoted to seeing Kyle and his associates behind bars, but I won't allow anyone to hurt Aurora, including her *ex*-boyfriend.

Jackson's father is fortunate to be the focus of our investigation. If he wasn't, I would've done much worse than dislocate his shoulder. His day of reckoning is coming soon—if we can get Jackson to cooperate, that is.

Charlie chews his bottom lip, his gaze fixed on the stairs, as if he's planning to bolt. "This cover only goes so far. If you touch me *intimately,* I swear to God, I'll throat punch you."

I input the code into the keypad and resist the urge to roll my eyes. "That'll compromise the case we've worked on for four years. Besides, you're not my type," I whisper.

When we enter, they're standing in the living room, facing one another. Aurora is hugging herself, and Jackson is holding his hands in a gesture of prayer. Their heads turn, and it's hard to bury my emotions with the tears in her eyes or the way she gravitates toward me.

Trembling, she wraps her arms around my waist and, despite my impulse to carry her out of here, I only furrow my brows and ask, "What's going on?"

"Do you knock?" Jackson cuts in, not allowing her to speak.

I ignore him and cup her face in my hands. "You want him to leave?"

She shakes her head. "No. I'm fine."

"Don't lie to me."

Agitated, he shifts his weight from foot to foot. "I'm not leaving. You'll have to drag me out of here."

I lose all my patience. "That can be arranged."

Charlie squeaks behind me, and I tone it down a notch.

"She's sick, and you need to chill the fuck out. I'm taking her to bed. Go cool off on the terrace." Without another word, I guide Aurora into her bedroom and shut the door. "Climb up and lie down."

She tugs off her hoodie, settles under the covers, then stares up at me. "I'm sorry. I hate being this way." Her soft voice breaks, and I get to my knees next to the bed.

"What way?" I wipe away her tears with my knuckles.

Her lips quiver. "Weak. Needy."

"You are not weak." The corner of my mouth twitches, and I shrug. "Needy, maybe. You probably couldn't survive on your own. What would you eat?"

She slaps my arm playfully. "Coffee."

"See? It's true." I chuckle. "Do you even know where your phone is?"

"Umm..." She glances sideways. "Next to the bath—I think."

I find it on the floor, underneath a towel. "You're lucky you're cute," I say, handing it to her. "Do you want me to stay?"

She offers a gentle smile. "No, go enjoy your boyfriend."

I want to tell her I'll be right outside. All she has to do is call for me. "Text me. Are you sure you're alright?"

"I'm—" *Fine*. She cuts herself off. "Why wouldn't I be?"

Oh, I don't know. Maybe because your ex is a controlling asshole and his father is involved in human and drug trafficking? Or because you pour all your energy into others, leaving yourself drained?

"Because you missed me. Obviously."

On my way out, I hold myself back and only give Jackson one warning. "Whatever toxic shit you've got going on in your head—keep it there. If you're not here to care for her, let someone else."

He raises a taunting brow. "Like you?"

I exit before I strangle him or blow my cover.

18

JACKSON

Every time I fuck up, someone else enters the chat. First Ethan, now Ricky. He may have a boyfriend, but it's clear he's attached to Aurora, and she to him.

I stand in her hallway, staring at her closed bedroom door. She's right behind it yet worlds away.

My chest feels tight, an iron fist wrapped around my heart, crushing me. A tremor runs through my fingers, and I clench and unclench my hands. My stomach is a knot of dread, churning and twisting with panic.

She won't forgive me this time.

She's different.

A fiery haze of rage blurs my vision, though not against her.

Me. Kyle. My fucked-up life. The thought of living without her.

It's torture.

My phone buzzes in my pocket, and I absentmindedly lift it to my ear.

Silence hangs heavy before his gruff voice breaks through the blackness. "Take a breath."

Air fills my lungs, the act of breathing labored. "Let me guess: Ricky called you." My words come out raspy and broken, and I swallow the thick lump in my throat.

"Yup. Told me I better get a handle on my boy or he was tossing you over the balcony."

My feet carry me away from her door, my paranoia compelling me to check the apartment for him. "He can fucking try."

Ethan ignores my agitation. "What's she doing?"

"Resting or sleeping in her room." I release an audible exhale. "Without me."

"You're still there. She's pregnant and sick, and as much as she tries to hide it, she's heartbroken. Focus on what you can do. What does she need?"

"A security system. Anyone could break in here."

"That's ironic. Did you test that theory?"

Is semi-forced entry and non-compliance in leaving considered a break-in?

"Wasn't necessary. I practically walked in."

"Sure you did," he says sarcastically. "Go make yourself useful. If you haven't noticed, she doesn't mind being spoiled."

An unexpected chuckle vibrates in my chest. I created a monster. "You're welcome."

We hang up, and I wander through the apartment, allowing my chaotic thoughts to settle. It's an open space with tall, industrial windows overlooking the terrace. Modern and well-appointed, but cozy.

She has stacks of fashion magazines on the coffee table and racks of clothes in the front room. Her favorite pair of Converse is lined up next to the door, and her worn leather jacket hangs on a hook.

A bottle of prenatal vitamins sit on the counter, sonogram pictures pinned to a corkboard on the wall above. I remove the tacks from one and hold the paper to my chest, tears prickling my eyelids—fucking depression.

I can't miss this. I have to do better. I have to get control of myself.

Carefully, I slide the photo into my pocket, being sure not to crease it.

I check out the food situation. The fridge is stocked with prepared meals with sticky notes on them. I pick them up individually, reading what can only be Ricky's handwriting.

Breakfast. Don't forget your prenatal pill and one coffee!

Lunch. Drink a bottle of water. Take a nap.

Dinner. Another water. Text me if you need me. I'll be close.

Snack. Go to bed! Don't sleep on the couch.

This fucking guy. His "I'll be close" comment seems suspicious, especially since he walked in on Aurora and me arguing.

I send a picture to Ethan.

> Can I fire him?

COACH

No, that's his job.

"He's a little too good at his job," I grumble.

After I search her entire apartment, order groceries, and put them away, there's nothing else for me to do. The place is spotless; Aurora has never been messy.

I stare out the window, restless, at the bleak, rainy night. Does it ever stop snowing or raining in New York? Why would she want to stay here? She loves the ocean.

Is it work, or is she avoiding LA...and me?

That depressive thought leads me back to her door, and I quietly turn the knob.

Warmth fills her room, the fireplace casting dancing shadows on the white walls.

Snuggled in a blanket, she sleeps soundly, her arms wrapped around a fluffy pillow. Thick lashes rest on blotchy cheeks, her full, red lips slightly parted.

She's so fucking beautiful.

I slide my phone from my back pocket, snap a picture, and share it with Ethan.

COACH

As much as I appreciate pics of my girlfriend, please tell me you did not break into her room like a stalker!

Not your girlfriend. You're just the rebound guy.

I smirk, all too pleased with myself as I update his contact.

REBOUND

A high percentage of women marry the rebound guy.

Plopping down on the floor, I lean back against her bed.

Where'd you read that, Cosmo? And I'll kill you first.

REBOUND

Whatever magazine my future wife was featured in.

Doesn't matter. You'll die far sooner than I will, old man.

REBOUND

Not with all the shit you put in your body. Think about that next time.

There won't be a next time.

REBOUND

You're right, because I'll lock you in a shitty rehab and send you pictures of our wedding.

REBOUND

And honeymoon.

Fuck off.

Wait. What kind of honeymoon pics are we talking?

REBOUND

None of my dick, if that's what you're asking.

I stifle my laughter to keep from waking our girl.

> I wasn't! Jesus, Coach. Gross.

REBOUND

In all seriousness, she better be happy when you return her to me.

> Yes, Dad. 😊

19

AURORA

A SEDUCTIVE, MASCULINE COLOGNE, ONE I KNOW INTIMATELY, rouses me from sleep and releases a flurry of butterflies.

For a fleeting moment, I let my walls down. I squeeze my eyes shut and inhale deeply, allowing his scent to set my skin ablaze. Memories take me back to the night our worlds collided, the first time I breathed him in, thinking he smelled like sex in a bottle.

He was unlike anyone I'd ever met—a hurricane of chaotic energy and a whirlwind of unpredictable passion. The intense force that is Jackson O'Reilly utterly consumed me.

Tears well, and I let go of my illusions, facing the painful reality. It's impossible for me to have him this close. He'll break through all my defenses, and I can't keep allowing him to rip me apart.

I open my eyes, and I'm greeted by a heart-aching sight—beautiful, tragic, and mere inches away.

He sits on the floor, legs stretched out in front of him, leaning against the bed. His arms are crossed over his chest, his head turned toward mine, as if he drifted off to sleep while watching me.

With no one present to witness, I let my gaze trace his features. Sharp jawline from chewing gum or sucking on Jolly Ranchers or from running his mouth. Straight nose, despite breaking it at least once that I know of. Perfectly symmetrical full lips.

His only blemish—or endearment—is a scar that runs through the arch of his eyebrow, which I've kissed hundreds of times.

I sleepily gaze at him, my fingers itching to run through his tousled, sandy-blond hair. It's always this way. My body and heart ignore my mind and crave him.

Bright-green eyes stare back in amusement. "What are you doing, babe?"

I snap my eyelids shut and feign sleep. "Hmmm?"

A low, raspy laugh. "You were gawking."

Pretending to wake, I yawn. "I don't know what you're talking about."

He gives me that crooked smile and brushes my hair away from my face, tucking it behind my ear. "I love you."

That breaks the trance. I believe he's sincere—at least when he's sober. That's the worst part. He could love, want, and intend to be completely faithful to me—until he's intoxicated. The Jackson here with me might not be the Jackson I get tomorrow, the next day, or even two months from now.

"Do you?"

The smirk fades. He straightens and rolls his neck, stretching from the uncomfortable position he slept in. "When have I lied to you?"

I sit up and hug my pillow to my chest. "Seriously? Other than the obvious? Every day. Your actions contradict what your eyes and words convey. You look at me as if you love me, and you tell me you love me, then you do some stupid shit to ruin everything. So, which is the lie? Were you punishing me for leaving?"

His shoulders droop. "I wasn't punishing you. I was protecting you. My life is just fucked up."

"How is cheating on me—" The pictures, the idea of him with someone else, flood my mind, and my stomach rolls. I scoot toward the end of the bed and shove him aside. "Move."

I race to the bathroom, nearly tripping over his boots, and

drop to my knees, expelling what little I've eaten the last day, if anything.

He lifts my hair above my head and rubs my back. "Have you called the doctor?"

His touch gives me goosebumps. Even when sick, he affects me. "Morning sickness. Maybe a bug. I see her in a week," I manage between bouts of nausea.

He helps me to my feet, putting an arm around me. I feel his rapid breaths brushing my ear, his heart thumping against my shoulder.

"It's not morning; it's nine at night. Can you get in sooner?"

I pull out of his grasp. "Please, stop touching me." The more he does, the weaker my resistance.

In a dramatic gesture, he throws his hands up. "Why? You never had a problem with me touching you before."

I splash water on my face and rinse my mouth. After toweling off, I shoot him a glare. "That was before you touched someone else."

He rushes toward me, pointing a finger. "There's not a single photo of me touching anyone!" He slams his fist on the vanity. "Stop saying that."

Blowing out an exasperated sigh, I twist my hair into a bun. "I'm not doing this with you, Jackson. I'm not dissecting every picture. We never discussed being exclusive, and I don't want this."

"The fuck we didn't," he says with a tight jaw and balled fists. "And if the words weren't explicitly stated, they were strongly implied. This has never been casual. I didn't cheat on you. I *wouldn't* cheat on you."

I tilt my head. "What if the roles were reversed? What if I were pregnant with *your* baby, and it was Ethan getting drunk, high, and photographed with other women? Would you want that near your child?"

Rarely is Jackson speechless, but he stands before me, lips parted as I exit the bathroom.

On my way out of my room, I snag my hoodie and throw it on. This old building uses radiators and fireplaces; there's no central air. It takes time for the fireplace to heat the open space, and I don't like the smell of the radiator.

I chose a prepared meal from the fridge, only to have Jackson snatch it away.

"Sit. I ordered groceries. At least let me take care of you."

He sets down packages of cheese, fruits, and vegetables on the white granite island, and I perch on a barstool, facing him. In faded denim and a rumpled T-shirt, he moves with quiet efficiency. He's always loved to cook, and it reminds me of old times.

A mask of grim concentration settles on his face, and he drops the knife on the cutting board, abandoning my favorite cheese.

He places his palms on the island and glowers at me. "That's not a valid argument. Ethan wouldn't be in the picture if you were pregnant by me." He picks up the blade, slaughtering my poor pepper jack with far too much aggression. "I'd murder anyone who came between us," he says under his breath.

I make a mental note not to discuss other men while Jackson wields a knife.

He places sliced cheese on a plate, and I pop a piece in my mouth.

When I think the conversation is over, he peers up with glassy eyes. "You'd have nothing to worry about. I'd never leave your side. We'd be staying wherever you wanted until I got my trust fund and we bought a house. I'd play out my contract and be done."

He's given this some honest thought.

"That's...a lot to unpack." I mull everything over while picking at the food. "You'd quit playing?"

"If you wouldn't travel with me," he says with certainty. "I won't leave you to care for an infant alone, and I can't picture myself only seeing my child a few months out of the year. I'd go nuts."

Perhaps it's selfish of me, but I can't help but think—how ironic?

"You'd give up hockey for a baby but won't give up partying for our relationship? You realize you require one before the other?"

"I gave up partying before the season."

I scoff. "A dozen photos say differently."

"Are you ready for me to explain?"

I hesitate. "As ready as I'll ever be."

Jackson comes around the island, sits on the barstool beside me, and hands me his phone. "These are texts I received from Kyle after I relapsed."

I read through them, not fully understanding. I expected Kyle to be involved; he always is, but not until they discuss the baby do I begin to grasp the gravity of the situation.

> You manipulated me into meeting with you, knowing I'd relapse. Threw some drugs and half-naked women at me and took pictures to fuck my career and relationship, all to avoid me paying child support?

"Kyle took the pictures of you?" I ask, astonished.

Jax nods. "And sold them."

My head spins. I place the phone on the counter and my palm to my queasy stomach. "But I'm not seeking child support. Nor would I, especially from you."

"I know, but he isn't aware of that." He covers my hand with his and cradles my baby bump. "Remember the plan to portray me as the father?"

Icy dread freezes the air in my lungs. "We can get a paternity test. I'll stay in New York. I don't want your money."

He cups my face in his hands. "You don't need to convince

me. I'd happily give you and the baby everything you ever wanted."

Given Jackson's thoughts on quitting hockey, he'd spoil a child with more than money...*completely disregarding Kyle.*

The pieces come together, making sense of the madness. Jackson will have a family that won't include his father, because that abusive asshole is never coming near me or my baby. That day at the penthouse, Kyle witnessed his biggest fears becoming reality—Jax getting sober, choosing me, creating a life outside of him and drugs.

My eyes brim with tears. "How did he manipulate you?" I ask, referring to the text.

He pushes his fingers through his hair and draws a deep breath. "When my mother died, I inherited all her wealth."

I furrow my brows, my brain having trouble connecting the dots. "Okay...?"

He lowers his gaze and takes my hand, rubbing circles over my knuckles with his thumb. "Because of my mental health and addiction, Kyle controls my inheritance. I used it to purchase the house in Santa Monica. I've never accessed the funds before and didn't think it'd be a big deal."

Exasperated, I cock my head. "You already bought the house?"

"Yes," he waves me off, "but wait before you get pissed at me. It gets worse."

What could possibly be worse than the situation we're in?

"Kyle threatened to contest the purchase unless I met with him. He wanted to party in Vegas. I refused but arranged it for him. When I tried to blow him off that night, he said he'd ruin you, me, and Ethan. He claimed he had pictures. In hindsight, I should've told you both. I shouldn't have gone, but it was late, and I didn't want to burden either of you with my problems."

"Pictures?" My throat tightens, and I struggle to articulate the word.

He brings my trembling fingers to his lips, his gaze filled with regret. "Kyle had photos of you and Ethan kissing in a diner downtown."

Breakfast before we went to Santa Monica. We were swept up in the moment and careless.

The tremor in my hands works its way through my body. "Did you tell Ethan?"

"Yes. He's only mad I failed to call him and played into Kyle's games."

"You may not have wanted to burden us—which is bullshit, since we were supposed to be in a relationship—but you also didn't want us to find out about the house." Hot tears spill down my cheeks, a salty burn against my heated skin. "Kyle took pictures of Ethan and me, and it didn't cross your mind he'd do the same to you? Fuck, Jackson."

Defeated, he rests his elbows on the island, drops his head into his palms, and scrubs his eyes. "You're right. I fucked up about the house, but I wasn't thinking straight that night in Vegas. My memory is spotty, and I had no intention of drinking or using ever again."

He leans back and empties his pockets on the counter— wallet, keys, cash, Jolly Ranchers, sonogram pic—and hands me a crumpled piece of paper.

I unfold what appears to be lab results, but, unfamiliar with the medical jargon, I glance at him in question.

"I tested positive for GHB, the date-rape drug."

The words on the page run together, and the world around me teeters.

"He wanted to end our relationship, make it appear as if I was incapable of handling my trust, get me in trouble with the league—maybe even send me back to the hospital—forcing me to depend on him."

I stand on unsteady legs, both physically and emotionally drained. I spent my days hating Jax for relapsing and hating myself for leaving. I couldn't eat, couldn't sleep—I was destroyed.

Then, there's the nightmare he endured.

For what? Because Kyle opposes me and won't let Jax go?

His arm comes around my waist and draws me between his knees. "Where are you going?"

A choked sob escapes me. "You should find someone your father approves of. Your life would be a lot easier."

His expression hardens. He glares at me through glassy, bloodshot eyes. "I don't give a fuck about Kyle. I hope he drops fucking dead. I want a life with *you*, no matter what it takes. I'm not leaving, and I won't let him separate us."

21

JACKSON

AURORA HEADS TO BED, TELLING ME SHE NEEDS *SPACE*. THAT TERM isn't part of my vocabulary, but since she hasn't kicked me out, I let her go.

I focus on what I can do for her.

It's late evening in LA, and I text Ethan with an update.

> She's still throwing up and barely eats.

REBOUND

> Bring her home.

My initial thought is: Home is wherever she is, but that's not accurate.

Home is where the three of us can be together and explore this situationship, a place where she and our child are safe and Kyle doesn't exist.

For now, that'll have to be frigid New York with fucking Ricky, not Ethan.

I listen to Aurora move around her room while I clean the kitchen, racking my brain on how to fix the distance between us. Since I'm sleeping on the couch, I search for the thermostat to take the chill out of the air but don't find one.

Her bedroom light is on, and I figure not having heat is a solid reason to interrupt her space.

Despite myself, I respect her privacy and knock.

She answers the door in an oversized team T-shirt, *Coach* printed on the breast. What a possessive asshole. I need to step up my game.

Her nipples peek through the fabric, and with great effort, I look away. I'm already in enough trouble.

"Hey...where's the thermostat?"

"There isn't one. There are knobs on the radiators, but please don't turn them on. They smell." She crinkles her nose.

"The what now?" I ask with lowered brows, clueless how the fuck a radiator works in a house.

Her face brightens, and she giggles, the sound warming my heart. Maybe I'll survive in New York after all.

She steps back and points to the wall. "This here, rich boy, is a radiator."

I enter her bedroom and stare at the painted metal contraption. "In my defense, I've seen this before, from afar, probably in a museum, but I didn't know they still existed in the wild."

Her laughter fills the air, and I breathe it in, allowing its energy to flow through my veins and bring me back to life.

I slide my phone from my pocket and sit on her bed. "Let's ask the old man. He lived here, right?"

With an excited grin, she climbs behind me and wraps her arms around my neck. "FaceTime him."

Jesus, fuck. I would've dragged him here if I knew he was the key to getting Aurora to touch me again.

He answers with his typical scowl, but as soon as he sees her, his expression softens. "Hey, baby girl." His gaze runs over her, ignoring me. "You wearing my shirt?"

Bringing the collar to her nose, she inhales deeply. "It doesn't smell like you anymore."

His lips tug into a rare smile. "Come home, and I'll give you as many as you want."

My eyeballs might roll right out of my head. "God, I hate you."

It can't be true, because with them flirting, Aurora's tits

pressed against my back, and her mouth an inch from my ear, I'm getting hard.

I adjust my pants, and he smirks with a devilish glint in his eyes.

"Did you call to show off my girlfriend?" he asks.

"No, I require your ancient knowledge." I briefly switch the camera view to the radiator. "She says this smells when she turns it on."

He bites his lips and raises his brows. "You think just because I'm thirty-five and grew up in the city, I know how to use a radiator?"

I stare blankly. "Yes...?"

He chuckles and shakes his head. "You two are fucking twins." Then, he sobers and sighs. "Don't turn it on. Looks like you got the landlord special. It could be burning off dust or mold."

Aurora and I share an expression of sheer horror.

"Is the fireplace gas or electric?" he asks. When we fail to answer, his thumbs move across the screen. "I'll text Ricky to check if the apartment has working carbon monoxide detectors. If not, and that's the reason you're sick..." His nostrils flare. "Whoever owns the place better say their fucking prayers."

"Ricky is a medic; he'd know if the gas was making me sick," Aurora states confidently.

"Of course he is," I mutter. I must be delusional, because I'm certain her arms tighten around me.

We hang up with Ethan, and she moves away, creating an emptiness inside me.

The silence is thick with unspoken emotions, and I swallow the painful lump in my throat. "Can I stay with you? Or is that pushing it? I promise not to do anything."

She holds my gaze, her anguish mirroring mine. "I have a lot to think about."

"What's there to think about? I love you, and you love me. Did you not read the part of Kyle's text where I *didn't* sleep with anyone?"

Torn by indecision, she twists the hem of her shirt. It takes a special person to love someone as fucked up as me, and I know she won't refuse me—not when I'm this close, not if I grovel hard enough.

"I want you so fucking bad." My voice is strained, and my vision blurs with tears and pain, my head throbbing from holding it all in. "I'll get on my knees and beg. Please, Aurora."

She crosses her arms under her chest, highlighting what I'm already struggling not to stare at. "Will you leave if I say no?"

"Probably not. I'll sleep on the floor."

"Then why did you even ask?" A hint of a smile dances on her lips. "Switch off the lights."

I hit the light and watch with longing as she pulls back the covers and crawls underneath.

She furrows her brows. "Shut the door."

"Does that mean I get to sleep with you?"

"Are you waiting for a formal invitation? Would you rather sleep on the couch?" Again with the banter.

I scramble to close the door, undress to my boxers, and climb into the king-size bed beside her, leaving little room between us. Her scent lingers on the pillows, and I can't fight back the heartbreak.

A week without her was a slow death. Now she's next to me, but I'm not allowed to hold her. It's fucking torture.

The headache worsens, and I throw my arm over my eyes. I haven't slept in a day. My body is exhausted, as if I played the longest, most brutal game of my life, and tears run down my temples.

Her fingers weave through my hair, and relief washes over me. She's my drug and my cure. Her touch calms me, and the chaos in my mind fades.

"What do you need?" Her voice is far gentler than I deserve.

"This." Then, my shit emotions have me adding, "Even if we're only friends, I can live with that. I just can't live without you."

The lie tastes bittersweet on my tongue. Yeah, I'll take being friends over her shutting me out, but I'd fight like hell for more.

I can't bear the thought of sitting on the sidelines, watching her and Ethan build the family I fucking want.

"We'll never be friends." She exhales deeply. "You know that. I refuse to live with the drugs and alcohol, and everything that goes along with it. I care about you, but my child deserves better." Her voice breaks. "*I* deserve better."

22

AURORA

It's quiet—far too quiet. It's the type of silence that equates to loud minds, and in the darkness, I find it easier to let my guard down, to reach across the void between us.

Jackson lies rigid on his back, his arm shielding his eyes. I lie on my side, facing him, and run my fingers through his soft hair. The weight of his pain is palpable, and the compulsion to care for him, to ease his torment, is visceral, a primal urge etched into my very being.

"Can we start over?" he asks, his voice gravelly. "Can I show you, before the baby comes, that I'll stay clean? I'll keep away from Kyle. I'll live with you in New York and won't leave your side."

If only life were that easy.

"That's not realistic. You have hockey, and every time one of us travels, I'm going to worry you're getting high and screwing around with someone else."

He throws his arm back and hits the plush headboard. "Stop fucking saying that. That isn't who I am. Besides, I've been suspended, pending league investigation." He rolls toward me, glides his hand up my neck and into my hair. "*Please*, Aurora. You are my best friend. I can't see a future without you. Give me one more chance."

His skin burns hot against mine, and I melt into his touch.

What's wrong with me? I should be running in the other direction, demanding he leave. He won't, but, still...I shouldn't want this.

"Are you keeping anything from me? If we were to start over, is there anything I'd find out?"

He hesitates, and my stomach sours.

"Maybe."

"Jackson..." I say in warning.

With a reluctant sigh, he places his forehead on mine. "That night, at Kyle's party, when I saw you with another guy and threw a bottle at him, it wasn't only because I was wasted and jealous. It was because the men around Kyle are sick; they're dangerous. I was pissed—at Emily, at me, at fucking life. I could've killed someone. I nearly did, and my reaction put you on Kyle's radar. He had something more to control me with..." He shakes his head, as if clearing the memory of one of the most horrible nights of my existence. "None of that matters. It's his fucked-up society I refuse to be a part of, and I need you to understand it's safer if you don't know."

~

Ricky

MY PARTNER and I exchange a glance as we listen to Jackson's confession.

"So you won't tell me?" Aurora's tone is heavy with disappointment, and it pulls on my heartstrings. We're all lying to her.

"You don't need to be tainted by this shit. Believe me, it's not knowledge you want to live with."

I can't blame him there. I also wish she wasn't a part of this. She's too innocent, too naïve.

Aurora and Jackson fall silent, and we remove our headphones.

"So he knows...which we figured. How could he not?" Charlie chews on his lip and stares out the windshield.

I nod in agreement. "But he's not involved."

Charlie's gaze snaps to mine, and he raises a finger, indicating he's about to spew a lesson. "Oh, Jackson is involved, whether he wants to be or not. How is organized crime identified, tracked, and ultimately dismantled? The money trail. Not only is Kyle using Jackson's fortune to bankroll his extravagant lifestyle, but he's also likely money laundering. A police commissioner's salary alone isn't enough to afford multiple properties, a yacht, a jet, and endless vacations—not when he failed to marry into wealth and politics. Is it financed with corruption or his son's assets?" Excitement brightens his expression. "So Jackson can run to New York, but..."

"His father will never let him go," I finish.

"Correct. Stick to Jackson like glue. Become his best friend." He waggles his brows. "Or Aurora's."

"We're already good friends." Because she believes I'm her gay bodyguard. Wait until she finds out I'm very much *not* gay, have seen her naked, *and* I'm investigating her boyfriend—not precisely him, but close enough—she'll never forgive me. "And Ethan is his."

I rub my sore eyes and reflect on everything we heard tonight. Something doesn't sit right. A knot of anxiety twists in my gut, and fragmented thoughts linger just out of reach.

"You think Kyle is actually worried about child support?" I ask.

He shrugs and presses his lips together. "It's money he thinks he's losing."

"But to ruin his son's entire career over a percentage of his paycheck? That seems extreme."

"Jackson said Kyle wanted to maintain the trust by depicting him as mentally unstable." He drums his fingers on the steering wheel. "Still, he could've done that without jeopardizing Jackson's substantial income. He's losing more money in the long run."

"Exactly." The puzzle pieces come together, and my exhaustion fades into eagerness. "A few things are clear—Kyle wants

Aurora and the baby out of the picture, and he wants to retain control of the trust."

Charlie gasps, and his eyes widen comically. "I bet if Jackson gets married or has a kid, he'll gain access to his inheritance... Although Kyle's primary focus seems to be the baby."

"It won't happen, but say Aurora goes to court for child support..."

My partner grins, and he rubs his palms together. "They'll dig into Jackson's financial records."

"Bingo. Kyle risks losing his capital while also being exposed for mismanaging his son's funds."

"At the very least." Charlie slaps the dashboard in victory. "Fuck yeah! What'd I tell you? The money trail!" He grabs his phone from the cup holder. "I'm on it."

My gaze wanders to her bedroom. "The gas isn't making her sick," I voice my thoughts. "It's either a cold from being out with Ethan or the pregnancy."

"If it were possible to get someone pregnant twice, that big fucker could do it. Jesus, that man can fuuu— Ow!"

"Shut your trap and work."

He massages his bicep, where I landed a solid punch. "What the hell was that for?"

I shoot him a piercing glare, not an ounce of fatigue in me after remembering their fuckfest. "This is an undercover mission, not porn."

"It's not pornography! We're unable to see anything. It's ASMR, and you're just jealous. Go get laid, you oversized bear. Stop thinking with your dick. They should've put me on Aurora. I, for one, don't find her attractive. She's needy and pouty." He puckers his bottom lip in mocking. "Great to look at, but damn, she can't even walk the street without having a panic attack."

His tirade is so over-the-top, I burst into laughter. "Oversized bear? Really? Is that the best you could come up with? This is New York City. Any woman would be scared to walk the street. Plus, she's sensitive to sound, something I'd expect you to empathize with."

"Whatever." He rolls his eyes and returns to his phone. "She plays on your hero complex, and you love it. You'd pick her up and carry her around like a fucking child if you could."

"You need to stop listening while I'm in there." I reach behind the seat, grab two waters, and hand him one. "Maybe it's you who needs to get laid."

"Anyhow," he drawls. "Don't let Daddy Dom move them to a new apartment—I'm tired of installing mics—and seriously," he stares at me intently, "since protecting women and children *is* our job, that baby is Kyle's biggest threat. He doesn't know it's not Jackson's, and he thinks it'll cost him everything, maybe even a prison sentence. It's concerning he'd go to such lengths to keep anyone from his son's trust and financial records."

23

JACKSON

Before I even open my eyes, I'm assaulted by the sounds of the city and the same unnatural glow we fell asleep to.

"Fucking New York," I groan and pull the pillow over my face.

No sun to warm your soul and no ocean to get lost in. Who could possibly enjoy this shithole?

Despite the unrelenting lights and the constant noise, I slept—actually slept—without nightmares or waking in panic. My head no longer throbs in pain, and I no longer have the urge to tear the skin from my bones.

Just lingering depression, but that bitch never leaves. Her claws are embedded deep, poised to drag me back into a dark abyss at any moment.

I sense Aurora's absence. The space beside me is cold; if she were here, she'd be curled up next to me, head on my shoulder, leg between mine.

I can't remember if we fell asleep that way, or if she gravitated to me during the night, but I vividly recall the weight of her body upon me, her fingers in my hair.

That's how she is. When she loves, she loves with every fiber of her being.

Whenever we argued, I'd still find her on my chest in the

morning. If I hadn't abandoned her at the height of my addiction, she would've never left, never achieved her dreams.

A part of me understood that pushing her away was necessary to overcome our codependency. But for me, breaking free from her wasn't possible then, and it's not possible now. I was dead inside the entire time we were separated, and I refuse to go back.

I redirect my thoughts to what Aurora needs. Is she sick? I don't hear her in the bathroom.

She's probably eating one of Ricky's damn prepared meals.

I leap out of bed and dash toward the door, eager to slap the food right out of her hand.

The moment I exit the bedroom, seductive music fills the air, emanating from the living area.

Okay, I can get down with this.

I envision cooking Aurora breakfast, wrapping my arms around her from behind as she eats, caressing her tiny baby bump, inhaling her sweet vanilla scent—

My feet come to an abrupt halt.

Her back is against the brick wall, her neck arched, and her mouth open in pleasure, as if someone were on their knees, their face buried between her thighs.

She's doing a photo shoot. In the living room. In lingerie.

What a fucking way to wake up.

I only wish I had my phone to send Ethan a pic.

Captivated, I watch the photographer move in, focused entirely too much on her full tits. She tilts her head, bites her bottom lip, and gazes at the camera with hooded, lusty eyes.

God. Damn. I need to buy every photo. No one else should see her in black lace, looking like an orgasm personified.

"Wow. I guess now, we know why she keeps you around." That voice, nails on a chalkboard, shifts to Aurora. "I hope you had him tested before you jumped back into bed with him."

Cue record scratch. My worst nightmare is here—the wicked witch of the west.

Emily's thirsty gaze traces the contours of my nearly-naked

body. My excitement dies along with my morning wood, and my hands shoot to cover myself.

Cheeks flushed, Aurora narrows her eyes at my diminishing erection, then at her ex-best friend. "Emily—" she starts.

"Fuck you," I snap, unwilling to let Aurora bear the weight of my mistakes.

Emily's face lights up; she's delighted to push my buttons or have my attention, not sure which. "No thanks. *I* have standards."

That makes me scoff. "Really? You've fucked half the hockey team. What are your standards? A jersey and a padded bank account?"

"A clean dick," she taunts me with a smug smile.

I step forward, not giving a damn about my undressed state or the photographer gawking, only about defending my relationship. "I haven't been with anyone except Aurora in over five years, so get off my *clean* dick."

Emily rolls her eyes. "Yeah, okay, Jackson. Save your breath. *I'm* not stupid."

I don't miss her low jabs at Aurora, and it's the last thing I'll tolerate. She can talk shit about me all she wants, but not my girl. I come at her, finger pointed. "That's the second time—"

"Get out!" Aurora's exasperated tone cuts through the air like a sharp blade.

My heart skips with fear and regret. I should've shut my mouth and walked away. I'm the one who convinced Emily to return—and when I say convinced, I mean paid—and here I am, fucking it all up again.

I face Aurora, ready to fall to my knees and beg for her forgiveness, but for once, it's not me.

She glares at her assistant with outright murder in her eyes. "Leave."

A mocking cackle, sharp and brittle, escapes Emily's lips. "Are you serious?"

"This is my place. I'll have whoever I want here. I'll *fuck* whoever I want. It's none of your business. You've dropped off the collection, and now, you can go." At that, she turns her back and grabs a black satin robe.

Damn, Aurora is fucking hot when she's angry at someone else.

Emily stands stunned, mouth hanging open—that makes two of us—before she shakes her head, gathers her belongings, and walks out.

"Jackson!"

Fury dances in Aurora's eyes, and my dick twitches.

"Yes, babe."

"Put some clothes on."

"Come here." Before she can refuse me, I draw her into my chest. "Good morning. You're fucking hot when you're jealous. Have you eaten?"

She shoves my shoulder. "You're impossible."

"And you're irresistible." I lower my voice for only her to hear. "Can I pin you up against the brick like that and eat your sweet little cunt?"

"Jax! Go get dressed." The tension has left her body, her voice playful and pleading.

"Kiss me, and I'll go get dressed before you murder someone."

She rises on her toes, gives me a quick peck, and pulls away. "Clothes. Now."

I spin around and head directly to the bedroom, my hands shielding what's only hers.

24

AURORA

ETHAN AND I DON'T TALK MUCH, JUST A FEW DAILY TEXTS AND A call here and there. It feels odd compared to Jackson, who constantly needs attention, but I tell myself he's busy, making his first season remarkable and dealing with Jax's public relapse.

So I'm surprised when my phone buzzes with a FaceTime request in the middle of the afternoon when I'm about to nap on the couch.

"Hey, baby!" Ethan's face transforms into a grin that lights up his spectacular gray eyes.

He's wearing a tie, beard neatly trimmed, and behind him is a whiteboard of hockey jargon, once again reminding me of his dedication.

"Hey, yourself. This is rare. To what do I owe the pleasure?"

"The pleasure is all mine, but I, ah, unfortunately need my overpaid captain, and the pain in the ass is not answering my calls."

"You didn't even call to talk to *me*?" I pout and feign outrage. "And here I was, missing you."

"Yes, I did, you little brat." He traces his thumb along his bottom lip, the corners of his mouth betraying a pleased smile. "But this is kind of urgent."

I roll my eyes—only because I know it irritates him—and yell into the kitchen, "Jax! Your boyfriend is on the phone!"

Ethan grumbles something about me *regretting my attitude* as Jackson saunters into the living room, wearing loose basketball shorts and a T-shirt. He returned his rental car this morning and brought his bags in while I worked. I should've locked him out, but honestly, I'm sick of being miserable.

Fucking Jackson and my damn bleeding heart.

I peer up at the man in question. "Coach wants to talk to you. He's on FaceTime."

He sits next to me and greets Ethan with, "Hey, fucker."

Then, to my utter astonishment, he effortlessly lifts me onto his lap, wraps an arm around me, and takes the phone.

It shouldn't surprise me that Jackson has resumed our relationship as if nothing occurred, caressing my baby bump and planting gentle kisses on my neck while I struggle to keep my walls up.

"I got some bad news." Ethan rakes his fingers through his thick, wavy hair. "The league made their decision. Twenty. Games."

"Holy fuck. What happened to four games for first-time offenders?"

Ethan gives him a pointed stare. "You know very well this isn't your first offense."

Jax waves him off. "First *official* offense. The board knows no different."

"They do. People talk, and you don't have..." Ethan trails off.

"The protection of my father?" Jackson finishes with an arched brow.

"Or," I cut in, "Kyle is in their ear, and he's pressing you."

Clenching and unclenching his jaw, Jax nods in contemplation. "Twenty games is a killer for the team."

"Kyle did tell me to enjoy my last season." Ethan rolls his lips. "A disastrous first year is sure to put me on the chopping block."

The three of us fall silent, and I hang my head. If this suspension hurts the team and Ethan, Jackson will break. He'll give in to Kyle and return to LA, promising things won't change between us, then grow cold. It happens every time. Kyle always finds a way to get what he wants.

Waves of nausea churn my stomach. My cheeks warm, and my eyes well up.

I twirl the frayed edge of my sweatshirt and focus on taking deep, slow breaths. Collecting myself, I swallow the lump in my throat and blink away the tears. My gaze lands on Jackson's hand cradling my abdomen, fixating on the tattoo on his ring finger.

Daylight.

I trace the words, the ink still raised and fresh.

Rough stubble grazes my cheek before the raspy sound of his voice fills my ear.

"I love you. I love you. I love you," he repeats until I glance up, his brilliant green eyes mirroring my torment. "You're my daylight. Always. I'll fix this."

Yeah, that's precisely what I'm worried about, but before I can express my concerns, he turns to Ethan. "You want me to negotiate with Kyle? Get him to talk to the board?"

Ethan recoils. "Fuck, no. I have a plan. I'm appealing, meeting with the president, and even if he won't reduce your suspension, I can coach." He smirks, full of confidence that borders on arrogance.

I can't stop the chuckle that bubbles up. "You definitely have a knack for being assertive and achieving your goals."

That smug smile spreads into a knowing grin. "I always get what I want. Remember that."

They discuss the appeal and other hockey nonsense, and I rest against Jackson's chest, my eyelids growing heavy, this baby urging me for a nap.

Jax clears his throat, jolting me from my sleepy state. "Since we're all together, I'd like to chat about the bodyguard. I propose we get rid of him. He's not needed while I'm here, and I'll be here a while."

The lighthearted mood crumbles, and I turn sharply to face

him. "Where the hell is this coming from?" I shake my head. "No."

Green eyes narrow, full of baseless suspicion. "Why?"

"You've been here for a whole five minutes. I'm not tossing my friend aside because you've returned."

Ricky was here for me when no one else was, and call me crazy, but I don't trust Jax yet, not while Kyle is putting pressure on him.

"You tossed Emily out without a problem."

"When my bodyguard stares at your dick, then we'll talk."

"Aurora, watch the attitude," Ethan interrupts.

I glare at him. "No." I can't explain why I'm being so resistant—maybe I'm overtired—but giving Ricky up is out of the question. "He's not waltzing back into my life and telling me to get rid of people."

Jackson chokes, his eyes widening. "The fact that you're so defensive and attached to him is reason enough."

His voice is raised, and he's doing this in front of Ethan for a reason, hoping to gain support by playing on Ethan's strict side —and it's working.

"He's got a point, Aurora," Ethan agrees. "Listen for once."

My temper flares. Listen? My whole life, I've listened and minded others.

"Says the man whose wife called while we were in bed together. Don't lecture me on other people until you block her from your phone."

"She's not my wife." His words are clipped and sharp, his tone a low growl. "And don't forget what happens when you run that smart mouth, baby girl."

Done with this conversation, I break free from Jackson's hold.

"Where are you going?" he asks with an offended scowl.

"To take a nap," I say over my shoulder. "This is leading nowhere. I worked this morning, and *you two* are not telling me to fire *my* bodyguard."

25

RICKY

MY BODYGUARD. FUCK. AURORA HAS NO IDEA WHAT THOSE WORDS do to me.

Charlie gnaws on his lip. "He's perceptive."

"No, he's insecure and threatened," I correct, a grin still plastered on my face from her refusing to let me go. "He never wanted her to have friends."

Friends would convince her to leave. I would if it wasn't for this case.

"Try to be nice to him." Charlie raises his hands in a placating gesture. "You can do that, right? Otherwise, we'll have to fabricate a scenario requiring your protection. Then, Daddy Dom Ethan will move them, and I'll have to install mics again. Not to mention, command is breathing down our necks."

I shake my head at his anxious ramblings while we ride the elevator to Aurora's apartment. "Kyle's threats are a reason for me to be here."

"But they don't know we know, you know?"

His nervous energy is palpable, and I grab hold of his shoulder.

"Take a breath. Your words are jumbling. Your only task is to sit there and look pretty."

"I'm not pretty. I'm the opposite of pretty. Aurora and

Jackson are pretty. They're probably two of the prettiest people I've ever seen."

Charlie was burned in a bombing while we were deployed overseas. His scars are hidden, but it's something he's self-conscious of.

"That's not true." The elevator pings, and in jest, I say under my breath, "Get your shit together, or we are *so* breaking up."

Unlike the stairs leading to the back hall, the elevator opens into a brick foyer, overflowing with designer clothes and shoes. I take a deep inhale of Aurora's vanilla-and-jasmine scent, and my shoulders relax instantly. It's bewitching.

"Jesus. Who needs this much clothing?"

Charlie hovers behind me. I think he finds comfort in being concealed from society as a special agent, locked in the van with his computer tech, watching and listening. I'm certain he only talks to civilians when he goes for coffee—that's if he can't get it delivered.

"She's a model, remember?"

I hang my jacket next to Aurora's. She's clean and tidy. It's one thing we have in common, perhaps our only similarity. Where I'm hard, she's soft. I'm stoic, and she's bubbly. I'm standoffish, and she's affectionate.

I remove my boots and set them under the wooden bench, and Charlie meanders to the clothing, touching the more delicate items. He's a starved kid in a candy store, and judging by his wide-eyed gaze at the lingerie, he might be a virgin.

He holds up a pair of red lace thongs. "Do you get to see her in these?" he whisper-yells.

My face flushes, and my body breaks out in a nervous sweat. "Put those fucking down," I grit through my teeth. "I will rag-doll your skinny neck."

He snickers, drops the underwear, and toes off his shoes. "Maybe she'll model something for us. How did you get her naked, exactly?"

If it wasn't for the smirk he's failing to hold in, I'd kidney punch him right here and now. I need no reminder of Aurora naked, water glistening off her body... Jesus.

She believes I held that towel open for her when, in reality, it was a strategic placement. Even pregnant, she's a knockout. That, or she unlocked another new kink.

"Do you wanna be beaten by an unhinged hockey player? I won't stop him."

"I love getting you riled up." His chest shakes with silent laughter. "Your face is the color of those sexy-as-fuck underwear."

God help me through this night.

The living room resonates with the sounds of a televised game, Jackson watching from the couch while playing on his phone.

"Hey, man." I lift my chin. "Jackson, this is Charlie." I motion between them. "Charlie, Jackson."

My partner steps forward and raises his hand in a stiff wave. "Hi," he squeaks. "I know who you are. I mean…I don't *know* you. I saw you here the other night and on TV…" He catches himself babbling and lowers his arm to his side. "You look different in person, though."

Jackson's skeptical gaze bounces between us. "Yeah, the skates and equipment make me appear bigger." His lips curl into a tentative smile. "Sorry to disappoint."

"No!" Charlie slaps his chest dramatically. "I'm not disappointed! You're huge. Not as huge as Ricky, which I like, you know, because he's my—"

I fist the back of his shirt and force him into the armchair, shutting him up before this gets any more awkward. "Ignore him. He's starstruck." I glance around the open space. "Where's Aurora? Is she still sick?"

"Taking a nap. She worked this morning."

He returns his attention to the hockey game, dismissing me. His indifference sets me on edge.

I head to the kitchen. "Has she been eating? Drinking enough water?" I call out over my shoulder.

She's a picky eater and forgetful, too focused on securing a future for herself and the baby. I'm usually the one who makes sure she eats, and after counting the prepared meals, it's clear she's been skipping some.

Jackson doesn't answer. I slam the fridge and march back into the living room. "Hey, has she been eating?"

Crossing his arms over his chest, he breaks away from the flatscreen. "Yeah, why?"

I'm getting the hunch he dislikes me, which is strange, since he gets along with Ethan, who you'd think was the greater threat. Besides their previous relationship, though, I've spent more time with Aurora than either of them.

"You've seen her eat three times a day? There are extra meals."

He narrows his eyes. "I can feed my girlfriend, dude."

His flippant attitude grates on my last fucking nerve. He wasn't with her every time she fell apart over him, wasn't the one to pick up the broken pieces, and wasn't the one encouraging her to get out of bed and put food in her system.

Yet, here he is, taking up space and oxygen.

"Are you sure, *dude*? Because you haven't cared for her in... ever."

That was harsh, but I'm feeling some sort of way between being separated from Aurora and the meal situation. Besides, a genuine friend would be concerned, right?

The air carries a nervous energy, or maybe it's Charlie. I practically hear him screaming, *What the fuck are you doing? This isn't part of the plan.*

Jackson glances toward the bedroom, his jaw pulsing as he seems to weigh the consequences of losing his temper. "I understand you're among the many people who hate me. I fucked up. I get it more than you realize, but treating me like shit doesn't make things easier on Aurora. If you have concerns, let me know, but I eat a lot, and she always eats with me."

Damn it, why does he have to be reasonable? He's trying to be amicable, and I'm not.

Before I can reply, Charlie cuts in. "Well said, my man." He releases an audible exhale and settles into the armchair. "I'm sure she's fine. I mean, she's what? A buck twenty-five? She probably doesn't need to eat much."

I fix him with a hard stare, frustrated he's making light of the situation. "She's pregnant and hardly keeping food down. Her doctor is concerned about her weight and blood pressure."

"Sure. Sure. But that was because of stress." Charlie gestures to Jackson. "He's here now. It's all good."

It's all good? Because he's here? What a load of shit.

"What are you talking about?" Jackson's brows furrow in confusion, as if it never occurred to him Aurora was negatively affected by his relapse. "When did her doctor say that?"

I scoff at how little he knows about the person he claims to love. "While you were off getting high and fucking whoever, I was here taking care of *your* girlfriend, and she's had to call the doctor several times. She collapsed into *my* arms the night she found out, and *I've* been the one—"

In two steps, he's in front of me, and we're chest to chest. I've got a few inches on him, more muscle, and I'm combat-trained. Yet, he isn't intimidated. He raises his hands, and I brace myself, certain he's about to throw a punch.

Instead, he motions to his face, challenging me. "Come on, big man. Take a shot," he taunts, his green eyes brimming with disgust. "Go ahead. You got the balls to run your mouth, so do something about it."

Charlie jumps up. "Okay, guys. Let's not fight."

I clench my fists hard enough to crack my knuckles. "You'd like that, wouldn't you? Better I hit you in the face than where it truly hurts?"

I want to knock him on his ass more than anything, the overwhelming urge vibrating in my taut muscles. He deserves it for everything he's done to Aurora, but I have a feeling she'd defend him.

If I touch him, she'll choose him over me without hesitation.

And Jackson knows it.

His mouth twists in a snide smirk. "Do it. Do what you need

to make yourself feel better, whatever gets you to shut...the...fuck...up." He leans in, accentuating each word.

I shove him with both hands. "If you hurt her again, I won't hesitate to end you."

It's not worth it. An altercation will only fuel the violence in his veins, nothing else.

He barely budges. He's an impenetrable wall of self-destruction, numb and reckless. "Get in line. You'll be waiting a while."

I sense movement behind me, and Jackson backs off, running his fingers through his hair.

Barefoot, Aurora enters the living room in a rumpled T-shirt big enough to be his and leggings—which reminds me, I need to find a studio with prenatal yoga. She enjoyed that when she was in Laguna.

I open my arms. She encircles my waist and peers up at me with drowsy eyes and sleep wrinkles on her cheek. "What's going on?"

Her hugs are my favorite, and the tension bleeds from my body.

"Ethan wants me to check the fireplaces and radiators." I tuck a strand of her messy hair behind her ear. "And I brought someone for you to meet—officially."

"He's cute." She smiles and whispers, "But he looks terrified."

Laughter bursts from my chest. Maybe I just needed a hug.

26

JACKSON

I WANDER INTO THE KITCHEN, A MINDLESS FOG OF BARELY-contained fury, teetering on the edge of mania. I need to busy myself or get the fuck out of here—far away from *Ricky*.

Reaching into a top cupboard, I grab two boxes of angel hair pasta and toss them on the counter.

I don't care if he has a boyfriend. He and Aurora are too close, and I'm about to lose my damn mind. Okay, I've lost my mind. The next step in my downward spiral is lashing out and destroying shit.

Like his brute face.

He's not Ethan. He doesn't want Aurora and me together. He hates me—I see it in his loathing blue eyes.

And seriously, blond hair and blue eyes? Tattoos and a bad attitude? Protective? What is this purgatory?

I hope he's illiterate and has flesh-colored facial hair.

The cutting board thumps onto the island, followed by the knife and vegetables. Aurora better have a blender; she hates chunky sauce.

I bet Ethan calls spaghetti sauce gravy. I bet he'd put a stop to their hugging.

Honestly, what kind of name is Ricky? He doesn't look like a Ricky. What's that, his gang title? His MC outlaw alias?

No. He doesn't wear motorcycle boots. *I* wear motorcycle

boots. He wears black combat-style boots—basic standard issue.

My brain is a familiar battlefield of intrusive thoughts, his words on repeat in the background.

While you were off getting high and fucking whoever, I was here taking care of your *girlfriend... She collapsed into* my *arms.*

The butcher knife slices through a tomato, cutting it in half with ease.

"In his arms," I mock, my face twisting in annoyance.

Fuck him. I'll slice his throat.

No, I won't. That'll make a mess, and Aurora will be pissed. The visual is nice, though.

I toss the tomatoes, garlic, peppers, and herbs into the blender. I stare at it all becoming a deep-red liquid, wishing it were Ricky's heart ripped from his chest.

Now would be a great time to lose myself in the oblivion of a bottle of what-the-fuck-ever I can get my hands on.

Instead, I'll make Aurora's favorite meal and pray for a food coma.

I might poison him.

My mother should've poisoned Kyle. She loved to cook and had plenty of opportunities.

It's never-ending negative thoughts on a loop, my insecurities adding their own bullshit. I'm warring with feelings of guilt and shame and anger and hopelessness. *Jealousy.* A toxic combination that has me ready to explode like a ticking time bomb.

I remind myself Aurora loves me—deep down, I know that—but here's the thing: it only amplifies my regret. She doesn't deserve to be burdened with my chaos.

But I don't want to be this way. If I had the choice, I wouldn't choose this damaged brain. I'll always be broken. I'll always be the harbinger of Kyle's manipulative games.

Unless he overdoses on the drugs he loves so much.

"Jackson?"

"Hm?"

"Are you making soup?"

Oh, shit. The blender. I take my finger off the puree button. "No."

She eyes me with suspicion. "Do you need a break? I can cook."

No, she can't. She's gorgeous and sweet, but wow, she's a terrible cook. Aurora is the only person I know who prefers raw foods over prepared meals. Of course, the only people I associate with are hockey players, and we eat a fuck ton of food.

I push aside the cutting board and lift her onto the kitchen counter, positioning myself between her knees and enclosing her with my arms. "I got it."

"Okay," she says in that gentle voice, running her hands over my neck and weaving her fingers into my hair.

She touches me, and my dick pulses—yup, definitely on the manic side—my breath quickening in anticipation of the pleasure only she can give.

Not that she'll give me any. The fact she's touching me is a miracle.

"Did your *friends* leave?" Nope, that doesn't sound bitter at all.

Our gazes meet, and I struggle to hide the darkness emanating from my thoughts.

"Yes. You can stop being jealous now."

I don't want to ruin this. I don't... "Where were you when you fell into his arms?"

She cocks her head, confused.

"The night I relapsed."

Her eyes narrow. "Are we doing this?"

"Tell me."

"It was four or five in the morning. I was in bed."

Adrenaline shoots through my veins. "With him?"

"He came into my room after my phone kept ringing." Her expression turns exasperated. "This isn't an argument you want."

∾

Aurora

JACKSON LEANS IN, our faces inches apart, a war raging behind his green eyes. "Ricky touches you more than his boyfriend. He doesn't look at you like a friend. He gazes at you in awe, as if you shit fucking rainbows."

Anticipation and fear pound in my chest. "You're getting worked up."

"You think?" he asks sarcastically.

"Jax—"

"Him or me? Who do you choose?" His eyes search mine, vulnerable but cold.

My impulse is to choose him, a rambled apology on the tip of my tongue, ready to prevent an escalation.

But I refuse to tolerate this behavior any longer.

"What's happening right now? Is this truly about Ricky? Or us?"

"Choose." His features and tone become harsher. "It's playing with my mind, watching you two, knowing he was here when I wasn't."

I shake my head and glance away, trying to avoid the outburst I sense is coming. "No. I'm not choosing."

"Are you fucking kidding me? Or are you hiding shit from me?" His nostrils flare and his chest heaves. He's on the verge of crashing. "I'm here. You don't need a bodyguard. You don't even need to work. We should be home with Ethan."

I push his shoulder, wanting to escape, but he doesn't budge. His arms cage me in, fingers gripping the edge of the granite, biceps bulging.

"Let me go," I say, steady and firm. "I'm not hiding anything. Maybe you believe that because it's who *you* are, but I've done nothing wrong. I tried to give you everything—"

His hand moves swiftly, and I flinch. That fist has smashed through walls beside my head. This time, he's only gesturing angrily. Still, it's intimidating.

"You don't think I know that? You think I wanted this?" He releases a shuddering breath, and his raised voice softens. "I'm sorry. I'll take it down a notch. Are we together? Can you give me that at least?"

With Jackson, it's all or nothing, and nothing isn't an option. Still, I'm not sure I'm emotionally ready. I'm hesitant to slap that boyfriend sticker on someone who was just photographed with other women.

Boyfriend. That's...not right. The word is weak, utter bull-shit. We're ingrained in each other, despite my best efforts and the lies I tell myself. That's why it hurts so much, and perhaps he's feeling it too, with Ricky, although it's unwarranted.

"Ricky has a partner, and we're only friends. I understand what you're going through better than anyone." I stare point-edly into his troubled eyes. "When you disappear, when you hide our relationship—"

"That was before—"

"When you relapse, when you're with other women, it kills a part of me, a part of *us* we can't get back."

"I wasn't. With. Other. Women." Teeth clenched, he swallows hard, his throat clicking. "Stop saying that." His voice vibrates with raw emotion. "You wouldn't if you knew what I've been through." His eyes well up, and his jaw ticks. "Sex is warped inside my head." He taps a finger against his temple. "Except with you. I'm not attracted to random people, no matter how drunk or high I am. I don't even *like* anyone other than you. How could I possibly *touch* someone else?"

Dread washes over me, as if icy flames scorch my skin. A bone-chilling horror coils tight in my stomach, leaving me jittery.

Only weeks ago, he told me he didn't ghost me, that he overdosed after hurting me. It took months and another argument for him to admit that.

His mother's death. Kyle's torment. I realize how little I know of his struggles, of what's buried underneath the anger and addiction.

One thing's for sure: he's trapped inside his head.

I cup his face with trembling hands and run my thumbs over his cheekbones. "You're okay. *We're* okay." A painful tightness grips my throat, my voice barely a rasp. "Even when I'm too afraid to say it...I love you. I will *always* love you. Ricky has a partner. He's not interested in me. No one is taking me from you—*you're* in control of losing me."

His defenses crumble, and his shoulders slump. He shuts his eyes and presses his forehead to mine. "I'm depressed. My thoughts are racing. I got a taste of you again, and I don't want to go back to starving. I don't want to lose the only thing I have."

His words hang heavy in the air, but they're not true. Ethan cares about him, possibly as much as he does me.

"We can work through this, but you can't yell or intimidate me. Our life will be more complicated with a baby. Think about it, Jax. Think about a child peering up at you."

A tear rolls down his cheek, and I hold on to the hope we've reached a place that'll allow us to heal, that'll allow *him* to heal, and this night won't lead to self-destruction.

27

JACKSON

Tears sting my eyes. Fucking depression.

Aurora's fingernails glide over my scalp. "You're not on the ice, burning energy and relieving tension. You don't do well cooped up. You need sunshine and the outdoors."

If she's trying to convince me to return to LA without her, it's not happening. "I need *you*."

"You have me. No one can replace you, Jackson O'Reilly."

Her voice is playful, her touch soothing. She's comforting me, as always, not getting rid of me, and the chaos in my brain quiets a bit more.

"Your intoxicating scent, that crooked smile, this mouth..." She tilts her head and places her lips on mine.

A flutter stirs in my stomach, and a chill runs down my spine. I let out a low groan, tangle my fingers in her silky hair, and deepen the kiss. She moans softly, and the heat between us intensifies. I clasp her thigh, bringing her closer.

"How about this?" She glides her tongue over my bottom lip. "How about you feed me your cock, then dinner?"

I pull back and stare at her in disbelief, searching her devilish eyes. "You think a blow job will make me feel better?"

She bites her lips to hide her mischievous grin, and just like that, the tension eases. We fall into place, Aurora and Jackson.

I nod, feigning contemplation. "You'd be right." I smile, dip my head, and place a kiss under her earlobe. "But I want more than you on your knees for me."

She wraps her legs around my waist and presses me tight to her center, only the thin material of her leggings and my shorts between us.

Our mouths meet in an urgent entanglement. Hips rock, craving friction, and she whimpers. God, I missed that sound.

I grind against her. "I want to bury myself inside you all fucking night." I need her—need that deep connection we have.

Yet, I can't shake the feeling she's only doing this to prove her love for me rather than her desiring me in this moment.

"Don't do this," I pant. "Not unless you truly want me, want us."

She answers by reaching her hand between our bodies to palm my erection.

An involuntary "fuck" escapes my lips, and my head drops back.

"Stop overthinking." She trails kisses and bites along my throat. "Do you want this or not?"

She slips into my shorts, and her fingers wrap around me, moving agonizingly slow over my length.

"More than anything," I groan.

She strokes me faster, twisting her fist, and my heart beats at the speed of light, breaths coming in gasps.

My body surrenders, entirely at her mercy. I grip the granite counter, rock-hard, aching, leaking. "You're killing me, baby. Please."

She takes me to the brink, knowing precisely what drives me crazy. I'm already on the edge, pleasure furrowing low in my stomach, my muscles tightening.

"Then give it to me, O'Reilly." Her voice is pure seduction, captivating me as she does the camera.

Her teeth sink into my neck, and I lose all restraint. I lift her off the island and set her on her feet. Our mouths instantly draw together in a messy kiss, and we stumble toward the bedroom. I lift her shirt over her head, and my gaze fixates on her breasts, overflowing from her black lace bra.

My lips part. "Holy shit, they're *huge*."

She chuckles at my reaction and reaches behind her. "It's the pregnancy."

Her bra falls, and my dick twitches. "Damn, we need to keep you pregnant."

I yank my shirt off and toss it aside. While I'm doing so, she drops to her knees, lowers my shorts, and grips my length. Her hot mouth engulfs me, and my breath catches in my rib cage.

Without hesitation, she takes me into the back of her throat, swallows, and my eyes nearly cross.

I cup the back of her head and flex my hips. "Look at me, baby," I command, my voice rough as gravel. "Look at what you do to me. You fucking wreck me."

Her caramel eyes lock with mine, brimming with lust and longing. She sucks and strokes in tandem. Her tongue swirls over the sensitive underside, and I recite my wedding vows, struggling to last until I can come inside her.

She moans with a mouth full of my cock, and my balls draw tight to my shaft.

"Don't make me come." I fist her hair, unsure if I want to push or pull. "I need to fuck you."

I step back, and just to drive me mad, she increases suction until I pop free from her lips.

"Come here," I growl and lift her to her feet.

Driven by a furious craving to find release within her, I spin us both toward the breakfast table. In a frenzy of motions, I bend her over and press her chest to the surface, careful of the baby.

I rip her leggings and underwear to her mid-thighs, too crazed to remove them entirely, and palm her luscious ass. The view from behind is glorious—soft curves, her glistening pussy peeking through.

"You're everything, Aurora." I trace my fingers up her spine and clasp her neck.

This position has me looming over her, my grip ensuring

she remains pinned to the table. Her leggings around her thighs further restrict her movement, adding an element of submission and vulnerability.

It's erotic and primal, just the control I need.

I notch the head of my cock at her entrance and thrust home in one firm, smooth stroke, eliciting a cry from her lips.

"Goddamn, I missed this pussy, baby."

Her walls clench. "Jax," she whimpers sweetly.

And my sole mission in life becomes making her soak my cock.

Reaching around, I rub fast circles over her clit while punching my hips forward at a harsh pace. She clutches the edge of the table, her face flushed with desire.

The sound of our skin slapping fills the room, and her ass ripples with each thrust.

"You feel so *fucking* good," I groan, on the brink of an orgasm once again. "I'm going to spend *every single day* filling you with my cum."

Her mouth opens on a silent moan, her body feverish, pussy so wet, her cream covers my shaft. I can't drag my gaze away—my hard, glistening cock sliding in and out of her tight, bare cunt, and fuck me, I need her to come.

I angle my hips downward and pound into her, matching my thrusts with the movement of my fingers. "Give me more. I want you dripping from me."

She pulses around me, releasing a strangled cry of pleasure. Her cunt becomes a vise grip, and every stroke has waves of ecstasy shooting through my veins.

My pace turns erratic, my dick unbearably hard. I tip my head back, and the orgasm hits like a bolt of lightning.

I slam into her one last time, my vision darkening, a broken "fuuuuuck" the only sound to escape my clenched teeth. My brain has lost all ability to speak coherent words.

My body collapses over her, my forearms taking my weight. My lips find hers, kissing her as I gasp for air, my cock jolting deep inside her.

She runs her fingers through my sweaty hair, and my senses slowly return, along with my doubt.

"You never said we're together." The thought leaves my mouth.

"What?"

"Say you take me back. No ultimatums. No one foot out the door. I fight for you, you fight for me."

She doesn't immediately answer, and panic splinters in my chest.

"I'll fight for you as long as you fight for *us*. There's not just me anymore." She peers into my eyes. "Do you want to be a part of this baby's life?"

She's focused on the baby. I'm no longer her number one, but I can live with that. I love him. He's mine too.

"Yes. Absolutely. One hundred and fifty percent." I place a gentle kiss on her lips. "Because I'm taking half of Ethan's claim."

She giggles. "No, you are not."

"That baby is inside you, which means it's mine too."

"You're insane."

"Certifiably—we know this—but I'm yours."

With a soft smile, she sighs. "You are."

That's all I need to hear. My heart is whole. "I love you. I love you. I love you." I repeat the words as I trail kisses along the delicate curve of her neck.

"I love you too," she replies. "But I'm about to drop to the floor if you don't feed me."

My lips curl into a stupid grin. "I'll feed you for the rest of my life."

"Sounds good. Now, get off me, you Neanderthal."

<u>Ricky</u>

I'll never eat in that kitchen again.

I yank the headphones from my partner's head. "Stop

listening! You think he'll scream Kyle's secrets while five inches deep?"

He chokes on the coffee he just brought to his lips. His face turns red, and he pounds his chest, grinning from ear to ear. "Five inches?" Tears run from his eyes, and he brushes them away, struggling to rein himself in. "You've got it bad. He's six-three. He's at least seven to eight. Everyone knows every inch over six foot is another inch of dick."

Despite being agitated, my brain attempts the math. I blink and blink again. "What?"

"It's true. It's science."

"No, it fucking isn't."

Still...I'm about six-six, measuring in at... Do piercings count? No, piercings don't count. Carry the one... That can't be right. Fuck it. Either way, science says I'm bigger.

"See? You're trying to work it out in your head, aren't you?"

"Doesn't matter. Stop listening."

28

ETHAN

THIS APPEAL HEARING IS SIGNIFICANT—NOT ONLY FOR THE TEAM, but for me personally.

I promised Aurora I'd look after Jax, and I failed. That night, exhausted from the game and sex with Aurora, emotions running high, I showered and went to bed without checking on him. When the plane landed, he said he was tired, and, given his illness, I believed him.

This is my chance to right my mistakes and restore our trio.

While I wait for the meeting to begin, I tap my pen on the provided legal pad and reflect on Jackson and Aurora. They're like twins. The more I know them, the more I realize how alike they are, particularly how they bust my balls. There's the nonstop banter, same facial expressions, clingy-ness, and that freaky communication with their eyes.

They're reliant on each other. There's no happy Aurora without Jax and no sane Jax without Aurora. I need them both, and they need someone to care for them. I have no clue how they survived together for two years on their own.

I abandoned love a long time ago. Instead, I prioritized my career, determined never to live in poverty or hopelessness again. My life revolved around hockey. Wash, rinse, repeat. My reward was the win. I didn't need anyone or anything, and I wore it like a badge of honor.

Most days, loving Aurora scares the fuck out of me. I can't admit it to myself. That'd make it real, a weakness in my well-constructed armor.

And yet, I'm in a threesome—is that what it's called?—with a baby on the way, and I don't regret it. I miss them, actually.

I'm standing at the cliff's edge, staring down at the mesmerizing waters, considering the exhilaration of the plunge, knowing damn well I might drown. Even the breeze at the top is tantalizing, tempting me to take the jump.

Who am I kidding? I'm already falling.

Without her—or *them*—my days are dull.

They're on my mind before I open my eyes. I wake early to adjust for the time difference and send Aurora good morning texts, and then I stare at my screen, hoping she'll respond. I eagerly await pictures from Jax, grinning when I receive one.

Getting out of bed has become difficult. They seem to be the energy in my veins, and my career is a nightmare, thanks to the piece of shit who just walked through the door—accompanied by the league president. Great.

"What the fuck is he doing here?"

Heads snap up from their phones. I know I should remain professional, but this motherfucker hurt Jax, ruined our relationship, and hired someone to follow Aurora. He brings out the violence in me.

Kyle straightens his tie and sits on the opposite side of the conference table. "I'm here to represent my son."

Is he serious? I pin him with a glare. "Nope. His agent is representing him. *I'm* representing him. *You* shouldn't even be able to refer to him as your son." I take a deep breath and attempt to gather my composure. "He doesn't want you here."

His face twists in anger. "You don't know what he wants."

I pick up my phone. "How about I call him?"

Of course, when I call Jackson, he doesn't answer. Typical.

"Let's move on." Kyle's fake-ass voice has enough saccharine to rot teeth. "Shall we, gentleman?"

Robert, the team owner, and Colby, Jackson's agent, glance at me with raised brows, seeking my response.

"Hold up. I know where he is." I'm already calling Aurora, my hands trembling with fury.

"Ethan!" she answers excitedly, her beautiful face appearing on the screen.

Damn it, I hit our last call, not realizing it was a FaceTime.

"I need to talk to Jackson. It's important."

She peers up and off to the side. "It's your boyfriend."

The heat of embarrassment radiates from my cheeks, but my lips don't get the memo and smirk at the brat.

My captain's shit-eating grin fills the screen. "That was quick. Miss me already?"

"I'm in the meeting we talked about..." I fix him with a pointed stare that sobers him.

"Sorry," he mouths.

"Do me a favor: look at the people in attendance and tell me if someone doesn't belong."

"Okay..." he drags out, his brows furrowed.

I turn the camera and scan the room.

When I land on his father, he shakes his head. "Hell no."

For all to hear, I clarify, "You don't require or want Kyle at this hearing, correct?"

Jax gives a curt nod. "Correct."

"Are you in agreement with the plan we discussed earlier?"

"Yes." Agitated, he pulls at his hair. "You have the power of attorney?"

That sets Kyle off. "Clearly, you can see there's more going on here."

He thrusts a hand in my direction, and I end the call. I don't need Jax's temper disrupting this appeal, and I don't want him to be affected by his father's manipulation tactics.

"No further argument." The president raises his hand. "We're all adults here. Please leave. I'd like to get started. My plate is full."

Kyle shoots me a scathing look and storms out the door, slamming it behind him.

"I've always hated that creep," Coby mumbles.

The hearing goes well. Jackson's twenty-game suspension is reduced to nine, with the agreement I'm his sponsor until the end of the season. When he returns, he's to live with me, travel with me, and see a therapist. If he tests positive again, he'll receive a mandatory one-year suspension.

Now, I only have to convince our girl to come home...and stay home.

Walking out to my car, I'm flooded with relief, and my thoughts turn to my next pressing issue: preparing for our little guy.

I'm nervous about our upcoming doctor visit in a few days. Aurora is nineteen or twenty weeks along now and still sick, and I haven't been to a single appointment with her.

I can't believe we're having a baby. It blows my mind. I'm not at all ready. I won't even have an extra bedroom after Jax moves in.

Fuck, this is about to get weird. I can't imagine sleeping with Aurora while Jackson is in the other room. Or the opposite—Jackson with Aurora. Jesus, that's fucked up.

Despite being lost in thought, I immediately spot Kyle, casually leaning against a sleek, all-black SUV beside mine. He's engrossed in his phone, the sunlight catching the sheen of his thinning hair.

I scan the parking lot, assessing my surroundings. There doesn't seem to be anything suspicious, and he appears to be alone. Considering his desperate attempt at controlling his son, though, I'm leery.

"Can I help you?"

I approach my silver Porsche Cayenne, a new purchase rated safe for Aurora and the baby. I rarely drive, but I can't picture putting a car seat in an Uber. Jackson has plenty of vehicles, but I'd like to provide *something* other than DNA.

Kyle glances up, silently observing me until I face him from the other side of my vehicle.

He slides his phone into his pocket. "What do you want with my son?"

"I want the same thing you should: for him to be healthy and successful."

"Jackson is unwell, delusional. He thinks he's in love. He's being taken advantage of, and she's affecting his game." His tone is placating and fake as hell.

Does this asshole think I'm an idiot? Is this some divide-and-conquer method of manipulation? Has he forgotten the times I kicked him out of my locker room? I know who's affecting Jackson's game, and it's not Aurora.

"Who's the one taking advantage of him, Kyle?"

He stands straight and balls his fists. "You know very well who!"

I remain relaxed. He wouldn't dare come at me—not in public, particularly considering the fifty-pound muscle differ-ence. I'd have him asleep on the concrete with one hit.

"The only person I see taking advantage of him is you."

He scoffs. "I see you're as whipped as he is. The two of you are going to bleed him dry."

How long did he expect to keep control of Jackson's money? Did he think if he kept fueling his son's addiction, he'd always be the trustee? That no one would send Jax to rehab? Not him? Or the team? Or a judge? Boy, did I disrupt his plans.

Dread flutters in my chest. What if he never intended for Jax to get clean? What if he wants him in a grave next to his mother? Disgusted, I push the thought away.

"I'm guessing since you know which car is mine and you had me followed, you likely ran a background on me, so you know I don't need or want Jackson's money. That's you."

"He's petitioned for you to take ownership of the house he attempted to purchase—"

"There is no *attempted to purchase*. The sale was completed. Whether you have legal control of the house is to be deter-mined. I have lawyers as well. You're not playing with an amateur, Kyle. Your best option is to walk away."

A deranged grin takes over his features, crinkling his dead eyes. "You'd know about properties in trust, wouldn't you?" He cocks his head. "Or is it a shell company?" Given the smirk on his face and the glimmer in his eye, he assumes he's uncovered some deep, dark secret.

And he'd be correct, but he's wrong if he thinks I give a fuck.

I roll my neck and shoulders. "You got something to say?"

"Everyone thought your father turned FBI informant to save his wife, but he really flipped to save your mother, didn't he? The FBI discovered his mistress and threatened to use her at trial, right? She would've been thrown to the wolves, and the FBI would've appropriated the properties he was hiding in her name. Your father took a deal in exchange for life in prison. Who does that?"

A man in love, apparently. I wouldn't know—I've never met him. His imprisonment destroyed my mother. The only thing he saved was his empire, which I want no part of.

"If that were true, I wouldn't need Jackson's money, would I? And you'd be smart to leave me the fuck alone."

His face contorts, and his eyes fix on me with a hateful gaze. "I will—when you prove the baby is yours."

"The baby is none of your fucking business, and you'd do well to remember that."

"It is my business. I have control of my son's assets. She was his six-figure call girl. You can't tell me she doesn't want money. If it's his, I'd be willing to negotiate. He's not ready for a child, and it'll ruin both their careers. I'm sure you don't want someone else's kid."

No. He better not be suggesting... "What are you implying?"

"There are *other* options. We can work together."

He doesn't want Jax healthy. He doesn't want this baby born. If he'd drug his son...what else would he do?

My body shakes, rage begging to be released. I press my fists into the hood of my car, stopping me from doing something that'd undoubtedly get me both arrested and fired.

When I speak, my tone is lethal. "That baby is mine. *She* is mine. *My life.* Touch her and lose yours."

Before I make things worse, I get into my vehicle and drive away. At the first stoplight, my fingers fly across the screen:

Do not let Aurora out of your sight. Jax either.

RICKY

Kyle?

Yup.

29

AURORA

We enter the doctor's office, and nervous energy emanates from both Jackson and Ethan. Jax is enthusiastic, bouncing on his feet, while Ethan appears terrified, his hands stuffed in his pockets.

I bump my shoulder into his. "What's wrong?"

He clasps the back of my neck, his thumb gently caressing. "Nothing, baby."

I guide the way to the reception window, aware of the curious gazes. There are many reasons to stare—LA's infamous hockey player being one, the three of us together another.

At the window, I introduce myself and reach into my bag to retrieve my identification and debit card.

Dr. Z's receptionist, Cathy, takes my ID and hands me an iPad to complete the electronic medical forms.

"Do you have your insurance card?" she asks.

"I don't have insurance." Unlike in the past, when I couldn't afford to see a doctor, I don't feel embarrassed. "I pay out-of-pocket."

Jackson's wide-eyed gaze snaps to Ethan, then me. "What?"

Here we go...

My face heats. "It's fine. I got it."

"Absolutely not." Ethan snatches my debit card before I can hand it over and pulls out his wallet.

"You don't have to do that."

His eyebrows nearly hit his hairline, his stormy gray eyes thunderous. "Yeah, I fucking do."

Thankfully, Cathy interrupts. "Which ultrasound would you like?"

Jackson's face lights up. "What are our options?"

"The various packages are displayed on the window." She points to the glass in front of us. "We have standard 2D, 4D, and 5D with 8K enhancement. You can even opt for a video."

Mesmerized, my boys gape at the different ultrasounds.

I stifle a chuckle. "The Wellness package is fine. Thank you."

"No, no, no." Jax shakes his head. "We want the Grand Premiere package with 8K and video." It sounds like he's purchasing a car, and given the cost...

Cathy giggles—*fucking giggles*—at his eagerness. To her credit, I don't know if I've ever seen him smile this much. Every time I catch a glimpse of him, my heart flutters.

"There's more to see if you get the enhancement after thirty weeks when the baby has more fat," she explains.

"Can we only get it once?" He cocks his head, as if he doesn't understand why anyone would limit themselves.

"No. No, of course not," she stammers. "Today is an important wellness ultrasound, but you'll have other ones."

"Okay, we'll get it then too." He gives her a dazzling grin that has her blushing.

I take a seat and fill out the forms while Ethan pays an outrageous amount for a twenty-week ultrasound.

Jackson sits next to me, his gaze glued to the questionnaire. "How come it asks how often the baby moves?"

"Some women feel movement by now, but it's normal not to. It's hard to tell."

His brows pinch in concern. "Are you sure?"

I give him a reassuring smile. "I'm positive."

"Good. I can't wait."

His wistful tone breaks my heart. *God, please don't take this away. Just let him be happy.*

"Really, Aurora?" Ethan drops into the seat beside me. "I asked you for one fucking thing: to support the baby financially." He lets out a frustrated huff. "You've been paying thousands of dollars and never mentioned it to me?"

He strokes his beard, his signature scowl firmly in place. He's cranky. Maybe it's tension or lack of sex. Our flight was delayed because of a snowstorm on the East Coast, and I was dragging when we arrived at his apartment. We cuddled and passed out, only to wake up to a fully energized Jax, who doesn't even drink coffee.

I squeeze his hand. "It's okay. It's my baby too."

He grips my cheeks, puckering my lips, and plants a loud, smacking kiss on me. "No. It's *not* okay."

I finish the forms and return the iPad. Once I'm back, I hold Ethan's hand and trace the prominent veins. I had no idea hands could be so sexy.

It's not long before we're called back, and I cringe when they take my weight.

It gets more awkward when the doctor enters the room and does a double-take. "Wow, who do we have here?"

"This is Jackson, and this is Ethan, the baby's father," I reply in an attempt to simplify our unique relationship.

"Okay, so boyfriend." She gestures to Jax, then to Ethan. "And baby's father. Is that right?"

"Close enough," I answer as Ethan says, "We all live together."

"Oh...*oh*!" she exclaims, struck by realization. "I get it."

Who knew the three of us were living together? Ethan, apparently.

She reviews my medical record and asks the typical questions before getting to the more pertinent material. "Any dizziness or fainting?"

I shift, and the damn paper crinkles underneath me. "Once."

"What was happening at the time?"

My heart rate spikes. "I was under a lot of stress."

"Job related?"

Jesus, she doesn't quit. "No...ah...relationship stuff."

She glances between the guys. "Would you like to talk alone?"

"I'm fine." Why is it so hot in here? My face is on fire. "It's better."

"Good, because there's something else we need to go over."

Fuck, I knew this was coming.

"Would you like to discuss *that* alone?"

Ethan collars the back of my neck in an unmistakable gesture that he's not leaving. I peek up at him, and his stern expression says precisely that. I glance at Jackson. His eyes are filled with remorse. Still, he brings my fingers to his lips, easing some of the fear racing through my veins.

"No, it's okay. They can stay."

"By this stage of the pregnancy, I like to see over ten pounds of weight gain. You've gained around five. You've gained less than a pound since I saw you last."

"I've been eating." It comes out in a whisper, and I attempt to swallow the golf-ball-sized lump in my throat. "But I'm throwing up nearly every day."

Jax caresses my hand. "It's true, and not only in the morning."

"Unfortunately, that's a myth." She scrunches her nose in apology. "Try frequent small meals, find what you can keep down, and get plenty of rest." She punches something into the iPad. "I'll have the nutritionist contact you."

All I can manage is a nod.

"Now is not the time to restrict calories."

"I'm not, I swear. I had a rough few weeks. I've been sick and sleeping a lot." My eyes well up. Harming my baby is the last thing I want.

"The baby needs nutrients to develop and grow, which he'll take from you if you're not replacing what's required. That leaves you tired and depleted. He'll be growing rapidly from here on out. You need to rest and eat properly."

Ethan answers with complete confidence and a hint of bite. "She will."

"Other than that, your blood pressure is a tad high. It could be dehydration or stress on the body, but we'll continue to monitor it. Now, it's time to see your baby." She smiles. "The tech will be in soon."

Once the door shuts behind her, Ethan captures my chin, bringing my face to his. He remains silent, but his piercing eyes tell me everything. He's pissed.

"I'm eating. I promise." My voice trembles, and a tear rolls down my cheek. "Ricky prepares meals and Jax cooks."

"You have one month in New York. *That is all.* By your next appointment, you will be under my roof. Am I clear?"

I don't hesitate. "Yes."

Do I have a choice? He looks downright murderous. It's kind of hot, though.

"Good girl." He kisses my forehead then glares at Jax. "And you..."

"I know. I know. I have no intention of leaving her side. I'll ensure she eats, rests, and is blissfully happy."

30

ETHAN

"HE'S SO TINY." JAX WATCHES THE ULTRASOUND VIDEO ON HIS phone for the millionth time on our way to eat. "You can see his heart beating."

The three of us are in the back, Ricky driving. I attempt to feel jealous of Jackson's excitement over this pregnancy, but I can't find it within me. He's fiercely happy, and I don't have the heart, or lack thereof, to extinguish that. With everything that concerns Aurora, he's one hundred percent invested. Why wouldn't I want that? She needs our support.

All went well with the ultrasound. The baby is perfect, measuring slightly bigger than expected, making me feel terrible for my behavior. I've turned into an irritable bastard since my run-in with Kyle. It doesn't help that I haven't told either of them about his threats or my own father. I've been tight-lipped about many aspects of my life.

Aurora smiles at Jax, her head on his shoulder.

He kisses her forehead then whispers, "I love you. I'm sorry...for everything. I promise I'll do better."

Fuck, if that doesn't make me feel ten times worse. Jackson has done a lot of shitty things, but he owns up to his mistakes, and he'd do anything for her, including quit hockey.

Yet, here I am, giving her what little I can spare when it's clear she needs more. *They* need more. I have all this guilt and fear burning inside me. For fucking up with Jax. For not providing for her. For not protecting them both. All of it, tearing at my soul every day.

"I know. I love you." Her words are full of confidence. Something between them has changed. *She's* changed. Maybe because she knows, without a doubt, that he returns her feelings—another thing she lacks with me.

Aurora is forced to hold back, although I can read her like a book. She gazes at me with adoration, clings to me as if she needs me, and submits to me as if she's mine.

But she doesn't share those sentiments with me. She thinks I'm not ready for them, and I made her feel that way. I told her as much.

Jackson might be a hothead, but he never lets a moment go by without telling her he loves her or misses her or whatever puppy-love bullshit he's on. Except it's not puppy love or bullshit. He wears his emotions on his chest for all to see.

I refuse to be a sappy, lovesick fool, and my bond with her may never compare to his, but Aurora and I share *something*.

She goes to kiss him, but before she can, I wrap my arm around her and pull her away. "Enough. You've been with him for a week. It's my turn."

Jax crosses his arms over his chest. "You had her last night."

Their flight arrived late, and all I got was a sleepy Aurora. Not that I'm complaining—I'll take her in my bed in any shape or form.

"We were sleeping." I give him a half-hearted glare. "And only for a few hours before you woke us, seeking attention."

He shoots me a cocky smirk. "You're lucky I wasn't in bed with you. I thought about it many times."

Jesus, he's not lying. He has no boundaries.

In response, I lean down and capture Aurora's lips, flipping him off with one hand and cupping the back of her head with the other. Unspoken words linger on the tip of my tongue, but it's not the time, not while her boyfriend is mean-mugging me, no doubt.

Breaking the kiss, I brush my fingers through her hair. "I've missed you so fucking much. Spend the night with me." Then, I add, for him to hear, "Just us."

He shakes his head. "Not happening, asshole." Given his ridiculous smile, he's enjoying this.

I slump my shoulders and glower. "You always going to be a cockblock?"

"Your cock has done enough, homewrecker."

It's hard to keep a straight face with Aurora's giggles and the way he grins at me. *Grins*, as if we're best friends. As if he didn't shove me, his eyes filled with rage and loathing, only a few weeks ago.

"I'm being serious, dickhead. We have a lot we need to talk about."

He motions between us. "So talk. Fuck for all I care, but she's sleeping with me." He echoes my words, lowering his voice to mock me.

I am *not* finding this jackass funny.

Shit, I am, and I've never been more annoyed with myself.

"Don't test me, Jax. I'll bend her over the table while you eat your Lucky Charms."

"That's disgusting, Coach. I'd never eat Lucky Charms." That damn smart mouth of his.

"I'm going to kill you," I say with a chuckle. I can't help it.

Jackson

OUR GIRL TIPS her head back, laughing—*really* laughing. This is the happiest I've seen her in a long while, and I've *never* seen Coach this happy.

That sums it up. It's decided. We are now in a relationship, and there's no arguing otherwise. It's fate.

And his comment about bending her over the table might have made me hard.

Time to have some fun.

I pop a Jolly Rancher in my mouth and stuff the wrapper in

my pocket. Threading my fingers through Aurora's hair, I bring her gaze to mine. "Come here."

My voice is raspy, and she bites her bottom lip to hide her naughty smile. She doesn't need to read my thoughts—the mischievous glint in my eyes gives me away.

I move toward the center of the seat while guiding her to straddle me.

"Wanna make out?" My tone is playful, but I'm one hundred percent serious. I'll be the devil who leads them to sin if it brings the three of us closer.

I palm her ass and adjust her over my erection. Her lips part as her fingers glide up my neck and weave into my hair.

Ethan settles into the leather seat, and I sense his penetrating gaze.

I shift my hips, seeking friction. "I dare you to share my Jolly Rancher with the old man."

He scoffs and shakes his head, but he doesn't turn away.

I twirl the candy with my tongue and place it between my front teeth. Aurora accepts the challenge, but just as our lips brush, I suck the Jolly Rancher into my mouth and deepen the kiss.

Our tongues intertwine, and her body surrenders to mine.

Everything disappears: my coach sitting next to me, Ricky, the fact that she's stealing the Jolly Rancher from me...

With a triumphant smile, she pulls away and glances at Ethan, her lips swollen and cheeks flushed. Not hesitating, he grabs her jaw and draws her in for a hard kiss.

Their tongues tangle, and I glide my hands under her hoodie to palm her full, round breasts and pinch her peaked nipples. She whimpers into Ethan's mouth while thoroughly enjoying my cock pressed against her.

I most definitely did not have my girlfriend riding my lap while sucking face with my coach on my bingo card for this afternoon, or even this year. Still, it's the *three of us*, and I'm so fucking hard.

I'd do anything to slide into her wet cunt right about now.

I sink my teeth into her neck, then whisper, "Baby, I want you to ride me," while flexing my hips.

Ethan bristles and growls, "Driver," reminding me we have someone else in the vehicle.

"Fuck..." I drag out the word, heavy with disappointment and, okay, some pouting.

I fix Aurora's hoodie and reluctantly drop my hands to her waist.

Fucking Ricky, always ruining everything.

Ethan adjusts his pants, and a laugh bursts from my chest.

"You look dazed and smitten, Coach."

Again, I get the middle finger. He leans back, and Aurora rests her cheek on my shoulder, facing him.

"You like this?" he asks, brushing his fingers through her hair.

He's so close, I can feel the heat radiating off his body.

"With all of us?" Her voice is vulnerable, and I place a reassuring kiss on the top of her head.

"Yes, my dirty girl. Do you want that?" His words are blunt, but amusement laces his tone.

My heart races in anticipation of her answer. The thrill-seeker in me, the part always chasing a high, wants nothing more than to explore this *relationship*.

She nods.

He kisses her forehead, mumbling, "Me too."

"Ricky," I call out, not wasting a minute. "Change of plans. Take us to my Laguna Beach penthouse, please."

My lips are streaked with sugar, the inside of my boxers are sticky, my heart is content, and my mind has never been clearer.

Only one thing... "Who has the Jolly Rancher?"

Ethan sticks the candy between his teeth. "Why? You're not getting it back."

Jax instructs Ricky to take us to his Laguna Beach penthouse, and I'm struck by the reality of having responsibilities. I'd love to remain in this lust haze with them, but unfortunately, I have an entire organization to answer to.

The media doesn't give a shit about me, or even me and Aurora, they go feral over Jackson O'Reilly, and I dread what the team—or worse, *management*—will speculate if pictures of us ever surface.

I know exactly what they'll speculate because I'm thinking it myself. A coach sharing a girl with his captain is both unfathomable and really fucking hot. I've never been so hard in my life, which seems to be an objective Aurora surpasses every moment we're together.

But I need quality time with her—for more than sex. They leave in two days, and I have to spill my guts.

"There's a lot to discuss."

"We can do it there." He waves me off.

"I don't have clothes." I admit, it's a weak argument.

"Borrow some of mine. Today's a good day for you to take a break for once." He gives me a pointed stare over Aurora's head, where she naps on his chest.

I release a long breath. Fuck, I hate when he's right.

"The team will be fine," he reassures me with that devilish smile.

~

"Jesus." We step into Jackson's over-the-top cliffside penthouse, and the word slips from my lips, my eyes unsure where to focus.

This is not a penthouse; it's a mini mansion.

Aurora gazes dreamily out the floor-to-ceiling windows overlooking the infinity pool and the Pacific Ocean. "It's ridiculous, isn't it?"

Ridiculous doesn't even cover it. The view is breathtaking, especially with her in it.

"Why are we moving into my apartment?" I ask no one in particular.

"Because it's closer to the arena." Jax shrugs. "We can stay at my downtown penthouse. It has plenty of room."

I'm curious to know his definition of *plenty*.

Aurora shakes her head, the sky creating a stunning backdrop behind her. "No thanks. I won't go back there." She turns toward the hallway. "You can live there."

I'm fond and proud of this new version of her. She expresses her thoughts openly, and not only to me. I'd love her no matter what—*oh, fuck, there it is. The actual words.*

I can't even remember what I was thinking. These two have me losing control.

Jax slips his phone from his back pocket. "Not without you," he yells after her. "I was planning on selling it anyhow." His fingers move across the screen; no doubt, he's contacting someone to list the property.

Not sure what to do with myself, I marvel at how the two-story structure is built into the cliff, the entire west side glass. "Who designed this place?"

"I worked with an architect. The ocean is Aurora's favorite;

it soothes her. I wanted to ensure she'd see it from every room." Still engrossed in his phone, he gestures toward the pool deck that rivals most five-star resorts. "Upstairs isn't quite finished. It'll be a studio with a saltwater, coastal view bath."

Insecurity slams into me, bruising my ego and filling me with self-doubt. What the hell does Aurora want me for? He essentially gave her the damn ocean.

"How much space do you need?" It comes out more bitter than intended.

He glances up, searches my irritable expression, and sets his phone on the counter. "As much as it takes for me not to hear you jerking off while I'm fucking my girl." He gives me that smug smirk.

Not one to back down and already on edge, I let my temper flare. "She's not yours. I don't see your ring on her finger, unlike my kid inside her."

His amusement dies. He removes his bag from his shoulder and tosses it to the floor.

For a moment, I think he's about to come at me swinging. You never know with Jax, and, truth be told, I deserve it for that comment. I'm a real prick sometimes.

Instead, he crouches and rifles through his backpack, pulling out a black velvet box.

No fucking way.

He stands and rolls it in his hand. "That's an easy fix. I've been carrying it around since I found out some married asshole knocked her up and took off."

My face heats, and I ball my fists. All the while, Jackson smiles, showing off his perfect teeth.

I might break a few. The fucker delights in taunting me.

Aurora wants the three of us together. I've stated from the beginning that I'd accept their relationship because she loves him and can't seem to live without him. He's the only one with an issue, although he enjoyed that make-out session. *He* instigated it and was ready to take it further.

My brows knit deeply into a scowl. "What is your problem?"

His smile morphs into a deranged grin, and honestly, I'm not sure if he wants to kill me or fuck me.

"No, seriously."

"My problem is you throwing your kid in my face whenever you can. It's not healthy, Coach. We're supposed to be a throuple. How will that make our son feel if you're constantly putting down one of his dads?"

I'm too old for this. I drop my head and pinch the bridge of my nose. "I can't deal with you."

"*Me*? You're uptight. It won't kill you to enjoy yourself. When was the last time you took a vacation? Or went swimming? Or watched something other than hockey?" He draws in a deep, theatrical breath. "Are you this uptight in bed?" Then, he lowers his voice. "Do you even eat pussy?"

That does it. My lips curl into an involuntary smile, and I lunge to swat him.

He ducks, laughing and hollering like a child. "Stop it! We're in a relationship! This is domestic violence!"

"Enough, you two," Aurora calls from the hallway. "If you're not making out, you're arguing."

Jax scrambles to stuff the ring in his bag.

"She has a point," Ricky grumbles from behind us, carrying in Aurora's bags before he takes off for the evening.

I could've carried them, but he snatched them first and insisted.

All my grievances disappear, however, when Aurora walks out in the skimpiest bikini, one that barely covers her ass and boobs. Even *Ricky* chokes and stumbles over his feet.

She pauses, hands on her hips. "Let's settle this so you two stop bickering."

My gaze moves lower to her adorable baby bump. "Settle what? I'm settled. Jax, are you settled?"

"Yeah," he mumbles, his stare fixated on her glorious tits. "But I'd agree to anything right now."

Same.

"I'll make this easy for both of you. I'm pregnant. Get over it. It's not a competition; it happened." She narrows her eyes at me. "Ethan, stop gloating about it and relax. And Jackson," she says through clenched teeth, "stop tormenting our sugar daddy. You'll scare him away."

I'm not their sugar daddy—*obviously*—nor does he stop tormenting me.

"Do you ever see the sun, old man? You're blinding me."

I might strangle him.

They're both already in the pool. I had emails to return and meetings to reschedule. Aurora is hanging off him, her smooth, tan legs encircling his waist and her arms draped over his shoulders. Her long, dark hair cascades down her back, her white triangle bikini top transparent in the water, her breasts in his face.

He shoots me a knowing, shit-eating grin.

This is awkward. I must really love Aurora—there it is again —because I'm standing here in baby-blue swim trunks with bright-pink rubber ducks printed on them. And no, I don't see the sun. I'm always working.

I'm also not a twenty-five-year-old professional hockey player who could grace the cover of *Men's Health* magazine.

Someone kill me now.

Thank fuck I still work out with the team and have some-what of a natural tan.

I come to the edge of the pool and stare him down. "Thanks for the swim trunks, asshole. Don't forget we live together."

"No worries. They didn't fit me—a little snug, if you know what I mean—but they seem to fit you well."

I glance down at the obvious bulge in the tight-as-fuck shorts, and I'm not even hard. "I've seen you in the locker room. Don't embarrass yourself."

His eyes go wide, and he gasps in mock horror. "That's nasty, Coach. Damn."

"Can you please stop calling me that?" Could he make this situation any more uncomfortable? This is Jackson, so...

"Do you prefer old man or Da—"

Aurora covers his mouth to shut him up. He retaliates by dipping her into the water, and she squeals. I've never seen them this happy, smiling and laughing this much, Jax in particular.

Suddenly, it hits me: this is how he treats those he likes. He's teasing me, but it's not malicious, not unless I deserve it.

He has grown since I started coaching, but he's not playful with others on the team. Grant might be the only exception, and Killian, our goalie he's close with, is a loner himself.

Jax refuses to let people in. Everyone he trusts is in this penthouse, and I hope what I have to tell them doesn't fuck this up.

I dive into the pool and shake the water from my hair.

"I want one of those giant pink flamingo floaties," she tells Jackson.

He drops a peck on her lips. "You can have whatever you want."

Crouching behind her, I sink my teeth into the curve of her shoulder. She shivers and leans into me. While they continue to talk, I wrap my fist in her hair and trail kisses along her neck.

"When we have a house, we can do this all the time."

Her breathless words give me pause. She never explicitly agreed to living together. The last I was with her, she'd insisted on staying in New York.

"That sounds so good," Jax groans, his mouth on hers.

My chest swells. Holy shit, this is my life. A house. A baby. Aurora. Jackson. It hits me, really hits me. "I'd love that," I whisper.

And I love you.

32

AURORA

Maybe it's pregnancy hormones, or perhaps it's the attention of two attractive men. Whatever it is, being with them is not only electrifying, but fulfilling in a way I've never experienced before, as if the shattered parts of me are finally mending.

A rough palm glides up my torso to cup my breast, and I rock my hips, moaning into Jackson's kiss. Their hard bodies and erections press against me. Fingers pinch my nipple, and a shudder runs through me.

"Are you cold?" Ethan's hands move to caress my arms. "Let's get you out. You have goosebumps."

He withdraws, and I let out a whimper of disappointment.

The temperature is in the seventies, and although the sun is setting over the ocean, the water is heated. I'm not chilly.

Jax brings us closer to one of the swim-up canopy beds—and I feel it.

I gasp and clutch my stomach, which terrifies him.

He sets me on my feet and looms over me, cupping my lower belly. "What's wrong? Are you hurt? Did I do something?"

"Wait. Wait. I think I felt it."

Ethan rushes over, panic etched on his features. "What is it?"

I grab his hand to place it where mine was, and there it is! A flutter, then a distinct push or roll.

His jaw drops, and his brows shoot up. "Is that...?"

"The baby." Tears prickle my eyelids. "He must like the water."

Jax positions his fingers beside Ethan's. "For real?"

We all go silent, eagerly waiting. The gentle flutter-roll happens again. My gaze meets Jackson's, and the emotion in his glassy eyes crushes me.

A gorgeous smile spreads across Ethan's face, revealing that dimple, and he clasps the back of my neck. "Holy fuck. We're having a baby."

My heart hammers and my lips tremble. "Yeah, we are."

Jax leans down and rests his forehead on mine. "Today is one of the best days of my life. Thank you."

His voice breaks, and I want to cry harder. Despite everything, moments like these are why I love him.

He straightens to his full height. "I need to make sure the pool temp isn't too high."

"It's not," I say with a chuckle. "It's perfect."

"Still, I have to feed you...and him." He runs his fingers through his wet hair. "This is so very real now."

"Yeah, no shit," Ethan mutters, his tone sullen.

"You okay?" I ask.

He tilts his head skyward and releases a heavy sigh. "We need to talk."

The mood shifts instantly, unearthing the deep-seated anxiety I had managed to bury.

∾

Ethan

WRAPPED IN A TOWEL, Aurora climbs into the outdoor canopy bed. I sit beside her, and she glances up at me with unease, searching my expression for any hint of betrayal. I know what she's thinking—that I've been unfaithful, or I'm still married, or I got someone else pregnant, or some other outrageous nonsense.

Jackson places a tray of food on the mattress and grumbles, "You're the worst buzzkill."

"This pertains to you too, dickhead." Bile rises in my throat, and I swallow it down. "Your father waited for me in the parking lot after the suspension hearing."

"Great." He frowns and plops down on the other side of our girl. "What the fuck did he have to say?"

Aurora clutches the towel, and I reach for her hand, laying it on my lap.

"He said some shit—"

"What kind of shit?" he demands, his body tense, shoulders squared.

I should've talked to him first, without Aurora, but it's too late now, and I need her to trust us. I can keep Kyle's threats to myself for now. That way, I'm not setting Jax off and worrying her.

"He's been doing his research," I say, steering the conversation. "Has he contacted you?"

"Just his usual fuckery. He wants to negotiate, which means he wants money, but the law firm I hired doesn't think that's necessary. It's my fucking inheritance."

I nod in understanding. "The sale of the Santa Monica house is finalized. My lawyer is waiting on confirmation of whose name the property is in—yours or the trust's—or if it even matters."

"I signed the papers. I'll text Kyle letting him know I'm moving in, see how he reacts."

One thing I can say about Jackson is he's not afraid of confrontation, though that's typically how he gets himself into trouble.

If his father ever showed up while Aurora was home alone... Just the thought has my stomach churning.

"We need to be certain he has no control over the property. I don't want him anywhere near there."

Aurora shrugs. "Let's live here."

"No." Jax's knee bounces. "You adore that house—the nursery, the backyard, the beach, the pool. It belongs to *you*." He clenches his jaw, the muscle pulsing. "I have a team handling it, but knowing Kyle, he'll drag his feet. I'll talk to him. Whatever he was planning, it failed. We're together. I'm returning to hockey. I'm clean." His gaze connects with mine, unsure and hesitant. "I have people to vouch for me if he tries to prove me incompetent." He takes a steadying breath. "He'll negotiate."

"Jax…" I don't know how to tell him the only thing Kyle wants is for Aurora and the baby to disappear—and that ain't fucking happening. So, I move on, deciding to protect them myself. For them, I'll do anything. "There's something I've been keeping from you, from everyone. Something your father discovered."

Aurora slumps and groans. "Please don't say you have another wife or kid."

"Or husband," Jax adds.

I shoot him an icy glare. "No, I do not have another wife, kid, or husband, idiot."

He arches a brow. "Boyfriend?"

"Fuck off. I'm being serious." Before he can intrude further, I gather my nuts and face Aurora. "My father is a turned FBI informant serving life in prison. I've never met him, few people know, and we don't share a last name."

They exchange a wide-eyed glance before staring at me with mirroring shocked expressions.

"He made a deal to keep my mother out of his trial." My heart races, and I feel a ramble coming on. "She was his mistress and pregnant, and his wife's family would've killed her. Only my father's brothers and the FBI knew. She waitressed at the diner I took you to," I say to Aurora. "That's how they met. Shorty, the owner, was my uncle, unbeknownst to me then. After my mother died, he told me about my father and how they'd hidden assets in my mother's name in a shell company. Somehow, Kyle found out." I scrub my fingers through my hair. "I was somewhat close to Shorty. He's deceased now, and my lawyer is one of the other brothers, but other than that, I don't communicate with them."

Though that's about to change.

"Holy shit, dude." Jax roars with laughter. "This is the best day ever. I can't even put into words how ecstatic I am that you have flaws." He shakes his head and smiles. "I didn't think it was possible."

Aurora furrows her brows and asks the obvious: "What did he go to prison for?"

I glance at Jackson, who understands better than anyone how grating it is to answer for the sins of your father. It's much worse for him. I never knew the man whose shadow I'm running from—Jax can't escape his.

His gaze shifts uncomfortably. Lying hasn't worked out well for him, and I find it within myself to shake off the unwarranted shame.

"Racketeering, arson, money laundering, and six counts of murder. The media dubbed him *Iron Eyes*."

33

RICKY

Aurora has been avoiding me. Since she and Jackson reunited and he expressed his suspicion of me, she has kept her distance. When I reach for her, she pulls away. No hugs. No little touches. Nothing.

It pisses me off far more than it should. This was inevitable. I'm not who she thinks I am. I'm not her gay bodyguard or anything else. I'm an undercover agent, and she'll hate me when she finds out I lied to her.

When this case is over, I'll move on.

At least, that's what I tell myself.

I try to remain invisible and focus on work, but it's hard to ignore Aurora making out with two guys right in front of me. In any other scenario, I'd leave, but I'm stuck watching, envying. What? I don't know.

She's not mine, and she'll never be. Yet, I like caring for her *a lot*, especially when we're alone. Plus, I'm attracted to her, even when she's with others.

What a mindfuck. I've never been this lost and confused.

I expected to hear them all fucking tonight, but Aurora's asleep, resting after a long day and late night. Shortly after, Jackson and Ethan started arguing.

I lean against the kitchen counter, casually drinking a bottle of water while they fight on the patio.

Our mics are mounted on the house. The wind off the ocean is too strong to catch what they're discussing at the edge of the property, but whatever it is, they don't want Aurora to overhear.

Ethan is gesturing animatedly, and Jackson is struggling. He's pacing and tugging at his hair. This can only be related to Kyle.

Regardless of Jackson's bravado, he fears the backlash of alienating his father. He still believes if he plays Kyle's games, he'll have the freedom to live his life. It's utter bullshit. Kyle will never let him go. He's too valuable.

My phone pings with a text, and I set the water bottle on the counter.

CHARLIE

Aurora was researching Iron Eyes an hour ago.

> Shit, Ethan must have told them.

CHARLIE

He thinking of using his father?

> Has to be. Flag the Rikers registration system in case he decides to visit.

CHARLIE

Got it.

We easily bugged Aurora's phone; she forgets it everywhere. We'd love to get our hands on Jackson's, but he keeps it close and hardly uses it. Smartphones hold significant data, such as locations and contacts, and his could provide key information to advance this case. We can track his device, but that's about it.

Now, it appears we need to track Ethan too. The last thing we want is the involvement of another organized crime group. The Rossi family is relatively small and tight-knit, but their assets are considerable—they own a vast portion of New York City real estate. Their reach is substantial, with ties to the Cosa Nostra and marriage alliances with the Bratva.

Vincenzo "Iron Eyes" Rossi won't tolerate anyone threatening his grandson, even if he and Ethan are estranged.

I tug my dog tags free, adjusting the chain. They settle on my chest with a clink, and I fist the metal before shooting Charlie a text.

> I need to step in before Ethan does. You got me.

CHARLIE

I got you. Good luck. He might kill you.

> Which one?

CHARLIE

Both.

34

JACKSON

A HARSH, COLD WIND WHIPS AROUND US, EMBODYING ETHAN'S icy glare. "This is the best option, Jax, at least until the baby is born."

I clench my jaw and grind my molars. I'm sure to have a headache after this. "I have a plan. Will you fucking listen to me?"

"Your *plan* is to keep her by your side. He harmed her while you were there." He spits each word as if I don't know. "This is *my life* we're talking about." He gestures with his hands in emphasis.

"It's my life too!" Heat creeps up my neck and face. My head swims. "I just got her back." In and out. In and out. Breathe. "Now you want to take her from me?"

He steps closer and clasps my shoulder. My impulse is to throw him off. I'm worked up. I can't stand anyone touching me, but right now, I allow it, and he squeezes, massaging the tense muscle.

"You'll be with her until your suspension is over. I know it's not long, but New York is the safest place for her. I have family there—"

"You haven't even met them. *They* could be dangerous."

"My uncles took care of me when I needed it." His grasp

shifts to my nape. "I'll have you there. You'll scope them out for me."

"What about me?" Ricky approaches, striding across the patio with his hands in his pockets. "I'm guessing this is about Kyle."

How does he always appear out of nowhere?

Ethan drops his arm to his side. "As always."

My head hangs in shame, and my gaze falls to Ricky's boots. His feet are shoulder-width apart, one slightly back, his posture defensive and ready for action.

It's inconspicuous, a false sense of security. That's how they're trained.

"*Come on, pretty boy. Fight me.*" The air freezes in my lungs, and my stomach tightens. That voice is only in my head, an echo from the past. It's not real. "*Fight me, pretty boy.*" It's the boots. The posture. It's not real.

"Why don't we go inside and talk?" Ricky suggests.

His tone is professional and placating, and it's all fucking with my mind.

In a hyperalert state, I follow them into the kitchen and sit at the table, Ricky across from me, Ethan beside me.

I slip my phone from my pocket and place it in front of me. Ricky does the same. He's mirroring me, another tactic they use to set you at ease.

This is an interrogation.

My instincts are never wrong. They have twenty-five years of acute conditioning.

I can't believe I didn't see it sooner. I was fooled by his Viking persona, preoccupied with how close he was getting to Aurora. Although I wanted to go to the police, I wasn't sure who to trust after the last time I opened up to someone, and I don't want one sitting at my kitchen table or living in my home.

Call me paranoid, but I grew up with dirty cops.

Dark rage builds in my chest. "I hired you to protect her."

My gaze connects with Ricky's, and something shifts in his eyes. Realization. Alarm. Guilt.

"He was disheveled and sloppy drunk, yet you let him in

without question. If you were truly thinking about Aurora's safety, that alone should've given you pause. You didn't come get me. You didn't follow him to the patio to ensure he wasn't a threat. How were you sure he was my father?"

Ricky's stare is unwavering. "I will always protect her."

Even if he is sincere, his loyalties lie elsewhere. I've spent my life deceiving others and dodging the truth—I recognize a non-answer when I hear it. If he's not one hundred percent here for Aurora, then he needs to get the fuck out.

I pick up my phone and lean back in my chair. "How about I call Kyle to join this conversation? Then you can ask him everything you want to know."

Ethan sucks in a deep, exasperated breath. "Jax," he snarls in warning. "What the fuck are you doing?"

With the number dialed, I turn the screen to face Aurora's supposed bodyguard. The room goes silent, and the first ring echoes. Ricky rubs his jaw, his hand covered in tattooed roses to conceal the scars marring his skin. It rings once more, our eyes locked in an intense stare-down.

"Son?"

Kyle answers, Ricky lunges for the phone, and Ethan dives between us, snatching Ricky's arm and preventing him from reaching me.

I hang up. That's all the confirmation I need.

"You're crazy, you know that?" Ricky's chest heaves.

Gaslighting. Yet another one of my father's favorite weapons. They're all the same.

"First, you think I'm after Aurora, and now, what? Kyle?"

Ice runs through my veins, my voice and fury escalating to a whole new level. "Oh my fucking God. Are you even gay?"

Ricky, or whatever his actual name is, glances at Ethan, and I know I've caught him. This is the reason I'm paranoid—I can't even trust my bodyguard not to betray me.

"*That's* what you're worried about right now?" he scoffs, daring to turn this around on me.

It grates on my last nerve.

"Yes, motherfucker, that's exactly what I'm worried about. A lying pig with no integrity taking advantage of what's mine. Nothing is stopping you from eye fucking her while she's undressing or touching her." My body quakes with anger, begging to be let loose. "You're not her bodyguard—you're here because you're after me!"

His brows shoot up, and he raises his hands in surrender, palms outward, fingers splayed. "No. That's not why I'm here—"

"Then why didn't you approach me?" My breaths grow shallow, my vision tunneled. "Why carry on this charade? You've read my history, right?"

A hand clutches the back of my neck, and my skin burns. I knock it away. A deep voice speaks, but I'm not there anymore.

After all this time, after all the abuse I've endured—myself and my mother—someone steps in, but it's not to help. It's to use me.

To manipulate me for their own benefit.

They didn't want to stop Kyle or any of the others when we were being fucking terrorized.

Ricky's face softens, and there it is. *Pity.*

I no longer see him—I see rage.

I see the anguish in my mother's eyes as she suffered trying to shield me, then the disappointment when I ultimately proved to be no better than the monster who tormented her.

Every officer who apprehended me and never once questioned my behavior beyond being a spoiled punk. Annoyed teachers who demanded my removal from their classrooms. Principals who delighted in punishing me—one even belonging to Kyle's band of sick fucks. Cops who attended my mother's funeral, eyes filled with guilt.

Intoxicated men who put their hands on me with that predatory gleam in their smiles.

I pounce, catching the corner of the table with my side. A sharp pain flares, but Ricky goes to the floor, the chair tipping and crashing beside him.

It's dark again, the demons laughing, the child crying.

He struggles beneath me. He's tough, but I've faced tougher.

I feel nothing but violence. The room spins. I grip his throat, put all my weight into it, and squeeze, refusing to let go.

My skin burns, and I throw my head back. "Don't touch me." It's monotone. I've checked out.

I'm floating in the afterlife, looking down upon myself, and I fucking love it. My veins light up with adrenaline and euphoria, and I breathe it all in.

No more hurt, only wrath.

I raise my fist, smiling. "I'm going to kill you."

His eyes widen, and so does my grin. I bring my fist crashing down, connecting with his jaw. Bone meeting bone reverberates through my arm.

The room erupts in chaos, the voices shouting. Another burst of pain, another, only feeding the madness. It feels good —better than good. Intoxicating.

There's something cathartic about pain and violence.

I unleash a flurry of blows, each fueled by a hunger for vengeance.

Blood drips to the floor. His or mine, I'm not sure. He yells, the vibration buzzing under my palm, but the thunderous pounding in my ears drowns out his words.

In vain, he attempts to pry my fingers from his throat and buck me off, but I lean forward and apply more pressure.

He chokes, his eyes water, tears running down his temples, and I relish in his suffering.

"*No one's here to save you, pretty boy.*"

"I hope you rot in fucking Hell."

A distant voice whispers, urging me to stop.

Stop.

"No."

Stop.

"No."

"Stop, Jax! Stop!" Aurora cries, her panic and fear breaking through the dark haze.

I release my grip. Ricky gasps, coughing. He shoves me off him, kicking and scrambling away.

The air is thick, the room still reeling, and I focus on my erratic heartbeat.

I rise slowly, pain radiating throughout my upper body. I flick the blood from my raw knuckles and watch it spatter across the tile, familiarity washing over me.

My head lifts, and my world tilts. Or maybe that's me. My gaze connects with Ethan's. His eyes resemble the gloomy shade of those New York storm clouds I despise. Ironic, since he grew up there.

I glance lower to the person trembling and sobbing in his arms.

Oh, fuck.

35

AURORA

MY BRAIN IS LAGGING. EVERYTHING IS MOVING TOO FAST, YET slowly at the same time.

Jax won't look at me, and nobody's talking. Ricky gasps for air, clutching his throat, while Ethan holds me to his chest.

"What happened?" I cry, shattering the silence.

Jackson spits blood in Ricky's direction. "Yeah, *Ricky*, what happened?"

Ethan moves forward, an arm out, ready to intervene if necessary. I try to break free, but he grips me tighter.

"Hold on. Jax, are you good? I need to know if you're calm. Do you need medical attention?"

"Jesus fucking Christ," Ricky snarls. "I barely touched him. I—"

"Shut the fuck up," Ethan cuts him off, tone low and menacing. "Your explanation can wait."

I'm so confused. I know Jax isn't fond of Ricky, but I've been careful not to trigger his jealousy. Although conflicted, I've kept my distance from my bodyguard, hoping Jax would come to realize he wasn't a threat.

But now Ethan?

What the hell happened while I slept?

"I'm good." Jax glances at me then averts his gaze. "I'm calm."

I peer up at Ethan. "Can I go, please? He won't hurt me."

He loosens his hold, and I dash across the kitchen, him right behind me.

Shivering, I wrap my arms around Jax. "What—"

His face contorts as he hisses in pain, and his torso tenses.

My eyes burn with tears. "Where are you hurt?" I gently take his swollen, deformed fist in my hands. "You need an X-ray."

"Already on it." Ethan rakes his fingers through his hair and lifts his phone to his ear.

Ricky grabs a hand towel from the counter and presses it to his bleeding lip. "It's broken. I can tell from here. Get some ice on it and a bandage. I have medical supplies in my bag."

It's unbelievable he can talk after the way Jax pummeled him. Still, he doesn't threaten to call the police. He moves to the freezer and scoops ice into a baggie. Whatever went down between them doesn't appear to be one-sided.

He hands Jax the ice. "Wrap it in your T-shirt."

I step back, allowing Jax to yank his shirt over his head, and I gasp when I see his inflamed and bruised ribs. I whip around to confront my bodyguard. "What the hell? Why?"

"That wasn't me!" he bellows, his voice raw, his face reddening further. "I went easy on him, for fuck's sake."

That may be true, but an unmistakable flicker of guilt passes over his eyes.

Jax sets the ice to his knuckles and grimaces. "I hit the corner of the table when I lunged for him."

Exasperated, I throw my arms up. "Why? What is wrong with you two?"

Again, nothing but dead air.

Then, Ethan says to Jax, "Doc is on his way. Get cleaned up. I'll handle this."

My frustration mounts. "Handle what? Someone start talking!"

Jackson's pained eyes finally meet mine. "Come on. We'll talk in my bathroom." He nods toward the hallway.

I follow him, and, perched on the edge of the spa tub, he

buries his face in his hands, his pinky not curling the same as the rest.

I hug myself. "Please, just tell me what happened."

His gaze lifts, heavy-lidded and full of regret, and a defeated sigh escapes him. "Ricky is not who you think he is. He's not your bodyguard. He's an undercover cop watching me."

The sound of static fills my ears. My mind jumps to the worst plausible scenario: Jax arrested. The floor gives way, and I stumble. He catches me and pulls me between his legs. My knees hit the floor, and I fall into him.

This has to be a mistake. Maybe I'm misunderstanding. "What?" The breathless word is barely audible.

"He's an undercover cop." He brushes my hair from my forehead. "He's not your friend. He's not with Charlie."

A sudden, sharp pain pierces my heart. "No." I shake my head. "He wouldn't... It can't be."

Jax holds my face in his trembling hands and stares deep into my eyes. "He lied to get close to you, baby."

Tears stream down my cheeks. "Why? He... The police are after you?"

"I'm not sure, maybe." He shrugs. "Ricky let Kyle into the penthouse. Didn't even question it. They could be associated with him or after information on him."

I clutch my tightening chest. "I don't understand," I whisper, my throat constricting. "What information?"

His thumbs glide over my cheekbones, wiping the tears away. "I'd hoped to keep it from you, remember? This is not..." His voice breaks. "This is difficult for me."

I grip his wrists. "Please, tell me."

Closing his eyes, he drops his forehead to mine. "Kyle has been involved in some messed-up shit for as long as I can remember." He swallows hard, his Adam's apple bobbing. "He's a part of this depraved society that hosts lavish sex parties for politicians and other assholes, with girls...and guys," he adds with a shuddering exhale. "They lure them in with drugs and celebrities. Some are sicker than others. For some, it's a lifestyle carried on outside the party."

I try to wrap my brain around it, but I can't, so I ask the obvious. "You've been there?"

He nods, and my world falls apart all over again. Of course he has. Although naïve, I've been to one of these parties. Emily brought me to prove a point. He was there, and he explained his reaction from that night. He said Kyle's men were dangerous.

But to be involved...in something worse than the pictures I've seen?

Fear clenches my heart and crushes the air from my lungs. "Why?" I sob.

"I didn't have a choice. I was too young to understand. When I could, I fought. When I was forced to, I got fucking wasted. It's not like I wanted to. I never took part..." He trails off, unspoken words hanging in the air.

Realization hits yet again, a previous argument echoing in my mind.

Stop saying that... You wouldn't if you knew what I've been through... Sex is warped inside my head...except with you.

"Aurora, stop! Look at me."

In Jackson's arms, she sobs inconsolably, gasping for air. He whispers reassuring words, but she's already in a state of panic —her breaths rapid and shallow, her complexion pale, her lips tinged purple.

I sit beside him, cup her tear-streaked face, and force her gaze to mine. "This isn't over. I have lawyers and connections. We'll fight whatever comes next. You hear me?"

Neither of them noticed I was leaning against the door-jamb, listening to the tail end of their conversation. When Aurora broke, so did my heart.

I realize she's focused on more than him possibly going to jail. She's thinking of him at these parties and devastated by all he's endured.

But I hate to see her like this; she was doing so well. It tears at my insides and makes me prickly. I prefer my mischievous, smart-mouthed girl.

"Baby, please," I soften my tone. "I promise I can protect him. I can protect you both."

She closes her eyes and shakes her head. Unable to get past her fear and anxiety, she starts to hyperventilate.

"Aurora," a rough, nasally voice barks.

Her attention snaps to Ricky, who stands in the doorway.

one eye nearly shut, swelling and bruising along his cheek-bone. The abrasion on his chin is raw, his lip split, and angry red marks crisscross his throat.

"Take a breath." He draws closer. "It's gonna be alright."

He crouches behind her as she sucks in air, and Jax stiffens. "I'll kick your fucking teeth in," he snarls.

"That was your one free shot for me not coming forth sooner. After this, you're dealing with a special agent, and I won't be easy on you."

My temper ignites, threats bursting from my lips without thought. "You touch him again, and I'll throttle you."

Ricky skewers me with a glare and dares to place a hand on Aurora's back. "I'm. Not. After. Jackson. I understand why you're pissed, but *I* was the one who helped her overcome her anxiety."

Fuck him. We've all done our part. "And ruined it. Good job."

Jesus, my captain is rubbing off on me.

He rubs her back with soothing circles. "It's okay. You're okay. Nothing will happen to Jackson."

"Wait." Jax lifts his palm. "Hold up. Special agent? Like the FBI?"

"I'm with Homeland Security. I'm a senior special agent working on a case involving Kyle and the LAPD. I'm not a cop, nor have I ever been."

Agent or not, Jax won't forgive Ricky's betrayal easily. If one thing sets Jax off, it's dishonesty and manipulation, which likely reminds him of his father. If Ricky were solely Jackson's body-guard, it'd be different, but fuck with Aurora, and you unleash a monster.

I can't say I blame him. Ricky has been with her under false pretenses for months. Was he *trying* to get close to her? He certainly wasn't getting friendly with Jax.

"I'm prepared to offer you protection for your cooperation —your *full* cooperation. I was *your* bodyguard first. *You* asked me to be hers, and I couldn't turn it down, nor could I chance being removed from this case. Either way, we can work together to put Kyle in prison, where he belongs."

Aurora's breathing slows, and she wipes the tears from her puffy eyes.

I open my arms. "Come here, baby girl."

She climbs into my lap, rests her head on my shoulder, and watches them.

Ricky grabs the wrapped bag of ice from the floor and offers it to Jax. "Ice it, and then I'll wrap it. Someone needs to teach you to throw a punch without breaking your fist."

Jax flips his hand over, his palm a bluish shade. "It's broken. Not much good the ice will do," he grumbles but ices his knuckles anyway. "I'll consider an offer when I see it on paper, and that's only after I get my trust. You're not seizing everything I have."

If I didn't know he loved spending his money on others, I'd assume, like everyone else, that he was superficial. He truly wants to give Aurora and the baby all he promised—the beach house, this penthouse, security.

"I can work with that—if nothing changes. You kick me out or go to your father, we're through." Ricky glances down at Jackson's swollen hand. "And you'll need that trust fund. You're never returning to hockey at the rate you're going."

Fuck me.

I massage my temple to ease the coming headache.

"Don't worry, Coach. As long as I can hold a stick, I'll play. I have plenty of time to heal, and this isn't my first fracture." Jax takes a deep breath and winces. "Ribs fucking hurt, though."

Fuck me twice.

How did I end up with the biggest pain in the ass in the history of hockey?

WHILE WE WAIT FOR DOC, Aurora showers, Ricky updates his partner, and I work through emails in Jackson's room.

It's getting late, and Jax rests against the padded headboard of his massive bed, icing his ribs. "Can you promise me something?"

"Yeah," I answer without missing a beat, lowering my phone to my lap.

"If anything happens to me, you'll take care of Aurora, no matter what."

My brows furrow. "Of course I will. Why?"

His gaze drifts toward the bathroom. "I'm going to petition to transfer the conservatorship to you and add your name to my accounts. Whatever is necessary."

Why does he sound defeated? "Jax—"

"Convince her to stay home. She'll listen to you. She doesn't trust me, but she'll trust you to care for her. Make sure she and the baby have everything." His eyes well up, and he drops his head.

I sit up straighter in the leather armchair. "Shut the fuck up. You're not going anywhere."

He faces the ceiling and blows out a long exhale. "I don't know what'll come of this."

"We'll work it out," I assure him.

"This," he circles his hand, gesturing to the three of us, "is temporary. If I'm not in prison or dead, the team will likely trade me once the season ends. If not, they'll let me go next year, and a few years down the line, they might release you too, because of all the shit I've done. What then?"

I won't accept that. The thought is instantaneous.

When did I go from desperately wanting a Stanley Cup to desiring a family? When did *this* become my priority?

"Pull yourself together and get back on the ice. Play with the same passion you did in your rookie year. Management wants you to sell tickets, to dazzle the media and fans. They don't care how you do it, as long as the team makes money. Fuck Kyle. Fuck what people will think. Play hard and win." I suck in a deep breath. "And if we end up separated, I'll be the biggest fan in your box, right there beside Aurora. Someone has to manage you, and I already spend most of my time doing so anyhow."

Are my eyes burning? No, they are not.

I expect a wave of regret or panic to hit me, but it doesn't come—instead, there's a sense of conviction. A weight lifts from my shoulders, and I feel...*unburdened*. Everything I said feels undeniably right.

Jackson blinks his tears away. I've never seen him at a loss for words. "Why? Why would you do that? You love coaching."

I chuckle lightheartedly at his dumbfounded expression. "Because I want Aurora—all of her—and she's not whole without you, and because you have *it*. You're naturally talented. Every part of you is made for the ice. You just need a team behind you."

"Wow," he breathes, taken aback. "Are you always like this, a coach? Is that *your* natural talent?"

I can't help the shit-eating grin that stretches across my face. He really is rubbing off on me. "No, my natural talent got your girlfriend pregnant." I grin wider. "You're welcome."

He returns my smile, the glimmer of light rekindling in his eyes. "And there it is—the reason I hate you. You're such a fucking asshole."

We both laugh, neither of us able to control it.

"Someone's exhausted." Ethan carries Aurora into my bedroom, her legs around his waist and arms encircling his neck.

He's smiling, but given Aurora's red-rimmed eyes, she has been crying in the shower, and he's trying to cheer her up. My gut clenches, a physical recoil, because I know I'm the source of her pain.

He drops her in the center of the bed with a bounce, making her giggle. His hands land on each side of her waist, and with one knee on the mattress, he bends down and kisses her.

Shirtless, sitting at the bedside, I watch the scene unfold with a sly smile. *I wonder when I should tell him...*

The warm fingers palpitating my icy ribs abruptly still, and I peer down to see Doc staring at Coach in utter shock.

Ethan is in a loose pair of gray sweatpants and a team T-shirt, his dark hair tousled, climbing into my bed to wreck my girlfriend—*our* girlfriend.

Although Doc doesn't know that.

He does now, and the look on his face is absolutely priceless.

My roar of hilarity grabs Ethan's attention. "Asshole, did

you forget we have company?" I ask between gasping for breath and wincing in pain from my body shaking.

Coming from my bathroom, on the opposite side of the room, he likely couldn't see Doc crouched, assessing my left side.

Our straightedge coach stands so quickly, I wouldn't be surprised if he strained a back muscle. Just as swiftly, he sits beside me, arms folded across his lap to hide his erection. His face flushes the color of my broken fist, and I tilt my head, erupting into more laughter, harder than I have in...I don't know when.

"I fucking hate you," he says under his breath.

"Doc, did I tell you about the time Coach got drunk and crawled into my hotel room?" I glance at Ethan with tears in my eyes. "Where were we playing...Colorado?"

"I'll break the other side of your ribs if you don't shut the fuck up," he grits through his teeth.

Aurora wraps her arms around my neck, pressing herself against my back, and whines, "You two always leave me out."

God, I love her. My perfect match.

"You wouldn't have to miss out if you came with us," Ethan replies, not helping the situation.

Naturally, my girl pounces on the opportunity to tease him further. She plants a lingering kiss on my neck, and goose-bumps erupt along my chest.

"Oh, yeah? What do you have in mind, Coach?" Her voice is pure honey, thick with seduction.

"Why are you two like this? Can't you be normal for five fucking seconds?" As if he wasn't the one intending to sleep in here tonight, because there's no way in hell he was dropping Aurora off and going to his own bed, not with that hard-on.

"Hey." I grasp his shoulder. "What did you tell me?" I pause for dramatic emphasis, fighting the urge to smirk. "Fuck what people think, right?"

"You know what? You're right. I'm trading you." He's got that death glare in his eyes, but humor glints in their icy depths before he turns away. "What's the verdict?"

Doc clears his throat and crosses his arms over his chest. "Fourth and fifth metacarpal bones are most likely fractured."

"They were previously fractured," I point out.

"Yes, which you never let heal properly."

I shrug. They'll heal during my suspension. If not, it wouldn't be the first time I've played injured.

Exasperated, Ethan releases a heavy sigh, puffing out his cheeks. "What do you suggest?"

"Soft cast until he sees the orthopedic specialist. A more permanent solution after the season."

I shake my head. "I'm not having surgery."

"Jax—" Ethan starts.

"I'm not." Our gazes lock. "I can't take narcotics, and the baby is due in March."

He nods in understanding. "Okay. How about the ribs?"

"Crunching where Jackson indicates it's most painful. Could be cartilage or a torn intercostal muscle, unlikely to be broken. All you can do is rest. I know you don't want anything for the pain, but over-the-counter meds won't hurt."

"I'm good," I mutter.

"What about the other guy?" Ethan gestures toward the guest room.

"No concussion symptoms. Swallowing and breathing sufficiently." Doc turns his attention my way. "Wanna tell me *why* you strangled your bodyguard?"

Ricky is far from being my bodyguard, and I scoff. "Nope."

"Do you want to talk alone?"

As much as I respect Doc—and I genuinely do, seeing as he's been nothing but kind and patient with me—I'm not sharing this. Hallucinations? Flashbacks? Blacking out? Yeah, Ethan will never allow me around the baby. "No, I'm fine."

"Are you using?"

Irritation swells in my chest, and I clench my jaw. "Fuck, no."

His tone softens. "Jackson—"

"He's not," Ethan cuts him off with a shake of his head.

"What happened was an isolated incident. Ricky messed with the wrong person."

That's one way of putting it.

38

ETHAN

What a fucking day. From seeing our baby, making out, sharing secrets, arguing, finding out Ricky is an undercover agent, Jackson snapping, to lifelong promises...this is life with Jax and Aurora.

And I've never felt more alive.

In my arms in Jackson's bed, Aurora gazes out the floor-to-ceiling windows at the moonlight over the rough waters.

Full of pent-up emotion, I tuck a strand of hair behind her ear and whisper, "You're the moon and all the stars in my sky, you know that?"

Of course, Jax can't stay quiet. "If you're *his* moon and stars, you're *my* sun and universe," he says, approaching the bed after walking Doc out.

"The universe includes the sun, idiot. Way to ruin my moment."

With that damn smug smirk playing on his lips, he drops his phone on the bedside table and crawls into bed on the other side of Aurora. The electric blinds close, and complete darkness engulfs the room.

Bedding rustles, and she's pulled from my arms. He wastes no time getting positioned between her legs.

"Jax," she chides halfheartedly.

"I just wanna taste," he says, his deceiving words muffled by the covers.

He's insane. *This* is insane. Still, I find myself capturing her lips in a messy kiss.

"Jesus, baby, you always taste so fucking good," he mutters from between her thighs.

I'm conflicted—my cautious brain battles with my hard dick.

Why do I crave this so much? I shouldn't enjoy another man being with the woman I want.

Her moans fill my mouth and erase all argument. Every whimper and hitched breath he forces from her sends a wave of raw desire through me.

I press my teeth into her bottom lip to ease some of the ache. "I hate this in the worst way."

But I don't hate it. I should, but I don't, because I've *fallen* for her in the worst way.

God-fucking-damn-it, I love her. I'd do anything for her—for *them*.

I can't imagine being with anyone different. It's unfathomable.

They've ruined me. No one else could evoke this desperate craving inside me.

I pinch her nipples and swallow her moans elicited by my captain, and she strokes my cock as if she's begging for it.

On a sharp cry, her lips leave mine, and her hand releases me, presumably to grasp Jackson's hair.

He always knows how to get her attention. Fucker.

I kneel beside her pillow, drag my sweats below my ass, and, refusing to be ignored, grab her chin. Before she screams his name, I have my cock stuffed in her mouth. "Suck."

She greedily pulls me in, hollowing her cheeks and gliding me along her teasing tongue until I hit the back of her throat.

"Fuck. I love how you swallow me whole."

Jax eating her out has me on edge; coupled with her pleading whimpers, I want to blow.

"You crying around my cock has got to be the greatest sound I've ever heard."

Her orgasm takes over, her body becomes pliant, and I use her mouth as my personal fuck toy. She writhes in pleasure, and my mouth waters to taste her, but for now, I settle for her sucking my dick as if it's her favorite meal.

She comes down from her high, and her breath slows. Her hands come to my waist, her nails biting into my skin, and her tongue circles the sensitive underside.

I fist her hair and work my hips, ready to unload in her mouth until...

The bed shifts, and Jackson says, "Baby, I need to be inside you."

I'm barely holding on, running through hockey stats in my mind to keep from coming.

Her body meets his and jolts with his thrusts, and the carnal sounds of him fucking her devour my sanity. I cup the back of her head, ensuring she stays in place, and thrust in and out of her mouth, seeking some semblance of control.

She moans and inhales me with renewed energy. Air hisses through my teeth, and my balls hug my shaft.

"Give me what I want, baby. Soak my cock," he groans.

Jesus, fuck, what is happening? I'm both jealous he's making her come a second time and so turned on, I'm about to come myself.

"If you come again on his cock, I'm shoving mine down your throat," I warn her, tightening my fist in her hair.

I'm positive I hear Jackson snicker.

She relaxes her mind-blowing suction and parts her lips, tempting me to follow through with my threat.

What's left of my control shatters, and my hips punch forward. "God, you drive me crazy." *Thrust.* "You like both of us filling you, baby?" *Thrust.* "Like being our dirty girl?" *Thrust.* "How about next, I fill your ass while he fills your cunt?"

This time, I'm certain Jax chokes.

Her throat squeezes tight, and I feel it down to my fucking

toes. Her body trembles, and she releases a strangled cry that vibrates through my balls.

My heart pounds an angry rhythm against my rib cage, my head dizzy with the frantic need to follow her release.

"*Fuck*...that's it. Milk my cock, Aurora, make me fill that perfect pussy, baby."

His fractured words are maddening, provoking a violent rush of possessiveness and arousal. Ecstasy rips through my veins and steals my breath.

Can you die from an orgasm? Because I just might.

"Swallow," I gasp, and my thrusts turn greedy.

My dick jerks over and over, and she swallows every drop until I'm wrecked and my body collapses.

"I BEGAN WORKING AS YOUR BODYGUARD FOR PUBLIC EVENTS," Ricky, if that's even his name, explains to Jackson, sunglasses covering his bruised eye.

We're slumped around the patio table, half asleep, diving into the breakfast Jax had delivered. It's too fucking early. I want to return to last night, when I had Aurora wrapped in my arms.

There's a slight breeze coming in off the ocean, and the air smells salty and crisp. I see why they love this place. I can picture us spending a lot of time here. *Our house will be just like this.* The thought has me smiling behind my coffee cup.

"I was hoping to get into one of your father's parties," Ricky slides the strawberries from his plate to Aurora's, "but it didn't happen."

Jax cuts into his French toast, piled high with whipped cream and berries. "Kyle would never believe I'd bring a guard to a party."

"True," Ricky agrees. "But Aurora would."

That catches my attention, and I set my fork down.

Jackson settles back in his chair and crosses his arms over his chest. "She's not getting anywhere near his fucked-up parties."

"I'm not saying that, but they could be in your suite together during games."

My stomach turns at the mere thought of Kyle being close to Aurora. "Absolutely not."

Jax returns to his food. "That's not even conceivable."

"*Hypothetically*," Ricky stresses. "What if we arrange an accidental meeting in your suite? Give him access, let him fill the room, and we show up."

"How would you go from being her bodyguard to attending his parties...*alone*?" Jax shoots him a sharp look.

"Aurora will bring a female agent to your game to catch someone's eye. We just need an in."

Every second, my irritation builds, and the crease between my brow deepens.

Jackson huffs. "You think I trust you to use my girlfriend as bait?"

Our girl picks her head up from my shoulder. "I'll do it."

"No," Jax and I say in unison.

"We want this to be over, don't we?" Her gaze shifts between us. "Kyle won't do anything at the arena, and it's safer than Jax going to one of his parties."

Of course she'd offer herself up, and that pisses me off.

"Stop talking," I snarl at her. "It's not happening. For either of you."

"Ethan—" she starts, but I was through with this conversation before it even began.

"That baby is mine." I point to her stomach, then to her chest. "*You* are mine. So let me make myself clear: you are *not* going anywhere near Kyle." I emphasize each word, my eyes boring into hers, daring her to cross me.

"Stop with the possessive bullshit," Ricky barks. "I can protect her. I'll be there as well."

"Like fuck you can." My head snaps in his direction. "Like you protected her when you allowed Kyle in here?"

His nostrils flare, and his voice rises. "I didn't think Kyle would harm her."

"You didn't think a man who abuses women would harm her?"

He has the gall to appear insulted and lean in opposite me. "Not his son's pregnant girlfriend!"

"What the fuck is wrong with you?" I rest my elbows on the table. "Did Jackson rattle something in your brain? Kyle abused his son and the mother of his own child." I inch forward until we're nearly face-to-face. "It's not fucking happening." I push my chair back and toss my napkin down before I wrap my hands around his throat and finish the job Jax started.

Aurora places her hand on mine and attempts to weave our fingers together.

I shake her off, stand from my seat, and mumble, "I have to go. We have a game tonight."

Every step I take toward our room intensifies my frustration. It occurs to me that while I'm at work, nothing is stopping her from going behind my back. She'll do it to prevent Jax from meeting with his father and possibly relapsing.

I'm folding my dirty clothes from yesterday when she enters and shuts the door.

"Ethan." My name rolls off her tongue in that uncanny way that's both pleading and adoring.

I swear, if she pleads with me to let her put herself and our child in danger, I'll snap.

"Don't do it, Aurora."

"We have time to discuss this. Jackson's next game isn't for weeks."

"There is nothing to discuss." I spin on her and wave my hands. "*Nothing.*"

"Can we at least talk about *us* before you leave?"

She's innocent and young, standing in front of me in an oversized T-shirt and tall socks, her hair bedroom messy. A part of me wants to lift her into my arms and carry her back to bed.

Another part of me, the one that's winning, is scared shitless. "Us? What the fuck is that supposed to mean?"

"*Us* right now doesn't feel like *us* yesterday." She twists the hem of her shirt, her head lowered. "Yesterday, you were in this relationship. Today, it feels as though you're running. I won't even see you for weeks."

That hits a sore spot. I have a tendency to run. From feelings. From emotions. From getting my heart trampled on.

She'd do anything for Jax, including defy me.

I want her, but I have to know I can trust her.

I need to be in control.

"Relationship? You have no concept of what it means to be in a stable relationship." *Especially one with me.*

She flinches, as though my words have dealt a physical blow, yet she swiftly regains composure, straightening her posture and squaring her shoulders.

"And you do?" She gives a cynical chuckle. "Because you were *married*? I'm sorry, but I'll choose this," she gestures in front of her, indicating our chaotic trio, "over your *marriage* any day."

She spits out the word *marriage* as if it's a joke, only adding fuel to my anger.

"You have no idea what it's like being married, what type of commitment it takes."

"Commitment?" she echoes mockingly. "Okay, Ethan." She nods in defeat, and her eyes turn glassy.

A sense of foreboding hits me in the chest, but I'm too much of a prideful asshole to admit she's right and fix this.

"I've *bled* for that man." She thrusts a pointed finger toward the door—toward Jax. "I've had my heart shattered and stomped on. I've spent sleepless nights worried about where he was, days wondering why I wasn't good enough. I've been through drunken rages and frightening hangovers." Tears cling to her lashes, and she sucks in a shuddering breath. "*That's* commitment." Her lips tremble. "It's not a ring or a piece of paper." Her tears spill over. "It's breaking yourself to put *them* back together, and you have no fucking clue what that's like."

She turns away, and I'm frozen in utter shock and stupidity.

When she reaches the door, she pauses and glances over her shoulder. "You're right about one thing. I've never had anything stable. But if stable looks anything like your marriage, then *fuck stable*. If that's what you want, then fuck you too."

If it were anyone else she was berating, I'd be so proud of her.

Am I resentful of everything she went through and continues to go through for Jax? Undoubtedly. Am I going to allow her to walk away from me? Nope.

In two steps, I'm in front of her, and she's backed against the door.

I grab her chin and force her gaze to mine. "If you defy me and meet with Kyle, I'll handcuff you to me. You won't leave my sight. When this is all said and done, we'll discuss *us*."

She twists her reddened face from my grasp and leaves the room without another word.

I stand there, dumbfounded. I know why I'm angry—I don't want her risking herself. I'll lose my fucking mind if something were to happen to her or the baby.

She's mad and hurt, and rightfully so. I flung my marriage in her face, and she caught it and threw it back at me ten times harder. That's what Aurora does. She hands me my ass tied in a pretty little pink bow with a note that says, *Nice try, asshole*.

On the way home, regret settles in. I was jealous and possessive, and I let my temper go unchecked. I don't want her around Kyle, that's a given. Yet, I can't help feeling envious of her unwavering devotion to Jax and her fierce determination to protect him.

It's almost hilarious how much of an idiot I am.

I doubt Aurora is laughing right about now.

40

ETHAN

By the time I get to the arena, I taste acid on my tongue, my stomach in knots, as if a snake is slithering inside.

Briefly, I worry I may have food poisoning. Doubt it. I didn't eat more than a few bites this morning. Maybe it's a stroke or a heart attack. There's no other rational explanation for feeling like death pissed in my veins.

It's impossible to concentrate on getting ready for the game. I can't think about anything other than how I let my fear and jealousy control me. I lost my head for five fucking seconds, ran my mouth as I always do when I'm in a panic, and now, I'm going to pay for it.

I tap my pen on my desk and rack my brain.

Aurora would forgive Jax immediately, but that's not how she and I operate. We verbally spar.

And then, it hits me.

She doesn't want another Jackson, you idiot. No one could put up with two jealous hotheads. What the fuck is wrong with me? I need to stop focusing on *their* relationship and consider the dynamics of *all* of us.

I reach for my phone, the compulsion for her stronger than my pride and this apparent stroke I'm having, and text Jax to bring me our girl.

He responds with a saluting emoji, no sarcastic remark, filling me further with dread.

I have two offices in this building. Today, I'm working within the locker rooms, and I sense Jackson's presence when the lull of conversation among training staff comes to a halt.

"Hey, man!" I hear Grant call out. "What are you doing here?"

Grant is the first player to arrive each day. Today, he's the only one here. I swear, he's a lost puppy without Jax.

I glance up from the financial sheets I've been absentmindedly examining, and my heart skips a beat when Aurora appears. She's wearing an oversized sweater *thing* that shows off her bare, tanned thighs and her favorite Converse.

"Coach is in a mood," says my captain, a smug smile plastered on his face. "Got into a fight with his girlfriend and has me playing wingman."

Aurora slaps his stomach, and he laughs.

"I'll be right back." He kisses her forehead. "You know where he is if you want to see him."

By *him*, he means me.

Jackson gives Grant a nod toward the door, and he juts his chin in understanding.

Our girl hesitates, her gaze following her boyfriend, and for a moment, I think she's going to leave with him.

"Aurora, my favorite team wife." Grant wraps an arm around her shoulders and pulls her in for a hug, distracting her.

"I'm not a wife." She shoves playfully at his chest.

"Semantics," he teases. "Can I touch our next superstar?"

He hovers over her belly, and irritation boils in my veins.

"No, you cannot," I yell out. "Not unless you'd like to be benched."

He retracts his hand. "Is he being serious?" he pretends to whisper. "Doesn't he know you belong to the team?"

She belongs to Jackson and me. That's it. Period. "Aurora," I growl, losing my patience. "Get in here."

Grant follows her in and sits on my couch. She pauses then moves to sit next to him.

"No." I reach out and grab her wrist. "You come here. Grant, get out of my office."

He ignores me and chuckles. "You might be worse than Jackson."

I pay him no attention and guide her between my legs. Intertwining our fingers, I hold her arms out and scan her stunning figure. "What are you wearing?"

"A sweater dress. I'm changing things up today, since I've been in nothing but team hoodies for the past few days. Not a fan?"

"I love it. It's a little..." I tilt my head to glimpse her barely-covered ass. "Short."

"That's because your son is making my stomach grow."

I don't know what that has to do with the length of her *dress,* but I'm fond of hearing her talk about what's mine. "Good."

"This is so fucking weird," Grant mutters, amusement lacing his tone.

I skewer him with my best glare. "Unless you want to be traded, get out and shut my door."

He leaves with a shit-eating grin, and Aurora settles herself on my desk.

I lean in and kiss her rounded stomach. "I'm sorry about earlier."

I go to run my palms up her thighs, but she halts my progress, weaving our fingers together.

Her gaze remains on our hands, her shoulders slumped. "It's okay. This is too much for you. I get it. I understand. You have work, and I'm a mess," she rambles anxiously. "I thought a lot about what you said."

I caress her belly, hoping to feel the baby move again. "And what did you think?"

"That you and I... We don't have to do this right now."

Typical Aurora. She'll give me up for my own benefit. It's

not that she's choosing Jackson. She's choosing my freedom—for me.

"And by this, you mean us?"

She nods.

"I was being jealous, baby. I was angry and jealous you always protect Jax. I knew what I was getting into, knew you loved him, but you volunteering to risk yourself pushed all my buttons. I was being possessive, that's all."

"You said we'd discuss *us* when this is all said and done." She repeats my words nearly verbatim, still refusing to look at me. "Did you mean our relationship? As parents? Or custody..."

I tilt her chin and force her gaze to meet mine. "Stop. You're overthinking. I was wrong and you knew it. You called me out on my bullshit, as you have every time since the day we met, and that's why I love you."

She stares at me until I realize...

"Oh, shit. I haven't said that out loud yet, have I?"

Her lips break into a soft smile, and she shakes her head.

"Well, fuck." I rake my fingers through my hair. "That wasn't exactly how I wanted to tell you...and not..." Jesus, I messed this up, and now I'm the one panicking unreasonably. "...while..." I exhale sharply.

"While we're breaking up?" she incorrectly finishes for me.

I scoff. "We are not breaking up."

"Or broke up, whatever," she mumbles and attempts to hop off my desk.

I grip her thighs. "Let me explain. Sit."

A spark ignites in her narrowed eyes. "I'm not a dog, Blackwood. I'm not at your beck and call, and I told you before, I'm not playing house until *marriage material* comes back around for you. Now, answer my question."

I stand between her legs and coil her ponytail in my fist. "I've had enough of your smart mouth today."

"Then answer my question. What did you mean? Did you mean a relationship—"

I tug her hair until she's forced to fall back onto her elbows with me leaning over her. Luckily, all I have are papers on this desk, and I don't mind if these print sheets smell like pussy. It's much better than despair.

"I meant, when you return to LA and everything is settled down, I'm going to teach you who's in control here. I should've bent you over my knee instead of arguing with you. It would've saved me some time."

∽

Aurora

ETHAN RELEASES my hair and grips my thighs, and there's no question where this is leading.

He spreads my legs wider and hauls me toward him. The action slides the hem of my dress up, exposing my black lace thong to his gaze.

He draws his thumb over the gusset. "You're already wet, baby."

Wasting no time, he roughly stretches the material to the side. His expression turns intense, and his eyes darken. "Is this for me, or did you let him fuck you again?"

I don't argue or hesitate, but I do sass him. Call me petty. "Someone had to make me feel better."

"Is that so?" He hastily undoes his belt and pants.

My desire amplifies at the clink of his buckle, as if some Pavlovian response. He falls over me, his weight on his forearm, and aligns himself at my entrance. "Wrap your legs around me."

I do, because this is Ethan, and although we're in his office, I might not walk out of here straight.

Then comes a gravelly, "I'm going to fuck the attitude right out of you," my only warning before he punches his hips and fills me to the brim.

A high-pitched moan slips past my lips, and he swiftly covers my mouth with his palm.

"Tell him thanks for the lube," he whispers next to my ear and slams into me.

I whimper beneath his hand and rock my hips, meeting his thrusts.

He does as he promised, fucking me hard and deep, his dirty words driving me to oblivion. "Who do you belong to, Aurora?" He moves his hand from my mouth to clasp my throat.

"You," I pant.

He continues his merciless pace. "Whose baby are you having?"

"Yours," I automatically respond.

"Whose pussy is this?"

"Yours."

"Who's in charge here?"

"You."

He pounds into me, his desk scraping against the floor. "Repeat that."

"You." My heart beats a frantic rhythm between arousal and the fear of being caught. "You're in charge."

His grip on my throat tightens. "You're mine. You will always be mine. Don't ever come to me trying to end things, understand?"

"Yes," I moan, each of his rumbled threats bringing me closer to the edge.

"The next time you're fucking him, think about me fucking your ass at the same time."

I'm so close, every dirty word from his mouth a heady rush.

"You like that, baby girl? You like the thought of both of us filling you?"

My legs tremble, and my neck arches.

"Answer me," he growls, low and menacing.

I squeeze around him. "Yes," I cry. "Please, E—I'm going to come."

"That's my good fucking girl," he punctuates with a hard thrust. "We're going to have you dripping from every hole."

Oh my God, I can't take it any longer. I fist his shirt, and I lose all thought, biting my lip to stop from releasing a string of cries that will make it obvious to anyone what we're doing.

"Fuck, baby, strangle my cock... Such a perfect fucking pussy."

His strokes become erratic. He bites into my collarbone with one last slam of his hips and pulses inside me.

The sound of someone beating on the door filters through our panting breaths.

"That's your boyfriend." He playfully slaps my ass, pulls out, and fixes my thong.

I rise to my feet on unsteady legs and adjust my dress while he puts himself away and buckles his pants.

"I love you." He places a tender kiss on my forehead. "I respect your relationship with Jax. You can do anything you want with him, or for him—unless it puts you in danger. Your safety is my top priority, above all else." He tilts my chin to kiss my lips. "Stop with the marriage shit. I'm not looking to get married ever again."

Well, okay, then.

41

JACKSON

Aurora pauses on the tarmac. "Wait. We're flying private?"

It took some convincing to get her to leave with me without seeing her grandmother and without Ricky.

We were supposed to fly out tomorrow morning but left tonight after visiting Ethan at the arena. He and Grant distracted her while I made arrangements.

I need time with her. Alone. I know Ricky will catch up. It'd be foolish for HSI not to be tracking our phones. He'll meet us in New York, blame my oppositional attitude, and not think twice about me abandoning him in LA. And if he does, oh well.

"Yeah, babe. The only alternative is renting a U-Haul and driving cross-country with all your clothes." Not fully truthful. I could book another plane to return, but again, I want her alone.

With her hand in mine, I guide her up the stairs into the cabin. Her eyes light up, glancing back at me in awe. I love it when she does that. It's my absolute favorite, like when she first saw the nursery in Santa Monica. It makes it all worth it— every penny.

I drop our overnight bags. Aurora will want the window, so I take the aisle seat. I told the booking agency we didn't need a flight attendant hanging around—just fill the fridge. I want it to be only the two of us for the next eight to ten hours.

Once the plane is in the air, I intertwine our fingers and bring her knuckles to my lips. "Hey, promise me something?"

She twists in her chair and faces me with furrowed brows, always suspicious of my antics. "What?"

"Promise me you won't cooperate with Ricky, no matter what he says or threatens. He's not your friend. He has one loyalty, and that's to his job."

Her brows furrow deeper. "But don't we want him to arrest Kyle?"

"Yes, but Ricky will do whatever is necessary *for the case*. He's proven that by lying to you, by pretending to have a boyfriend just to be close to you. He doesn't care about your safety. Promise me, no matter what, you'll refuse to cooperate."

Her gaze drops to our intertwined fingers. "Only if you promise me that anything you're planning—because I know you are—won't hurt you or separate us. Swear we'll be together."

Not wanting to make a promise I'm unsure I can keep, because I'll always protect her first, I go with deflection. "When did being together become so important?"

She narrows her eyes, and I try to hold a straight face, but a smirk sneaks through.

"Really?" She cocks her head. "You need your ego stroked right now?"

My smirk turns into a full-blown grin. "It feels pretty good, yes."

"Fine. In New York," she says with a hint of irritation.

"You want to be together?"

"Jackson," she warns.

I push my luck further and ask, "Like together together? Forever together?"

"I'm not speaking to you." She releases my hand and faces the window. "I know what you're doing, O'Reilly. You're avoiding my promise."

Damn, she's good. Not only did she catch me, but she also

didn't make *me* any promises. "I was only clarifying your stipulations."

She doesn't answer, and the pilot comes on overhead, announcing we can move around the cabin.

"Come snuggle with me, and we'll talk."

She removes her seat belt, and as she's climbing into my lap, the lights go out.

I recline my seat and hold her to my chest. My lifeline. My anchor. "I promise I'll do everything possible to avoid putting myself in danger or separating us."

Her fingers play with my hair. "Then I promise I will not cooperate with Ricky unless you're in danger or we'll be separated."

I shake my head. "No, Aurora. He'll leverage that against you."

She yawns, and her warm breath tickles my neck. "What are you worried about? Specifically."

"Kyle is focused on you and the baby. Ricky allowed him to hurt you, allowed photographers Kyle hired near you, and Ricky went with you to New York. Why? He wants to use you as bait when he's proven he can't keep you safe? No way."

After a long wait, during which I'm almost positive she's fallen asleep, she agrees. "I won't cooperate without discussing it with you or Ethan."

"He'll never let you do it, no matter what."

"I know." She yawns again, her voice distant. "But he'll fix it."

He may try, but this might be something not even Ethan Blackwood can fix.

I kiss her temple. "Sleep, baby."

She breathes evenly, and I stare at her utter perfection. Heart-shaped face, Cupid's-bow lips, freckles, thick lashes caressing her cheeks... All of it, perfect.

"You broke my heart today," I whisper, brushing my fingers through her hair. "I love you more than life itself. You're the light to my darkness, the only thing that keeps me fighting the demons in my head." Tears prickle my eyes. "I'll spend the rest of my life making up for those sleepless nights and the days you didn't feel like enough. I promise you."

Reaching into my bag, I fumble for the velvet box. One-handed, I manage to get the ring out and slip it onto her finger. A smile plays on my lips, picturing the fit she'll throw when she wakes, just as long as it's not the ring she throws.

I TRY TO STAY STILL, not to wake Aurora, but with my sore-as-fuck ribs, I can't help but adjust her in my lap. Plus, I only have one usable hand, making it difficult to play on my phone. I'm surprised I lasted nearly two hours.

"Sorry, I'm hurting you." Her bottom lip sticks out in a pout, her eyes half-lidded with sleep.

She's adorable.

"Not your fault."

She climbs off. "I need to use the bathroom anyhow."

I grab her hips to steady her. "Hold on to the seats so you don't fall."

She's not gone five minutes before she's back. Brows raised and face flushed, she holds her hand in front of me. "What the fuck is this?"

Though I've stared at the ring a hundred times, I pretend to study it closely. "It looks like an engagement ring."

Her arm drops to her side. "Jackson!"

"Okay, it's a tracker."

She glares at me, her hands planted on her hips. "I'm serious."

Fine, don't believe me.

Our eyes remain locked in a stare-down.

"I want a legitimate proposal, O'Reilly."

The corner of my lip twitches. "I gave you one. Not my fault you slept through it."

She crosses her arms over her chest. "What did you say?"

My touch is drawn to her belly. "I can't remember. Something about...I'm stuck with you. You're stuck with me. We might as well get married."

"So romantic," she deadpans.

"I thought so."

"Are you doing this because of the case?"

A scowl forms between my eyes. "No. I bought that ring when I moved you into the Laguna Beach penthouse."

"You were that sure of yourself, huh?"

"It's you or nothing, baby."

With a shake of her head, the ring still on her finger, she sits next to me. "You're insane," she grumbles.

"For you, yes. We've established this repeatedly."

She remains quiet for several long minutes, staring out the window while I stare at her impatiently.

Is that it? I'm literally on the edge of my seat here.

Finally, her head whips around. "I'll make a deal with you."

My heart stops. A deal means yes, because I'd agree to anything. My chest swells, and I can't breathe. I wasn't expecting yes. I expected to argue for eight to ten hours until I wore her down to a reluctant maybe.

The blood drains from my face, and my mind goes blank. "What?" The word is nothing more than air leaving my lungs.

"I have some questions." She leans back, her arms folded like an attorney about to cross-examine me on the witness stand. "What if you get bored?"

"Did you somehow forget about all the sex we've had lately? Or our sex life in general?"

"Point taken. What if you get sick of sharing me?"

My lips curl into a sly smile. "I'm quite fond of sharing you. It's making me hard just thinking about it."

She slaps my arm. "You know what I mean. What if you wake up one morning and want a normal relationship?"

I shrug, turning my palms up. "Where am I waking up? A psych ward after electric shock therapy? There's nothing normal about us. I love you. You love me. Ethan loves you. You love Ethan. We're having a baby. Then, we'll have another baby.

They'll both be boys and raised together as superstars, and Ethan and I will be forced to retire and coach them."

I don't miss the pleased grin on her face. She secretly adores the idea. She just hates being vulnerable.

"Wow. You have this all planned out. What if you dislike having a baby around?"

Apparently, we're playing twenty questions, and I rest against the seat, facing her. "I already want to quit so I can stay home and hold a baby we don't even have yet. I love him more every day. You two are the best thing to ever happened to me."

"What if I don't want another child?"

I roll my eyes. "Blasphemy. We're having a hockey team of kids. Next."

"Fine. You test me now."

"Is this part of the deal?"

"Yes."

I feign an exaggerated sigh. "What if I don't want to play hockey?"

Her answer comes immediately. "Then you'll need to get a hobby. You have too much energy."

"Okay. What if I lose all my money?"

"I'll go back to escorting." She grins because she knows it's bullshit, and probably because she's not worried. I'm glad.

"That's not even funny." Then, I ask, "What if I relapse?"

All humor leaves her face. "You won't." Caramel eyes stare into the depths of my soul. "If you do, I'm taking your money, moving to New York, where you hate the weather, buying premium season tickets to the Stars, and seducing my next husband with low-cut shirts and blow jobs."

Her tone is tart, but I know very well she'll punish me with something equally painful if I repeat my last relapse.

I slowly blink. "Wow. That's oddly specific. Any certain player you have in mind?"

She arches a brow. "Wouldn't you like to know?"

"Yes, I would. You're making that jersey—*the one you just happened to have*—more and more suspicious."

She cocks her head and gives me a mocking smile. "Actually, it was gifted to me."

Irritation swarms in my chest. "By fucking who?"

She ignores me, widening her eyes with a gasp. "Oh! Or maybe I'll go after their coach. Then, I'd have access to *all* the players."

Now I know she's being ludicrous.

"That's it. I'm calling Ethan. How does he punish your smart mouth?"

"I'm not telling you." She bites her lips shut.

And just like that, we're engaged—with the threat of her banging the entire New York hockey team if I fuck up. Which, of course, is a joke, because I'd commit murder first.

42

AURORA

I catch Jackson staring off at nothing, his bright-green eyes dark and empty. He's also gone through a bag of Jolly Ranchers on this flight. I want to ask what he's thinking—because I know he has a plan in that mind of his—but I don't want to ruin this moment.

This is our moment. Despite our public lives, we deserve something that's purely ours. Everyone deserves something special, and I can give that to Jax, even if we are young and dumb.

Who knows? This might all blow up in my face.

I glance down at the ring on my finger. It's not your typical engagement ring. It's a sizable heart-shaped diamond with swirls of gray and black—a smoky diamond. The top is brilliant, flawless. A dark storm encompasses the middle, and the lower portion is entirely black.

It's beautiful and unique and reminds me of him and, oddly, Ethan.

I lay my head on Jax's shoulder. "The ring is gorgeous. Thank you."

It's late, the tiny lights above just bright enough to see each other, giving a sense of whispering secrets in the dark.

His gaze meets mine, shimmering with affection. "It's meant to symbolize my heart wrapped around your finger."

I can't help but smile at his sweet words. "Ah, good one, Romeo."

He gives me that crooked grin. "I thought so."

"Honestly, I love it. Thank you." I hug him tighter, thankful there's no divider between our seats.

"You deserve nothing less." He leans down and plants a tender kiss on my forehead. "Plus, it had to be large enough to attract everyone's attention."

I burst into laughter, the sound echoing through the plane. It's such a typical Jackson response.

"There it is," I say, my voice laced with amusement.

"What?"

"Your ego. I thought you'd misplaced it for a moment there."

"Haha. Funny," he deadpans, his face devoid of emotion, making it even more hilarious.

Unfortunately, I have to break the spell. "I guess that means you want everyone to know?"

"That was the plan." He scowls, suspicion creeping into his voice. "Why?"

I sit up, my attention focused on him, and attempt to explain the whirlwind of my thoughts. "I hate everyone being in our business. The publicity. The paparazzi. I wish we could do something just you and me."

He takes a minute to consider. "You're way ahead of me. I didn't think you'd say yes, let alone start— Are you talking about the actual event? I'll do whatever you want. We can turn this plane around and go to Vegas tonight."

I narrow my eyes, shooting daggers at the thought of getting married where he relapsed. I hear the disapproving whispers, see the judgmental glances.

And if the media got hold of the pictures?

No fucking way I'm enduring that ridicule a second time.

He backtracks. "Shit. Never mind. Terrible idea. Never going to Vegas again."

My following words are hesitant and irrational, but fuck it.

"We could elope in New York. No one would know, save for me and you."

His face lights up, and his eyes widen comically. "Are you serious?"

"People will find out. I'm not ashamed of anything, but I'd rather start our life without listening to everyone's opinion on our engagement. Does that bother you?"

He stares at me, his chest heaving slightly. "Nope, not at all. I've already cleared it with Ethan."

I recoil, my brows shooting skyward. "Ah, what?"

He flattens his lips. "Oh no, you have that gleam in your eye, the one you get when you're about to tear my balls off." He raises his palms in a gesture of surrender. "You know, Ethan refuses to be married again. He sees marriage as a death sentence."

"Wow," I drag out. "I guess we'd better give him what he wants then."

"Nope." Jax shakes his head. "*Ethan* is the rebound guy, not me. Don't rebound me."

"I'm not rebounding you." I chuckle at his antics. "We're all in this together here."

I think Ethan secretly enjoys being the *other* guy, enjoys the taboo aspect of our relationship. It makes him feral.

If I marry Jax, Ethan will get to eat endlessly from his forbidden cake, and Jax will be over the moon. And I'll...get to do whatever I want.

This is a win-win situation—or incredibly idiotic.

Jackson's smile is devilish, his eyes full of mischief. "We're *definitely* in this together. Coach better take time off for an extended honeymoon."

"Does your dick-brain ever shut off?"

He glances down at said member. "Nope. Not with you."

43

ETHAN

The morning after Jax and Aurora leave for New York, my uncle wakes me up bright and early at five a.m.

His name is Rocco—I'm not even kidding. His law firm manages the real estate that is technically mine. His team also handled my divorce, and he *loves* to talk.

"What the actual fuck?" he says in greeting.

"I take it you received something from Jackson's lawyer?" My voice is husky, thick with sleep, and I clear my throat.

Rocco has been helping me with the Santa Monica property, and I *might* have asked him to investigate Jax's trust.

"Something? That's quite an understatement. Let's start with the property in question. It's in the trust's name. A real mystery, considering the trust was allocated for distribution at twenty-one and the beneficiary is twenty-five. I've found no explanation as to why the funds weren't distributed."

I sit up and roll my stiff neck. I miss Jackson's pillow-top mattress. "I'll tell you why: because Kyle O'Reilly is draining his son of every penny."

"There must be others involved. Tens of millions of dollars are unaccounted for. I received the original documents and an Affidavit of Change of Trustee, listing you as the new trustee. I'm filing it, along with a motion for a record of transactions. This is unbelievable."

The legal jargon is lost on me, but the missing money doesn't surprise me. "Will they allow it? The change of trustee?"

"They will, or I'll expose everything."

"That might be dangerous. Does the trust even exist if it ended on Jax's twenty-first birthday?"

"Yes. Kyle was the successor after Jackson's mother died. He never terminated the trust. We can take legal action against him for misappropriation of funds. It could become a lengthy battle, but I doubt it'll go that far."

"I'd rather not involve the courts." I'm not subjecting Jax to public scrutiny of his father's crimes, although that might become unavoidable, considering Ricky's involvement. "Why not demand he end the trust instead of transferring trustees?"

"Distribution will take months with a trust this size. We have to transfer deeds, accounts, and investments. It'll be quicker and safer on our side."

"Let's start on the Santa Monica property."

"That one's simple. It was purchased in cash. Once you're the trustee, you'll have control of the property and hundreds of millions of dollars, per my source."

"Well, damn." No wonder Jax spends money as if it's limitless. For him, it is.

"That doesn't even touch it. There are properties in California and Connecticut. A London flat. Heirlooms and investments. I researched his grandfather, Thad Jackson Vaughn. In the sixties, he achieved fame as an actor. He was a writer, philanthropist, and politician. His wife was an actress and singer. They had two children, Jacquelin and Thad, both named after him. Rather creepy, if you ask me. Thad Jr. died in a car accident when he was a teenager."

The word *politician* makes me suspicious, along with the accidental death. Jax's grandfather could've been associated with Kyle. Nothing would shock me at this point.

"This will sound strange, but who inherits Jax's money if something were to happen to him?"

"You're worried about him. I got you. It'd go to his successor, a wife or dependent. If there isn't one, then Kyle."

I already know the answer, but I ask anyway. "Say Jax had a claim for child support. Would they consider the trust?"

"Any good lawyer would, yes."

"Jesus," I curse under my breath. There's no straightforward way around this. Transfer the funds, and Kyle might go after Jax. Leave the funds, and he may go after Aurora. Either way, he's a threat to what's mine. "This is a clusterfuck."

"Why? Because you and Jackson are dating the same model?"

I scoff. "Stop stalking me, Rocco."

He chuckles, rich and hearty. "How's the baby?"

"Perfect. You understand my problem?"

"I sure do. What do you need?"

"Security for Aurora and Jax. They're on their way to New York, and Kyle has been having someone follow us."

"Are you serious? Why didn't you mention it sooner? Where are they staying?"

"Her Tribeca apartment— Oh! Which better not be one of ours with faulty radiator heat. She's been sick the entire time."

"You think I'd allow that? Your father would kill me. I'll find a place. Anything else?"

I take a deep breath, my heart pounding. "Can I see him?" There's a long pause, and my stomach sinks. Why do I even care? "If he wants nothing to do with me, spit it out."

"No. No. That's not it. I'm just stunned. I'll arrange it."

44

AURORA

I wrap in a blanket, climb onto Jackson's lap, and fall fast asleep.

A raspy voice rouses me, and gentle fingers stroke the side of my neck. "Hey, baby. We've arrived."

I groan. "I don't wanna get up. I'm perfect right here."

His chest feels safe and warm, and breathing him in shoots happiness straight to my brain. He smells like his usual irresistible cologne and a bit of me. It's heaven. Plus, my body is begging for rest, utterly drained. I could sleep for another eight hours.

He kisses my nose. "Our car is waiting. Once we're home, you can relax with me until your heart's content...after a shower."

I lift my head. "Are you saying I smell?"

"No." He chuckles. "But it's a thousand degrees under this blanket, and parts of me are sticking to other parts. I can't smell good."

"I've smelled your stench after games. This isn't even close, but we can shower together."

His impish green eyes light up with a grin. With his arms around my waist, he draws me closer. "I'm holding you to that."

Our lips connect in a slow, lazy kiss. It feels like new love, when you can't help but smile while kissing.

I brush my fingers along his sharp jawline. "We should leave, just the three of us. Stay somewhere for a while, where we can be anonymous. Spend our days in bed."

He places his forehead to mine. "We will, I promise. Anywhere you wanna go."

"Promises. Promises."

Our mouths meet again, this time with more heat, before he abruptly pulls away.

"Jesus, woman, you have to stop."

We're still grinning at each other when the hatch opens, and bright light filters through the cabin, shattering the spell we're under.

Hurried footsteps approach, and I recognize the familiar rhythm before his imposing figure appears, casting a shadow that obscures the sunlight.

Ricky glares at the two of us, and I break from Jackson's embrace, almost tripping on the blanket.

The swelling and redness around his eye diminished, revealing purple bruising underneath. There's a cut on his lip and another above his cheekbone.

A pang of guilt lances my chest, and I glance away, bending down and putting on my shoes. A few days ago, I would've hugged him. It feels awkward not to, but I don't know this person anymore.

"You could've told me you were leaving LA," his deep voice barks.

Jackson stands and collects our belongings. "Sorry. We stopped by the penthouse. You weren't there."

"Because I was hunting *you* down."

I step between them, eager to keep the peace. "We saw Ethan at the arena then grabbed an earlier flight. It was spur-of-the-moment."

Ocean eyes narrow. "I texted and called you."

"I've been asleep. My phone is in my bag." I checked it hours ago and messaged Ethan a few times, but that's it.

He leans in, expression stern. "And his?"

My mind goes blank with anxiety. "He...he's had it the whole time."

Jackson's arm comes around me. "Stop intimidating her. Your problem is with me."

The muscle in Ricky's jaw flutters. "You have family here."

Now, I'm utterly confused. My brows pinch, and I glance back at Jax.

He releases a reluctant sigh. "Ethan is being a controlling bastard. He texted me. His uncle sent someone to stay with us. I'll explain later."

Giddy excitement washes over me. I'm *obsessed* with the lore of the Rossi family. I've read everything I could find on Google. My grandmother loves true crime; she's going to flip her lid over this.

Two men wait on the tarmac, and they're undeniably Ethan's family. One is smiling, showing familiar dimples, and the other is scowling. The DNA is unmistakable.

I'm so enthralled, I almost trip down the stairs. Ricky steadies me with a hand on my hip as Jax carries our bags ahead.

Twins, identical, maybe around my age. They're decked out in black—T-shirts, jeans, boots, and worn leather jackets. One is wearing a baseball cap, but both are over six feet tall, with dark hair and eyes, muscular builds.

I can't stop grinning.

Jax juts his chin in greeting. "Hey. You must be security sent by Rocco. I'm Jackson." He gestures to Ricky. "The angry Viking is Ricky. He's Aurora's current guard." He shoots me a smirk. "And don't worry about her. She's nobody."

I bump his shoulder with mine and reach out to the twins. "Hi. Aurora."

"Like you need to introduce yourself. You're famous," says the one with the hat and a friendly smile. "I'm Desmond. You can call me Desi." He delicately shakes my hand.

"Yeah, Rocco talks about you nonstop," adds the other twin. "I'm Dante."

"Rocco is Ethan's uncle, the attorney," Jax clarifies then

shudders. "It's fucking cold out here. Let's get going before you're sick again."

"Are they staying at the apartment?" I ask. "We don't have enough room."

Unless Ricky is leaving, which wasn't the plan. Nothing was supposed to change...until he suggested using me to get closer to Kyle. Then, everything went sideways.

Dante twirls a set of keys around his finger. "We got a place for all of us. It's secure."

Now, I'm all discombobulated.

Before I can figure out what the hell is going on, Ricky places a hand on the small of my back and leads me to the passenger side.

Rounding the SUV, he leans in, whispering, "Jackson's phone is still at the arena. If he has another, it's not the one he had yesterday."

I stop, completely baffled. An icy breeze blows my hair across my face, and I lift my hand to tuck the strand behind my ear.

Ricky's eyes snag on the ring. His lip curls, and he shakes his head. "Tell him spousal privilege doesn't count in first-degree felony trials."

45

RICKY

THAT WAS HARSH AND HAD NOTHING TO DO WITH THE CASE, AND Aurora knows it.

"Fuck you," she mouths before she climbs in the backseat.

I'm lashing out at the wrong person. She's not my problem.

My problem is her boyfriend—sorry, her *fiancé*.

My problem is her thigh touching mine in the backseat and my skin vibrating with awareness.

My problem is now, I must contend with Ethan's family.

My problem is command breathing down my neck.

Since Jax is aware of the investigation, my team wants action, wants a plan in place before he runs to his father, which may have already happened.

I had a lot of time to reflect on my flight—six hours, to be exact. My gut tells me I pushed Jackson too far, drove him to negotiate with Kyle to prevent Aurora from being used as bait.

Jax sacrificed their relationship to keep her out of his father's depraved world. Why would he turn around and put her in harm's way? Even with two agents to safeguard her, he doesn't trust us.

He may have also leveraged the investigation, threatening to talk or turn over evidence if Kyle didn't leave Aurora and Ethan alone.

It's reckless, but above all, this trio will protect each other.

They'll do anything for one another. They've proven it repeatedly. Even Jackson's fuck-up was an attempt to protect Ethan and Aurora.

I tried to tell my team they were inseparable. The harder we push, the tighter their bond will become.

And I'm on the outside. I shouldn't care, but for some fucking reason, I do.

I'd go against my team to shield Jax from the legal consequences of running to his father, if I could. I'll keep my mouth shut concerning Ethan's family unless they're a danger to Aurora. I wouldn't hesitate to compromise my integrity for them.

Still, I'm on the fence. I'm at a loss. Jackson can't get me into a party, and I doubt he'll share evidence with me. I spooked them with my suggestion to use Aurora.

I can protect her. I'll *always* protect her, and that means protecting Jax as well.

Kyle isn't going anywhere. Eventually, we'll have another run-in, most likely during Jackson's first game back.

All I can do is lie low, be invisible and work on my relationship with Aurora. Right now, I'm the enemy. She won't speak to me unless necessary, and I didn't do myself any favors with that *spousal privilege* comment.

I miss the days when she was affectionate toward me, when she needed me, when I was the one who made her smile.

Jesus, I'm being overdramatic.

I didn't get where I am by not being able to shut off my emotions, but the switch short-circuited when I met Aurora, flickering between fuck this and fuck that.

And now, I'm in a car with two of the Rossi boys.

While we cram in the back, Dante drives, and Desmond faces the back seat, telling Aurora all about our new place.

One brother, Dante, is quiet, while the other loves to talk. Not just talk—he animatedly gestures with his hands, and Aurora giggles. She's smitten with Ethan's family.

"We only had one property available in the Fashion District. Pretty cool, though. Used to be an old factory loft. It's on the top floor, with a massive rooftop terrace." He extends his arms in emphasis. "And it has a gallery studio... I think that's what it's called."

He peers over at his brother, and Dante nods in agreement.

Aurora cocks her head, her brow pinched, her voice brimming with curiosity. "A gallery studio?"

"Yeah, a room of windows with natural lighting and a workspace. Hard to explain, but it'd be perfect for you. We could get some of those giant-ass mirrors if you'd like." Again, he talks with his hands.

My eyes gravitate to Jackson, and we share a glance full of suspicion. No way Ethan's family just *happened* to have the perfect studio space in the Fashion District.

"There are four bedrooms that used to be offices," Desmond continues. "The living area is so huge, you could play hockey inside, but the layout is strange. The galley kitchen is tiny, and we have yet to remodel."

Probably because they recently bought it. I bet they'd remodel if Aurora asked.

"I'm sure it'll be fine." She gives him a warm smile. "Only Jax cooks, and we'll be out of your hair shortly."

I have a feeling we won't be leaving anytime soon, not if Ethan and his family have anything to say about it.

46

ETHAN

"I *LOVE* THIS PLACE. IT'S PHENOMENAL. I COULDN'T DREAM OF A more perfect studio. It's better than Paulo's. Well, it could be. It's more of a blank canvas..."

In nothing but a towel, I sit on the bed, damp skin burning hot against the cool air of my bedroom, and listen to Aurora rattle on about the loft. The weight I've carried over the past few days feels lighter, the irritable snake in my gut less venomous.

This week, we're on the road, heading toward the East Coast. We have a game in Ohio, another in Montreal, and then two in New York.

All I think about is getting to New York.

"Please don't say that too loud. I don't need Jax buying more property."

I might own that loft, at least on paper, but I don't mention it. My family will spoil her either way. They've waited my entire life for this opportunity.

"He won't. He hates New York. But your nephews are so sweet."

She draws out the last word, and I can envision her pouty lips as does. Her excitement makes me chuckle, and I lie back and stare at the ceiling like a goddamn lovesick teenager.

"They said they'll move my clothes tomorrow," she continues. "And they have a warehouse. They're going to search for some big mirrors. They are *so* cute, too. They have your dimples."

"Wait. Who?" I have no clue who she's talking about, but they better be family. "I don't have any siblings, baby girl."

My father didn't have any children with his wife before he went to prison, which I learned from Google. She divorced him and remarried shortly after his incarceration.

Thank fuck my mother didn't have any other children. One was too much for her.

"The twins. Desi and Dante. They're a little older than me."

"So you automatically assume they're my nephews because they're your age?" I ask with mock indignation.

"Jackson said they're your family," she says, all innocent, a smile in her voice.

"I'm teasing. They might be cousins. I didn't interact with that side of the family outside the diner. The eyes would've given me away, you know?"

My mother's side lived in East Harlem. I wasn't close with them either, choosing to spend my time at school or the park. I learned to skate in a Harlem hockey program. Our apartment was between Central Park and Morningside Park on the Upper West Side, where I could play hockey, baseball, or basketball.

Sports kept me out of trouble, and I figured sports would be my ticket out of the city.

"That's sad. I hope our baby has your eyes."

She brings me back to the present, her words an ax to the sternum, cracking it wide to steal my heart.

My chest swells with so much love, it hurts.

That, or I'm having a heart attack.

"Jesus, I miss you. How are you feeling? Are you eating? What'd you feed my son today?"

"Your *cousins* ordered pizza."

"And you actually ate?" I highly doubt it. Her devotion to healthy food may rival her devotion to Jax, and she doesn't eat meat unless I feed it to her...

That'd be a great joke if Jackson wasn't part of the equation.

"I ate a margherita pizza with mozzarella, sun-dried tomatoes, and basil."

A grin spreads across my lips, although she can't see it. "Of course you did."

Clothing rustles as she shifts around. "When will you be here?"

"Why? You miss me?"

"Yeah..."

Her apprehensive tone has me sitting up. "What else, love?"

"I heard Jax and Ricky talking. You want me to stay in New York, don't you?"

"I want you to be safe."

"Is this about *us*? Is this about the whole marriage and commitment thing?"

She pauses, and I remain silent. I feel an anxious ramble coming on.

"I know you don't want to get married, and that's fine..."

Certainly doesn't sound fine.

"...you told both Jax and me that, but...are we still broken up?"

I stare down at my phone. "Say what?" Is this what it's like dating a twenty-two-year-old? "I thought we talked about this?"

She scoffs with theatrics. "We didn't talk. That was pillow talk, if anything."

I rub my eyes and take a deep, calming breath. "Let me get this straight. In your mind, we were not okay when you left LA? Because in my head, we talked, we fucked, and everything was peaches and cream or cum and cupcakes, whatever it is you kids say nowadays."

"Cum and cupcakes?" She giggles. "No one says cum and cupcakes."

"You just did twice, and you laughed. Now answer my question."

"But now I want cupcakes." She pouts.

"I'll bring you cupcakes."

"And cum?"

"Straight from the source." She's been gone for only a few

days, and my balls already ache. My dick wants nothing to do with my hand. "Now, answer me."

"I think we need time together, but that won't happen with your job and living on separate coasts."

Twenty-two, I remind myself, resisting the urge to throw my phone across the room. "Did I not say that before?"

"But now you want me to live here."

"Only until I figure out shit with Kyle."

I'm trying to protect Jax as well. If I can keep him away from his asshole father, it might prevent him from doing something stupid. He may not enjoy the winter weather, but he came back from New York happier than I'd ever seen him. Isolation with Aurora will do him good.

"How long is that going to take?"

I don't know, but I'm not telling her that. In her anxious brain, that could mean forever.

"Do I need to stalk you and break into your apartment for you to understand I'm crazy about you? We're not broken up. I meant everything I said. Now, if this isn't working when my contract ends, I'll figure something else out. Better?"

"No. You love your job."

"I also love you." It comes out of my mouth with no hesitation. "I have eighty-two games a season, and half are away. I have a stretch where I'm on the road for twelve days. Believe me, I've thought about how difficult this will be."

"You know I can't stay home, right? Not unless you want your life to be absolute hell for those twelve days."

"Oh, I'm banking on it." I'm banking on Jax forcing her to travel, and she'll do it because he needs her, and I need him.

I also need her. I'm just not at Jackson's level of dysfunction. *Yet.*

"What about when I can't travel because I'm too pregnant? The last I checked, you're away the entire week of my due date."

"That'll suck. Jax will go batshit crazy. We can ask the doctor about scheduling the delivery if you'd like. A couple of my players have done it."

"This is a lot of work, Blackwood. I can't believe you decided to use an expired condom, and now we have to schedule a baby in between hockey games."

Laughter erupts from deep within my chest. "Worth it. Best mistake of my life."

"Seriously, though, when will you be here?" There's that pout again.

"This weekend, love."

"And I'll have you all weekend?"

Jesus fucking Christ, my cheeks hurt from smiling. "I'm yours all weekend."

47

JACKSON

UNLIKE THE TRIBECA APARTMENT, THIS PLACE IS QUIET, TOO HIGH to hear the city or be blinded by the lights. I awake rested, with the most beautiful girl in my arms, who's currently sitting against the headboard, staring down at me with a bright smile.

She brushes her fingers through my hair. "You slept in. I didn't want to wake you."

I snuggle closer to her side and place a hand over her rounded belly. "How's my baby?"

"He hasn't woken yet, probably because he was up all night."

"He will once you eat." I pull up her shirt and kiss her stomach. "What's the plan for today?"

"Unfortunately, because of the nasty weather, and because I have a studio with a gorgeous view, we're doing a shoot here," she rushes out. "Before I'm the size of a blimp and creative angles and Photoshop no longer work, you know?"

I peer up at her and tug on a braid. "You will not be the size of a blimp. You're perfect. What time is the shoot?"

"In an hour." She grimaces.

I groan, not ready to get out of bed. "Okay, come snuggle with me then."

She slides in next to me, enveloping me in her jasmine-and-vanilla scent. I wrap my arms around her, close my eyes, and breathe her in.

Nuzzling my neck, she releases a satisfied sigh. "I love this. Everything feels surreal, like we're living in a dream."

I can't help but smile. "I love you. You're *my* dream."

We're in our own little world with Ethan's family. We spend more time together than ever, and I almost feel bad for returning to hockey. We won't find peace in LA, and soon enough, shit will go down with Kyle, and there'll be no peace for us.

~

AURORA DANCES around the kitchen in my T-shirt and leggings, brewing coffee.

I open the fridge and scan the food options. "You want me to make you scrambled eggs, babe?"

She scrunches her nose. "Too nauseated. I'll eat later."

"How about oatmeal?"

She pours coffee into a mug before she adds a diabetes amount of sweetener. "I'm craving those pastries Ricky gets, the ones with the strawberries and a flaky crust." She tips her head back and lets out an exaggerated moan. "Those are so freaking good."

I might crack a molar with how hard I clench my teeth. "In Tribeca?" I slam the fridge door shut, unable to hold in my annoyance.

She points a finger at my face. "Don't start, O'Reilly. You make my favorite dinners."

"I'm not going to Tribeca to get you damn pastries."

She widens her eyes. "Then don't!"

Desi pops his head in, interrupting our banter. "There's a blonde here with more clothes."

Aurora shoots me an uneasy glance. "That's Emily."

"You want me to leave?"

She wraps her arms around me and gives a quick hug.

"Nope. We'll be in the studio, and this is your place too." She grabs her mug of coffee, standing on her tippy-toes to kiss me. "Love you."

"Love you. Do *not* forget to eat, because I'm not going to Tribeca for fucking pastries."

I refuse. That's on him. He spoiled her.

She rushes out of the kitchen, her laughter trailing after her.

The twins, Ricky, and I sit in the living room in mismatched, worn-in chairs, eating donuts and drinking coffee —except me. That bitter shit is nasty.

I may hate New York, but nothing beats the donuts here— okay, the pastries aren't bad either.

Wait, are donuts pastries?

No, pastries have fruit, right?

Anyhow, my favorite is the donuts with chocolate icing and custard filling. I must have eaten half a dozen already.

Speaking of which... "Is there a gym you two go to?"

"Yeah, actually, it's a boxing gym," Desi replies. "You'd like it."

Dante cuffs his brother upside the head. "His hand is broken."

Desi retaliates with a punch to the gut. "They have other equipment besides the ring."

Ricky and I exchange an amused glance, and then his eyes dart to the side in a silent warning. The click-clacking of heels approaching is my only other indication before...

"Still suspended, Jackson?"

Life was going so well too.

"Still a bitch, Emily?" Ricky says, shocking the shit out of me.

She leans her hip against the arm of my chair, and my body radiates agitation. Why is she so close to me?

"Still spying for Jackson?" she spits back.

I scoff. *Nope, just the government.*

"He's got these idiots for that." Ricky gestures to the twins.

"We don't spy, we protect," Desi says.

"Others from Jax," Dante jokes with a side-eye at Aurora's supposed bodyguard.

"That's why there are two of us," Desi finishes.

I swear, they share one brain.

Emily gives the pair a once-over before she faces me. "My rent is due."

The audacity of this girl.

My gaze remains fixed straight ahead, on the sky out the window. "Aurora pays you, and I gave you enough."

She moves to stand in front of me, obstructing my view. "That wasn't our agreement. The agreement was that you'd cover my expenses in New York."

"I said *to* New York, to get established. Ten grand is plenty."

"I still have a condo in LA to pay for. You know, the one your girlfriend lived in after she caught you cheating."

This bitch knows just how to trigger me. "She's my fiancée, and she never caught me cheating because it didn't happen. I'm not arguing with you, and I'm not paying your rent. Aurora won't be working much longer. Stay in New York or don't. I don't care."

"Why would you pay her rent?"

Fuck me sideways.

Emily turns to Aurora, who's now standing in the living area, her hands on her hips.

"Because your *fiancé* promised to cover my expenses while I worked for you. He also promised he wouldn't be here, but like every other promise he's never kept, here he is."

Aurora's gaze locks with mine, and she cocks her head in an exasperated gesture. I give her a wink. She has to be used to my antics by now.

Desi leans over. "Did you and the blonde date?"

I scowl at him for even having the thought. "Fuck no."

"No, we've just known each other for a long time," Emily lies straight through her pearly white teeth.

"That's not true. I met you the same night I met Aurora."

"That you remember."

She's gaslighting me and trying to upset Aurora, and it's pissing me off.

"We didn't meet. Talk. Anything. You worked for my father. That means nothing to me." As if I'd *ever* be interested in something Kyle had.

Ricky sits up straight, and I see the moment it clicks in his brain. His gaze flashes to Emily, as if seeing her for the first time, then shifts to Aurora with...hurt?

He looks at her as if he already misses her.

"It doesn't matter." Aurora's brows knit together. "I want him here. He offered to leave, and I said no. He's not bothering you..." With a wince, her strained voice trails off, and her hand comes to the side of her stomach.

I jump out of my seat, my heart in my throat. "What's wrong? Are you in pain?"

Her face remains contorted. "A cramp...I believe."

My head and mouth spiral. "Should you have cramps? I don't think you should have cramps. You've been doing a lot. Fuck. The doctor said to rest. We're shit at this." I wave my arms around the room. "Everybody, get out!"

"They're probably..." Desi snaps his fingers at his brother. "What are those practice contractions called?"

"Braxton-Hicks," he answers.

"Yes, Braxton-Hicks. Our sister had those with her first baby. Perfectly normal."

"I don't think pain is normal. She shouldn't be working." I point to Emily. "You need to fucking leave." Then, to Ricky. "You fucking too."

He glowers at me from the other side of my girl. "What the fuck did I do?"

"You're...you." *And I see the way you look at her.*

Aurora places a hand on my heaving chest. "I'm fine. It's already fading." Her slightly elevated tone doesn't sound *fine*.

Desi shakes his head in amusement. "He's totally going to pass out when you go into labor."

"Or murder a doctor," Dante adds.

I ignore them and grab my phone from the end table to text Ethan.

Aurora tries to snatch it from me. "Don't you dare call him. He has a game tonight."

I spin away from her. "I'm not calling, I'm texting."

"Jax, no! You'll only worry him."

I do it anyway, knowing she'll listen to him, and maybe because I miss the big fucker.

> Your baby girl is having pains in her side. She thinks it's normal, but she needs to rest. She's working too much.

That'll do it. I sit back in the chair with a shit-eating grin as I search Google.

Bleeding? No, she'd flip out, and I'd know. It mentions Braxton-Hicks contractions and suggests warm baths and herbal tea.

Really? Herbal fucking tea? That's it?

Desi grabs another donut, this one fall-themed with unpleasant leaf-shaped sprinkles. "Our sister did yoga to help."

Aurora's face lights up. "Oh, I love yoga!"

"Shit," Ricky curses. "I was going to find a prenatal yoga class for you." He slips his phone from his pocket. "I'll do it now."

This motherfucker is always trying to one-up me, but I have more urgent concerns at the moment.

I reach out, guide Aurora onto my lap, and place my hand on her stomach. "Has the baby been moving?"

She settles into me and lays her head on my shoulder. "He will for you."

As we wait, a quiet lull comes over the room.

"Okay, well, about my rent..."

I am so looking forward to Ethan getting here.

"What's going on?" I ask, winded from jogging down the tunnel. I almost slipped and fell on my ass trying to get off the ice to call her.

"Nothing. I'm fine. I'm getting ready to do a photo shoot."

She's pushing the *I'm fine* a little too hard, her tone a little too light. It's difficult enough being separated from her. Having something happen while I'm away...that's my worst nightmare.

"No, you're not. Jax wouldn't tell me you were in pain unless it was true."

"It's normal, and it subsided."

I need to research some pregnancy-related stuff. We're pretty terrible at preparing for this baby. We're too busy. *I'm* too busy. There are two of us caring for her, and we're still failing.

I pace in the hallway. "Should you call the doctor and ask?"

"I will if it gets worse, I promise."

A female voice murmurs in the background.

"Who's there with you?"

"The boys and Emily. We're waiting for the photographer to arrive."

Emily and Jax, never a good mix. Then, something else occurs to me. "It's not that photographer you dated, is it?"

"I didn't *date* him. We went to dinner *once*, and I hated it."

"That doesn't answer my question, Aurora."

"No, it's not him. Don't be jealous, *Blackwood*."

"I've decided I'm not jealous. I'm territorial."

"That's not any better." She chuckles.

"It sure is. Jealous would be if someone else had you and I wanted you. That would be dangerous. I'm territorial because you're mine, and I want it to stay that way. No danger unless someone fucks around and finds out. See?"

Laughter rings through the line, and I breathe it in. I can't wait to get home—wherever *home* is.

"No one is encroaching on your territory, caveman."

"Better not be. Don't overwork today. They can come back tomorrow. You need to cut down. Remember what the doctor said."

"I *have* cut down. I'm lucky they accommodate my pregnancy *and* two demanding boyfriends."

My assistant coach waves at me, gesturing me toward the locker room.

"Okay, love. I have to go. We'll discuss this later. Send me some pictures. I miss you like crazy."

"Oooh, I got some good ones for you."

A few minutes after we hang up, she sends me a photo, and I walk straight into the player in front of me. He snaps his head around, but I'm too busy gawking at my phone.

She's in soft-pink satin lingerie, sitting on a bathroom counter, one knee raised. Her nipples are hard and pushing against the thin fabric, the slip just long enough to cover what's mine. She stares at the camera with a submissive, fuck-me expression.

It's beyond hot, but my favorite part is the pink ribbon wrapped and tied around her throat.

How is *this* my girl?

Good job, dick. You scored us a fucking trophy.

> Please tell me you have that choker.

BABY GIRL

I thought you'd like that. 😏

> God, you're incredible. When was this taken?

BABY GIRL

Six weeks ago, maybe. I just got the proofs.

> I'll be envisioning this all night. How am I supposed to concentrate on coaching?

> What do you think about during these photos?

BABY GIRL

You. 🌙

Fuck it. I'll meet the team in Montreal.

Once the game ends, I jump on a private jet to New York.

I have no idea how we'll keep this up without Aurora traveling with us, and I don't know what we'll do when she's unable to do so. But right now, I need to see her before I lose my mind.

In less than three hours, it's the middle of the night, and I'm stepping out of an Uber in front of an old building in the Fashion District.

Dante, per their texts, tosses a cigarette to the cement, putting it out with his boot, and lifts his chin in greeting.

"Don't you dare smoke around my girl."

He shakes his head vehemently. "No, sir. I'd never."

I give him a curt nod. "No need to call me sir."

We ride the elevator in silence, and I catch him peeking at me. "Whose kid are you? How are we related?"

"Our dad is your uncle, your dad's youngest brother."

Your dad. Not sure how I feel about that.

It's quiet for a beat, neither of us talkative. We kind of look alike—same wavy, thick, dark hair and athletic build, though I'm a few inches taller.

"What do you do for Rocco?" I ask to create conversation. "You seem young to work security."

"Property management." A smirk sneaks through his stoic expression. "Don't worry, I'm twenty-four and can handle myself. Same with my brother. We've been working for Rocco for nine years, know every business and tenant."

The elevator opens into a bare kitchen in desperate need of

renovation—white walls and cupboards, cracked tile flooring, mismatched older appliances.

Dante steps forward and unlatches the lattice gate. "We have yet to remodel. The place came on the market, and we scooped it up. It's spacious, got good bones. We'd been eyeing it for a while. We'll gut the kitchen and move it to the open living area."

"No, it's great. Thank you for doing this. Have they been any trouble?"

There it is—a dimple on the left side. "Not at all. They're a riot."

Sitting at a table, a kid who can only be Desmond rises and shakes my hand. "Wow. You're definitely a Rossi..." His beaming eyes dart to his scowling brother. "Sorry, that sounds stupid now that I say it out loud."

"Thanks, I guess." I smile genuinely. "How's my girl? Any more pain?"

"Just once."

"She's on her feet a lot," the more serious twin adds.

"That'll end. Any other issues?"

They both exchange a glance, and Dante juts his chin, prompting Desmond to speak.

"We found bugs in Aurora's apartment."

I furrow my brows. I didn't notice any when I was there. The place was clean. "Bugs? What kind of bugs?"

"The kind that listens in on people, not the creepy-crawly kind."

They were listening in on us. I rack my brain for anything damning, but all we did was fuck and fight. Who knows about Jax? His mouth never shuts up, but I doubt he was yapping about Kyle.

I shrug, too tired to give it much thought tonight. "Good to know."

Dante folds his arms over his chest. "Who's he watching?" he asks, his tone hard and eyes dark.

He holds my gaze. It takes me a beat, but I get what he's throwing down.

"Not you guys." *Or us?* "Sorry. Jackson's father. I'm not sure of the status of the investigation. I think they're waiting for Jax's trust to transfer."

"Good to know," he repeats.

"Tell me if it becomes an issue." I hike my bag higher on my shoulder. "Where are they?"

Desmond gestures to the doorway leading out of the kitchen. "They're in the only room on the right side."

My pulse races with anticipation. I can't wait to see her, to have her in my arms.

I quietly slip through the first door, but I should've known I couldn't sneak in on Jax. I should've known he'd be a light sleeper and wouldn't be keen on a large man entering their room.

His shadow springs upright, visible only in the weak glow seeping from under the door. "You got a fucking problem?"

"Did you miss me, asshole? Don't wake her."

"You're lucky." He flops back down. "Your size is similar to someone else."

I set my bag down on the opposite side of the bed.

Aurora moves toward Jackson, always searching for a body to snuggle with. I kick off my shoes and strip to my boxer briefs, my dick already excited.

I pull down the blanket and creep into bed. Fuck, just her smell has me throbbing. "You need to find another room."

"All the rooms are taken. You'll have to live with blue balls."

"Doubtful, cockblock."

She's lying on her side, sharing a pillow with him, her leg bent over his.

I brush her hair aside and kiss her nape.

"Jax," she whines with a hint of annoyance.

I silently laugh, my chest shaking, and trail kisses along the curve of her shoulder.

She pushes her ass back. "We just finished."

"Did you now?" I rumble, low and deep.

She stiffens then whirls towards me. "You're home?"

"I'm home, baby."

Her arms encircle my neck, her lips finding mine. *This* is my home. New York. LA. On the road. It doesn't matter, as long as I have her.

"How?"

"Hopped on a jet right after the game. Did you think I'd let you get away with those lingerie pics?"

"That's one expensive booty call," a voice grumbles behind her.

I tangle my fingers in her hair. "Ignore him. Kiss me."

She does, and our tongues intertwine, punctuated by her soft moans.

I withdraw and peck her lips, unable to stop. "You feeling okay?"

"Sandwiched between you two? Better than ever."

I grasp her thigh and guide her knee over my hip, pressing my needy erection against her. "I missed you."

She nips my bottom lip. "I see."

"Ugh," Jax groans with exaggeration. "You're not gonna let me sleep, are you?"

"Nope," I reply between kisses.

"Fine," he huffs with feigned reluctance. "Might as well join you."

"Don't say it like you weren't going to."

AURORA

THIS HAS TO BE A DREAM.

Ethan smells of brisk winter air and raw masculinity. I thread my fingers through his thick waves. He's had it cut. It's shorter on the sides and tamer on top. I trace his strong jawline, finding scratchy stubble.

His lips stretch into a smile over mine. "You checking me out, baby?"

"I liked the beard."

He flicks his thumb over my hard nipple. "It'll grow back."

Jax places open-mouthed kisses along my neck, his teeth grazing the sensitive skin, and a shiver runs down my spine.

Ethan's rough palm traces my curves and moves between my legs. His fingers glide through my slit. "Always so fucking wet."

"You're welcome," Jackson replies, a smile in his voice.

"At least you do something right," Ethan returns, quick with his comeback.

Jax's response is a silent chuckle and a bite to my shoulder.

There's nothing but kissing, rubbing, soft moans, and heavy breaths after that. Ethan alternates between circling my clit and fingering me while Jax cups my breasts and pinches my nipples.

The thought of taking them both has desire stirring low in my belly.

I trail my hand over Ethan's defined chest and abs to stroke his thick cock over his boxers. "Take these off," I whisper and push back against Jackson's erection. "Both of you."

Jax doesn't hesitate and strips without another word.

Ethan does the same, asking, "You want both of us?"

My answer is immediate. "Always."

"You tell me anytime if you need to stop, okay?"

I nod, and his hand moves to my throat, bringing me in for a hard kiss, our tongues entwining.

He pulls away and slaps my ass. "Be a good girl and face Jax for me."

I remove my shirt and flip onto my other side. Jackson grabs my chin and kisses me desperately, as if he's been waiting all night. I encircle his neck and tangle my fingers in his hair.

He raises my leg high on his waist, and in a single, smooth motion, he thrusts into me with a husky, "Fuck."

The bed dips, Ethan moves behind me, and then a slick finger penetrates my ass.

Jax never stops fucking me, teasing me, kissing me, the pleasure mounting as Ethan stretches me, preparing me to take him. One finger becomes two becomes three, and with Jackson sliding in and out of me and circling my clit, my orgasm climbs faster than ever.

I dig my nails into the hard muscle of Ethan's hip. "If you keep doing that, I'm going to come."

Fingers are replaced with the cold, wet tip of his cock, and I freeze.

"Just relax, baby." He clutches my throat and slowly presses into me. "I got you."

The head breaks through the tight ring, and I suck in a sharp gasp, clenching around Jax.

He releases a throaty groan. "Goddamn. You're crushing me."

Ethan pauses, allowing me to adjust to him. "Such a good

girl," he praises, his voice gravelly. "Taking both our cocks, letting us both fuck you."

Between his dirty words and Jackson's angled strokes hitting my G-spot while circling my clit, all I can focus on is coming. I'm not thinking about the incredible stretch—or maybe I am, and it only adds to the pleasure.

"Don't stop." My legs tremble, my head arching back over Ethan's shoulder, and I shatter, my entire body quaking. "Fuck, I'm coming."

"That's my girl." Ethan pushes into me with a low rumble. "Who do you belong to, Aurora?"

"You," I say automatically.

"Who else?"

"Jax," I whimper.

"Good girl," he punctuates with a snap of his hips. "You're ours. Don't forget that."

The farther he buries himself in my ass, the fuller and tighter everything becomes. I feel every inch of him, every inch of them both, only intensifying the climax, and I pulse around them.

"Fuck," Jackson rasps, thrusting hard and deep. "I can't take anymore. It feels too fucking good."

Ethan pulls out to the tip, then drives into me. "How much cum can we have dripping out of you over the next two days, baby?"

Jax clutches my thigh with bruising strength. "Not. Fucking. Helping," he grits through his teeth.

I have a vise grip on their cocks, the feeling so intense, I'm riding the precipice of another orgasm. That, or the last one never ended.

Needing more, I rock my hips. "Harder," I beg. "Don't stop."

They fall into rhythm, as if it's always been this way. The fullness of them both, the sounds of our bodies coming together, and their moans of pleasure have me hanging on the brink of oblivion.

Jackson's pace becomes punishing. "Ah, fuck," he groans, low and rough. "I'm going to fill this perfect fucking pussy."

I roll my hips, meeting their thrusts. My muscles tense, the air catches in my lungs, and wave after wave of ecstasy ripples through me.

"Holy fuck, I can feel you both coming." Ethan pounds into me, his voice strained. "Can I fill your ass full of cum, baby?"

"Yes," I breathe.

His teeth sink into my neck, and his cock jolts inside me.

The sensation of their hot cum and Ethan's claiming bite sends another shuddering climax ripping through me, and I can't contain my high-pitched screams while they piston in and out of me until the three of us are sated.

Jax flops onto the mattress. "Well," he pants. "*That* was fucking amazing. Pretty sure I'm ruined for life."

Me too.

AFTER THE THREE OF US SHOWERED AND JAX BRAIDED AURORA'S hair, it was pushing into the early hours of the morning. So when there's a sharp knock at the door and Aurora jolts awake, I'm not pleased.

"Oh, shit! I overslept." She goes to scramble off the bed, and her feet tangle in the sheets.

She falls forward, and her arms shoot out. I jump up, grab her shirt to stop her from face-planting into the hardwood, and yank her upright. I encircle her shoulders and draw her into my chest. Her heart pounds hard, and I can only imagine how high her blood pressure is.

"Slow down before you hurt yourself. They'll wait."

There's more knocking, louder this time.

Jax lifts his head. "Jesus, fuck. Hold on."

"We only have an hour," a snappy female voice answers.

"Be right out!" Aurora kicks her legs free of the bedding and heads to the walk-in closet.

I dig out a pair of sweats and a T-shirt from my bag and pull them on.

She comes out in cotton shorts and a sweater. "You don't have to get up. Sleep. You got in late."

"You were up with me, remember?"

"Oh, believe me, my entire body won't let me forget."

Jax throws on joggers and a hoodie. "I'll kiss it better later." He winks.

That image doesn't help my morning wood. He can kiss it better while she sucks my cock. That was pretty amazing last time.

Fuck, I need to stop thinking about sex before I pitch a tent.

We exit the bedroom to everyone gathered in the living room.

"Long night?" Desmond smirks.

The opposite of his brother's hard features and annoyed tone. "We tried to talk her out of waking you."

Emily gawks, her eyes wide and mouth hanging open. I remember her from the charity event, the woman at the bar. Her gaze brazenly drifts over me, same as that night. It's uncomfortable, even in my half-awake state.

The girls head to the kitchen, and I shoot Jax a *what-the-fuck* expression.

He puts his arm around my shoulders and lowers his voice. "Just wait until she makes an inappropriate comment about your dick in those gray sweatpants."

I shove him off, go back to the room, and dress for the day in jeans and a T-shirt. I'm meeting Rocco this morning anyhow.

When I return, Jax is sitting with the twins, a chocolate donut in hand. He's smiling and laughing, despite the others teasing him about his never-ending appetite.

I raise my chin at him. "You need to hit the gym."

"Bro, I was doing hip thrusts for an hour last night. I need a box of donuts to recuperate and a search party to recover my fucking soul."

I shake my head and turn away before he says anything more embarrassing. I'd be lying if I said I didn't miss his smart-ass comments, though.

Emily's voice hits my ears before I reach the kitchen, and I lean against the doorjamb, arms folded.

"That's not normal. Why don't you pick one? Stringing along two men is selfish. It's impossible to love them both."

Her words, although incorrect, awaken the snake in my gut.

I can't imagine Aurora choosing between us, can't imagine a world in which the three of us aren't together.

Aurora pours a cup of coffee, her back to me. "I do, and it feels perfectly normal." She turns toward the doorway. Her gaze wanders over my biceps, bulging in this position, and she tries to hide her smile by taking a sip from her mug.

I enjoy her devilish eyes on me; I revel in my girl checking me out. The other one? Nope. In fact, there's not much I like about Emily.

"What do you want for breakfast?" I ask Aurora.

Her lips spread into that naughty grin I love.

"Yeah, me, too. Go back to bed, and I'll make it happen." I've only been here a few hours, and, once again, I've transformed into my captain, letting shit slip in front of others.

Or maybe this is me, just less *uptight* and more comfortable.

Emily rolls her eyes. "Her other man went for breakfast, and hopefully, he'll return soon. We need to get started."

That puts a damper on my mood. "Who?"

"Ricky, the bodyguard who stares at Aurora as if he wants to join your orgy."

"Em," Aurora snaps. "Don't."

"Does your mouth ever close? You're as bad as Jax."

I say it as a joke, but it makes sense. She's extroverted, has no shame, and constantly runs her mouth. She probably spoke up for Aurora, talked her through her anxieties—and into things—and now, Aurora has us.

"Come sit with me." I motion towards the living room and walk away, not giving either of them the chance to argue.

I find an open recliner in front of the panoramic windows. Everyone is sitting in vintage upholstered chairs; in the middle sits an old trunk that serves as a coffee table.

The place has an industrial vibe, with exposed brick and ductwork. It's clean. Somebody painted, polished the floors, and found some furniture, but that's about it.

I set Aurora's mug on the table.

She clicks her tongue. "I need caffeine. Someone kept me up all night."

"Along with the rest of us." Desi yawns. "We're going back to bed if it's okay with you."

I nod, and they disappear down a hallway to the right, which I assume leads to the other three bedrooms. This place is impressive. It must span the entire floor of the building.

With my hands on her hips, I draw Aurora onto my lap. "You may need caffeine, but the baby doesn't."

She swings her legs over the arm of the chair and rests her head on my shoulder.

I press a kiss to her forehead and caress her stomach, eager to feel him move again. "You should cancel. Go back to bed. You need to rest." *And I need you.*

Emily sits opposite us. "We can't cancel. We were supposed to finish yesterday."

"I wish I had popcorn for this," Jax says from his seat beside me, a smile in his voice.

I'm tempted to keep quiet, but this girl grates my fucking nerves. Plus, I don't want Aurora working. She's mine. She should be in bed, resting and growing my son.

My eyes take on that stony stare. "You don't dictate her schedule. She'll work if she's well enough, and not for long."

Aurora snuggles into me further. "Everyone can stop. I'm fine. We'll finish today."

Emily meets my stare head-on. "You don't dictate her schedule either. That's Jackson's doing. You know, her *fiancé*."

"I'm well aware of who her fiancé is, seeing as we slept in the same bed together. If you think Jax is controlling, you haven't seen anything yet."

I thought a lot about Jackson and Aurora's engagement. It's not that I don't want a commitment. I do. It's that marriage isn't important to me. He'll cherish the shit out of being married to her. It would mean everything to him, and it wouldn't be right for me to take that away.

I'm jaded. The concept of marriage is tainted in my eyes.

I crave something deeper.

Jax can have his ring on her finger. I want her submission.

Aurora's body relaxes, her breathing goes steady, and I rest my head. If she falls asleep, I'm kicking everyone out and we're going to bed. The last I checked, it wasn't even eight a.m. We had maybe four hours of sleep.

"So let me get this straight." That annoying voice breaks the silence. "You're engaged to Jackson but having a kid with Ethan?"

Aurora answers with a sleepy groan. "Yes. Em."

"No," Jax counters. "We're *all* having a baby, and Ethan *may* have provided the DNA."

I jerk my head in his direction. "There's no question about it. I provided the DNA. We're not going over this again. You know what happened."

His eyes light up, that shit-eating grin on his face. "I do. She and I got into a fight. She rebounded with you, and you tried to get her pregnant."

Now I know he's fucking around, doing it to take the heat off Aurora and me. This is what he does—acts absurd in awkward situations.

"*Tried*? No, I *did* get her pregnant."

He crosses his arms over his chest, lifting his brows. "So you admit it was on purpose?"

My face heats, and Aurora shakes with laughter at his ridiculousness. I open my mouth to argue, but he stops me with a raised hand.

"Doesn't matter. The three of us are having kids. That's all anyone needs to know."

I cock my head. "Kids? Did I miss something at the last doctor's appointment?"

"He wants a hockey team of kids," Aurora clarifies.

My brain trips. It's far too early for this conversation. "Let's...take this one kid at a time."

I wouldn't deny him a child, but some shit has to change. When we're separated, I'm constantly worried. I can't imagine my anxiety after the baby arrives.

"If it's too difficult for you, I'll retire. I don't mind being a stay-at-home dad. You have no control over me fucking a baby into her."

"Jesus Christ." I shift under Aurora, my dick *firmly* on Jackson's side of the debate. "We'll discuss this later."

Emily gapes at us as if we've lost our damn minds—and we have, there's no doubt about it.

But nothing compares to last night. I'm itching for a repeat, and that *baby* comment has not helped.

The sound of the elevator rumbles through the apartment —the photographer and whoever else must be here.

I kiss Aurora's temple, my lips lingering. "I have to meet Rocco this morning. You better eat when food arrives and finish by the time I return."

She doesn't answer but moves my hand lower, and the baby brushes my palm. It's a light flutter, but I melt. I read babies learn and respond to our voices and touch this trimester— more reason not to be separated.

"I love you," I whisper.

"Love you." She places her soft lips on mine.

"This is *so* fucked up." Emily's voice raises, revealing her jealousy. "Jackson, I saw you shatter a bottle—"

Aurora breaks our kiss. "Em," she barks in warning.

"—*injuring* Aurora because a guy was *chatting* with her. But you allow your *coach* to be all over her?"

"What the hell is she talking about?" I don't recall anything about her being injured by Jax. Then, I remember her words: *I've bled for that man.* I thought it was a figure of speech.

"Nothing." She slides off my lap. "Em, stop or leave."

"Oh, you don't know? Jackson got angry and threw a bottle against the wall, aiming for a guy's head. It shattered, cutting the guy's face and neck. Luckily, Aurora shielded herself in time, because a large piece of glass embedded in her arm."

Our girl steps in front of Jax, always protecting him. "Leave."

Emily stands on high heels, but unfortunately, she doesn't exit. "Then he dragged her over the table and broke the guy's nose with his elbow for trying to stop him. He couldn't even see when Jackson punched him in the throat. The only reason he didn't kill a *senator's fucking son* is because his father intervened."

It all clicks in my head. Not that his response was appropriate, and I'm sure he was intoxicated, but it's not a surprise Jax was triggered by a predator taking an interest in Aurora, like the memory is triggering him now, driving him to his feet.

Aurora hugs his waist. "Ignore it. I'm okay."

He points a finger at Emily. "None of that shit would've happened if *you* hadn't brought her there. If you weren't such a jealous, scheming fucking whore, she would've never been with those people."

Jaw and fists clenched, Emily charges toward Jax, Aurora between them. "She also would've never seen you strung out!"

Aurora spins around, sways on her feet, then clutches her stomach, and the room erupts into chaos, *fast*.

I'm done, absolutely done.

Jax grabs our girl, and I get in front of her, in front of them both, knowing he's about to lose his shit. "Leave before I have you removed."

Emily narrows her eyes. "And who's going to remove me?"

"Me." Ricky enters my peripheral vision and snatches her arm, dragging her away. "Let's go."

She trips but manages to stay upright, her feet scrambling beneath her. "You can't touch me!"

"Wanna fucking bet?" he snarls, not letting up. "You came at the woman I'm protecting. I'll do whatever the fuck I want."

She struggles to free herself from his grip. "I'll fight back!"

He shoves her through the kitchen doorway. "And I'll put you in handcuffs."

Jax hovers over Aurora, tears in his eyes.

"I'm only nauseated," she assures him, her voice wobbly.

From behind, I cuff his rigid shoulder and clasp her nape. When he doesn't throw me off, I wrap my arm around his front and draw him into my chest. "You good?"

He releases a breath and nods solemnly.

Ricky returns from dumping the trash, his face flushed. He

glares at Aurora and points to the bedroom. "Get in bed." He lowers his hand and exhales. "I'll bring you breakfast and take your blood pressure."

Her gaze meets mine, seeking my response, as if I won't agree.

I release her neck. "Go."

Her shoulders slump. "I have to finish today."

"We'll see what your blood pressure says." I have no intention of letting her do anything. "Climb into bed with Jax. I'll bring you cupcakes after my meeting."

Once the bedroom door shuts, I find Ricky in the kitchen arranging her breakfast—a strawberry tart and a bowl of yogurt with granola, blueberries, and raspberries, a chocolate croissant on the side.

My God, can someone *not* spoil her?

"You know that's not your job anymore. You don't have to do that."

He pops the top off a steaming to-go cup of tea. "It was never my job."

I brush that comment aside. I lack the brainpower to deal with him right now. "Not that I'd ever let it happen, but you see why Jax can't be around Kyle or be put back in that environment, right?" Just the thought has my heart racing against my sternum. I should have someone check *my* blood pressure. "He'll relapse. He'll get wasted to get through it. It'll kill Aurora."

"I got you."

"He was a victim."

His eyes meet mine. "I'm not planning on using him—or Aurora—but he could give details of people and locations. That would help."

"I'll think about it. Don't let anyone up please. She doesn't need to be working. Is it always like this?"

"With Emily, yes. She goes out of her way to provoke Jax every single time. Other than that, no. He cooks and plays video games with the twins. They've talked about going to the gym. Aurora tinkers in the studio, reads, and naps. They spent a day shopping. They do well here."

That's what I was afraid of.

51

ETHAN

"You know, if you stayed in New York..." Rocco trails off.

We sit in a line of cars waiting to pass the Control Building at Rikers Island.

"I can't, and neither can Jackson. We both have contracts."

"The New York hockey team will take you back. They'd take you both. They'd be crazy not to."

It's not that I haven't thought about it. We'd have a semi-normal life here, far from Kyle and publicity. We'd be blissfully isolated for the most part, but... "I don't want to join the family business, no offense."

"None taken. You're right where your father wanted you to be. The war of his generation is over. No one is asking anything of you, but we enjoy seeing you."

After being cleared through the gates, we drive past the Control Building and Ward Visitation Center to the Men's Correctional Facility.

Barbed wire fencing surrounds the outside, and it's not much better on the inside. The group cells we pass in processing remind me of cages—humans confined in dingy cages.

Maybe this is why he never wanted me. This is no place for a child.

We sit on a bench bolted to the floor in a brightly lit room. I drum my fingers on the metal table, and my knee bounces.

Do I call him Vincenzo or Enzo? Certainly not Dad.

The door opens, and a man in an orange jumper enters. He has salt-and-pepper hair and pale skin, as if he hasn't seen the sun in years. He's several inches shorter than me and much less bulky. He appears healthy for seventy, not heavyset but not starved.

He looks older than the pictures I've found online, but there's no mistaking who he is.

The door shuts and locks behind him. No officer comes in, and he's not in cuffs as I expected.

He sits opposite me. "Wow. I never thought I'd see the day."

I nod, my head bobbing ever so slightly. "Yeah, me either."

We stare, taking each other in. It's strange seeing my eyes on someone else.

My father casually rests his cheek on his hand, elbow on the table, giving me his full attention. "So, tell me about your-self. Rocco says you're divorced, took a job in LA, and have a model girlfriend." He smiles, brightening his eyes. "Sounds glamorous."

He has my dry humor—or I have his, rather.

I scoff. "Not at all. Marriage wasn't for me. I accepted the coaching position to distance myself from my ex."

Rocco pushes his phone across the table to my father. "His girlfriend, Aurora."

I crane my neck to see a zoomed-in image of a bikini center-fold of hers. "Really? That's the picture you show him."

"I have a current photo." A wide grin spreads over his face. "Calm down."

He slides his finger along the screen, flipping through pics of Aurora, some professional, a few at the loft, until he lands on one of us from this morning. She's snuggled in my lap, my hand cradling her stomach, my lips pressed to her forehead.

"Where are you getting these?" I ask, unable to hide my annoyance.

"The twins. I wanted a photo with you two together."

It's the perfect picture, and Aurora would love it. "Send it to me then erase the rest. You don't need pics of my girlfriend."

My father chuckles, his deep, hearty laugh echoing in the small, barren room. "I see why the marriage didn't work. She's gorgeous. Young."

"Yeah, she's twenty-two."

"You love her?"

I answer without hesitation. "More than anything."

"How far along?"

"Five months."

"Know what you're having?"

"A boy."

His intense gaze never leaves me. "You turned out better than I could've imagined. I'm sorry about your ma." He inhales deeply and exhales slowly. "I really am. We tried to help her."

I give a half-ass shrug. "Yeah, me too. There was no saving her." Not while he was in prison.

It's twisted how fate works. Here I am, once again, attempting to save someone else from addiction. I couldn't save my mother—I wasn't enough—but I'll do everything in my power to stop from losing Jax too.

"You've got the job, the girl, and a kid on the way. What else?" he asks, his eyes glassy.

"It's...complicated."

"Love always is."

"She dated one of my players, Jackson. They were separated when she and I slept together, but they rekindled things before I knew she was pregnant. Long story short, the three of us are in a...relationship."

"A relationship...?" He scowls, his eyes darkening—another similarity.

The tips of my ears burn. I don't know why I care about what he thinks. He has no influence on my life, not when it comes to Aurora and Jax. No one does.

"As in, we're both with her. We plan on living together and sharing a future."

Understanding dawns on his face, and he strokes his trimmed beard. "I see."

"Like I said, it's complicated. Jackson has had it rough. His father is a corrupt police commissioner in LA. He thinks the baby is Jackson's. He's harmed Aurora while pregnant, threatened her, had us followed, confronted me about her and the baby, and you," I add. "He's destroyed Jax, and I...I don't know what I'm asking." Emotion grabs me, my eyes sting, and I lower my head. "For you to protect them, I guess." I blink away the wetness and swallow the hard lump in my throat. "I'll never ask for anything else."

Rocco slides over some documents I can't read.

My father's eyebrows shoot to his receding hairline, and he lets out a low whistle. "This his?"

"Yup. Met with him earlier this week." Rocco leans back and crosses his arms over his chest. "We're working on getting it in Ethan's name. He's engaged to Aurora, and eventually, he wants it split between the two, but ultimately, it'll be with us."

"Shit. Yeah, that type of money will corrupt weaker men." With a confident posture and a sly smirk, my father cocks his head at me. "So, you sought help from one criminal to deal with another?"

I match his smirk. "Pretty much."

They both laugh at my candor, and the tension melts.

"You care for him." My father doesn't ask it, only states the obvious.

"He's a good kid—crazy—but he loves hard."

"You get the baby, and he gets the marriage, huh?"

"Something like that. I don't need the marriage, just the girl. I never imagined having any of this, honestly."

He nods in contemplation then hands the stack of papers back to Rocco, simply stating, "Protect our investments."

My curiosity is piqued, but they dive into discussing business and family, and I remain quiet.

They casually chat and joke, as if my father hasn't missed a thing. Their relationship is close, and I find myself a little envious.

At the end of the visit, he gives me a firm hug. "I'll keep in touch with Rocco."

"I'll see you soon." The words fly off my tongue without a second thought, my voice strained.

He pulls back yet holds on. "You don't have to."

"I want to."

52

JACKSON

ETHAN IS QUIET, MORE SO THAN USUAL. HE RUSHED OUT OF HERE this morning before I could ask why he was meeting Rocco. If it were about money or the house, I think he'd tell me. It makes me nervous, but I trust Ethan. He'd never betray me.

We all end up eating dinner and watching a hockey game on the flatscreen the twins and I installed today. That was entertainment in itself, and it wouldn't surprise me if it fell off the wall.

Scratch that—Dante is an expert at every task he puts his mind to. Desi, however, is easily distracted, and somehow, we finished with more screws than we should have.

Even with Ricky here, I'm happy. Getting along with the twins is easy. Desi is unpredictable, and Dante is chill—they balance each other out, and it's great having people to joke with who don't judge my every move.

It's odd, but I'll miss Ethan's family when we leave.

Desi sets down his third bowl of chicken curry on the coffee table. "You like to cook? I figured you'd have a chef."

"No chef." I shrug. "My mother taught me to cook. It's peaceful, and I love food, so it's a win-win."

Ethan breaks from the TV to stare at me, and Aurora does the same. It takes me a second to realize...*I never talk about my mother.*

I glance away, and Ethan seizes the opportunity to bust my balls, finally shaking off his broody mood. One thing I like about him: he doesn't pity me. He has few outward emotions, and pity is rarely one of them.

"You sure you didn't grow up with an entire team of maids and butlers?"

"Staff wasn't allowed in the house, asshole."

Desi eyes me skeptically. "You do your own laundry?"

"Sometimes." The only reason I haven't done laundry here is because the washer and dryer are in the basement, and fuck that shit. I'm not about to piss my pants when a New York rat jumps out at me.

"Don't let him fool you," Ethan says with a smug smile. "The arena staff does his laundry. He doesn't even tie his own skates."

Everyone laughs except Ricky, who sits next to Dante, gaze fixed on the game, but I know he's paying attention.

He's not fooling me by biding his time, and he's not gaining my trust to use Aurora. I'll kill him first.

I've never actually killed anyone—not even Aurora's ex. I just gifted him a shit-ton of cocaine and fifty grand and let the LAPD do the rest. Not my fault he accepted and had prior charges. That's on him.

Given the chance, I'd happily expedite a few people into the afterlife. Ricky is lucky he's not one of them—yet.

I have no intention of strangling him again. I won't do that to Aurora. She'll see enough of me fighting when I return to playing hockey. Plus, my hand is broken.

Now that I know he's an agent and he keeps his mouth shut, he doesn't trigger me as much. It also helps that I donated his boots to the homeless guy who lives in our alleyway. It's winter. He needed them more.

It never stops slushing here. It's not even snow; it's rainy-icy-fucking-snow.

That vacation Aurora mentioned sounds better and better. When the season ends, I'm finding a secluded spot somewhere warm, and we're staying as long as possible.

Maybe we need a yacht. I'll have to ask Ethan. He shot down the private jet I wanted for away games, stating we're required to travel with the team. I'll amend that in my next contract, if there is one.

Aurora snuggles up to me on the couch, snapping me from my disordered thoughts that somehow went from laughing to murder to buying a yacht.

My brain has been tripping since the three of us had sex. I swear, I'm not having a psychotic break.

"That curry was fantastic. Thank you."

I kiss her forehead and notice her braids need to be redone. She would've taken them out before her photoshoot to give her those messy waves, but that never happened.

Not only can I cook, but I also memorized every food she won't eat, and I learned how to braid her thick hair. I'm not terrible in bed either. I'm an all-around catch, if you ask me.

Desi clears his throat. "Do you three always sleep together?"

Dante punches him in the arm. "Don't mind him. He has no filter."

Desi hits him right back. "I'm wondering if I need to sleep with headphones tonight. Not all these walls are real."

Aurora glances up at me with furrowed brows, and I shrug.

"They're temporary walls used to create rooms in open spaces." Dante points up. "Ours don't have ceilings."

My gaze gravitates to their side of the loft. *Well, fuck. Look at that.* "Definitely wear them. The old man snores."

Ethan's cheeks redden. "I do not snore, but this entire building will be awake if Jax is separated from Aurora. The last time he slept alone, he woke us up at the ass-crack of dawn like a toddler."

"We had a doctor's appointment, and I was eager to see the baby." And, okay, I wanted to prevent them from having morning sex, shower sex, or any other type of sex without me.

Aurora stands, collecting our empty dishes, and I gently grab her wrist. "Babe, what are you doing? We can get those."

She shoots me that sweet smile. "I'm going to the kitchen anyhow."

When she returns, it's with a pink box of cupcakes. She places it on the coffee table, opens the lid, and grabs a red velvet cupcake with white frosting and heart-shaped sprinkles.

I glance at Ethan with a blank expression. "Really? Heart-shaped sprinkles? Suck-up."

He flips me the middle finger.

Aurora has Ricky for breakfast, me for dinner, and Ethan for dessert. Now that she's not working—not that she knows, but Ethan is one controlling bastard, and I doubt she'll ever work again after this morning's uproar—there shouldn't be any issues at her next doctor's appointment.

Bringing the cupcake to her mouth, she takes a bite, frosting smearing her nose. Her eyes shut and she releases a soft moan, and my cock thickens.

I stare at her in awe. "When did you start liking cupcakes so much?"

She licks her lips and points to her belly.

My eyebrows raise. "The baby likes cupcakes?"

She nods, peeling off the paper wrapper and taking another bite.

A massive grin overtakes my face. "I knew that was my kid. Sorry, Ethan."

He glares at me without a trace of irritation. "Don't start that shit again."

After she finishes, I stoop to kiss her. Right before our lips meet, I playfully lick her nose.

"You did not just lick my nose!" She giggles and pushes me away.

"You're mine. I'll lick you wherever I want."

I prove it later that night, while Ethan is in the shower and we're in bed.

We kiss, and our mouths taste like vanilla icing. When I go down on her, her pussy is a combination of sweet and *Aurora,* and my dick throbs.

"You taste so fucking good. My two favorite flavors: cupcake and pussy."

"Jax." She stretches out my name.

Her warning tone turns into a moan when I suck her clit between my lips, flick it with my tongue, then bite lightly.

"Your pussy. Cupcake and *your* pussy."

She spreads her legs wider, and I dive in. I figure I have about five minutes to make her come before Ethan gets out of the shower.

Bonus points if she screams my name.

I flatten my tongue and tease her from hole to clit and back.

"Jax, please." She tugs my hair.

I smile, secretly wanting her to beg. "What, babe? Tell me."

She gives a tempting whine. "Make me come."

I fuck her tight cunt with two fingers, knowing the perfect spot to have her coming in no time. Then, I stop. "What will you give me?"

"I hate you right now." She rocks her hips with a whimper. "Anything."

"Will you let us fuck you again?"

"Oh, that's a hard bargain," she says, her voice dripping with sarcasm. "But sure."

With a silent chuckle, I concede. I pull back the hood of her clit and circle it with the tip of my tongue. She grows wetter, her juices flooding my fingers and mouth, and I leak precum in my boxers.

I work my tongue faster, alternating between sucking and nibbling.

She writhes underneath me, fisting my hair, and I know she's close.

I suck her clit harder, and she explodes.

"Oh fuck. Jax!"

Her cunt clamps down around my fingers, and a high-pitched scream fills the room. I don't stop until I have every drop of her orgasm, and her limbs flop to the mattress.

"Oh my God," she breathes.

Palming my aching erection, I crawl over her, ready to give her a second orgasm, when the bathroom door opens.

"Jesus Christ, you couldn't wait ten fucking minutes?"

53

ETHAN

I reach for Aurora. "Come here, love."

She moves out from under him, her face flushed and lips bright red.

With dramatic flair, he collapses onto the mattress. "Where are you going?" His voice is whiny, puppy-dog eyes aimed at our girl.

I'd expect nothing less from him. They're so alike, it's scary.

I smirk at his antics. "She needs to soak in the bath."

He has his ways of *kissing it and making it better*, and I have mine.

"We can't all fit into that bathtub."

He's not even joking. Hot tub, maybe. Tiny bathtub with him? Nope.

I smile. "I know."

The only thing semi-updated in this loft is the bedroom suite. Although not luxurious, the bathroom features a vintage clawfoot tub, most likely made of cast iron and too heavy to be removed. It's small, but it'll serve its purpose.

She climbs out of bed gloriously naked. Her baby bump grows more prominent every time I see her, her breasts larger and rounder. She's so fucking beautiful, my chest hurts.

I lead her into the bathroom and shut the door behind us. I hold her hand, helping her into the steamy water.

She peers up at me with those big brown eyes. "Bubbles?"

I grin at how adorable she is. "No bubbles. They might irritate your skin. Just Epsom salt."

I stopped at the store on my way home from the prison for cupcakes and Epsom salt. I've turned into such a romantic fuck.

There's an old wooden stool underneath the vanity, which I grab and set behind the tub. "Do you need me to take out your braids and wash your hair?"

She spins to face me, the water sloshing. "You're not getting in with me?"

I shake my head at the absurd idea. "No, my giant ass won't fit in there, love."

"Nonsense." She scoots back to make room. "Please."

She stretches out the word, and I lose all resistance. Jesus Christ, what has happened to me?

I drop my sweats and take my place behind her. Water tips over the side of the tub onto the floor, and she giggles. It's cramped, my knees bent and above the rim, but I'll do whatever the hell she wants—apparently.

She has me wrapped around her finger so tight, it's ridiculous. No ring necessary.

"I haven't been in a tub since I took ice baths after games." I guide her back against my chest. "This is *way* better."

"I bet we can make it even better."

There's a hint of flirtation in her voice, and I have to remind my aching erection that this is for her. No matter how much I want to palm her sweet tits and be inside her right now, this is for *her*.

Her hands glide over my hairy legs. It's such an intimate gesture, like nothing I've ever experienced—not only sharing a bath, but being this physically and emotionally vulnerable. She has my firsts in many ways and doesn't even know it.

I caress her stomach and cherish the feeling of our growing baby. "I'm so in love with you." The words slip from my lips, but I don't regret them. "I never imagined I could love anyone as much as I love you and our baby."

Her eyes glisten. "I love you too. I wish we could stay like this forever."

"Me too, baby girl."

We remain intertwined, and I realize I need more of this. I need her with me. I need to watch her grow with my child and not miss a moment.

"You feeling okay?" I ask.

"Absolutely perfect."

"Sore?"

"A little."

"The bath should help, but you need more rest. I'm serious, Aurora."

She emits a noncommittal sound. She may have my heart in her fist, but that doesn't mean I won't prioritize her well-being. If I have to force her to rest, I will.

"When do you leave for Montreal?" she asks, changing the subject.

"Tomorrow afternoon."

She stares up at me, sticking out her bottom lip, and I bite it. There's no reason for her to pout. She'll be with me.

She takes the bite as an invitation to climb into my lap. Silky thighs hug my waist, bare pussy sliding over my eager cock.

Her arms encircle my neck, and her fingers glide into my damp hair, tits in front of my face.

I stretch up to kiss her lips. "This bath is for you."

She glances between us, quirking a brow.

"Don't pay him any attention. He'd fuck you while you slept if I let him."

She grips my shaft then, giving it a smooth stroke.

"Aurora, no," I say with zero conviction. "You're supposed to be resting."

"I will rest..." Her fist squeezes me tighter, twisting over the head, "...on your dick."

Laughter rolls through me. I have a love-hate relationship with her smart mouth. "No, you will not."

She massages my balls with one hand while stroking me

with the other. The dual torture has my restraint crumbling. I palm both her breasts and squeeze them together, sucking and biting one, then the other.

Her hips rock while her hands continue their torment. I'm dying to plunge into her, fuck her hard and fast, but I can't in this position.

"If you want my cock, we need to get out." I give her mouth-watering nipples one last bite and pull with my teeth. "As much as I want you to ride me, there's not enough room in here."

I lean forward. Her hands release me and hold my shoulders, the steel bar between my legs trapped between us. Using the side of the tub for leverage, I stand, repositioning her so I have an arm underneath her before I step out.

In my haste to bury myself inside her, I forgot all about the water on the floor. I slip and nearly fall on my ass. She clings to me, thighs gripping my waist, and giggles hysterically.

"Fuck." My heart beats a frantic rhythm. "You're going to be the death of me."

I don't bother grabbing a towel. Only the bottom of her braids are wet, and we're about to get sweaty.

When I open the bathroom door and illuminate the bedroom, Jax sits against the headboard, playing on his phone.

"About fucking time," he grumbles with narrowed eyes and a tight jaw.

I wonder what he'd have done if I had fucked her in the bath. Pout like a toddler, probably. He's about to have an absolute fit when I leave with her tomorrow, or he'll insist on going.

Despite my desire to be alone with her, I am quite fond of threesome sex.

"Stay right there," I tell him.

His demeanor changes. His back straightens and his eyes gleam. He reaches over and sets his phone on the nightstand. I hit the bathroom light, and darkness shrouds the bedroom.

I place a knee on the mattress and set her on the bed, whispering, "Suck his cock for me, baby. I wanna fuck you on your knees."

She makes her way toward Jax, and I palm my needy erection, giving her time to get situated.

"Mmm... Fuck," he groans, and I take that as my cue to climb up behind her.

I notch the head at her entrance and slide into her gripping cunt, air hissing through my teeth. She's soaking wet, and this position has me driving deep inside her. I fucking love it, every tight inch of her.

She widens her knees and arches her back further, aligning us perfectly. My hips smack her ass and push her forward. She gags, her throat tightening around him as her pussy clamps around me, and both Jackson and I curse.

I do it again and again, our damp skin slapping. She moans, the sound muffled by his cock. I angle my hips downward to hit her G-spot and snake my arm under her to roll her clit with my fingers.

She whimpers and meets my hard thrusts.

Ecstasy courses through my veins, and even with Jax in the room, I can't stop the dirty words from escaping my mouth. "Such a good girl. You take us so fucking well. Come on my cock, baby, while you suck his. Give it to me."

It's not long before her cunt locks on to me, and she milks me for all I'm worth.

My hips punch forward, my head falls back, and the orgasm hits hard. My dick jerks, unloading deep inside her.

Between the three of us, it's a symphony of groans and moans. There's the occasional "Fuuuuuuck" and "Swallow my cum" and "So fucking good."

Music to my ears.

54

ETHAN

Aurora sleeps soundly. She had a long day, and as soon as Jax fixed her braids, she passed out.

She's on her side, her head on my chest, her leg between mine. I lie on my back, my arms bent underneath the pillow so Jackson can be close beside her. It's an awkward position, but once I fall asleep, I'm good.

But tonight, I'm wide awake. My mind keeps replaying the prison visit.

The place was deplorable. Picture an arena after a playoff game—floors black with grime, sticky from who knows what. I'd rather not contemplate what I stepped in.

Scuff marks marred the bland gray walls, and ceiling tiles were missing or rotted. Alarms blared incessantly, punctuated by the shouts of staff and inmates.

If I had visited as a child, I would've been scared shitless. Not that my actual childhood was much better, waking many mornings terrified my mother was dead.

The bed shifts. "Dude, I can hear you thinking from over here," Jackson rasps.

"Sorry." I don't know why, but I feel the urge to tell him. "I went to the prison today with Rocco. Saw my father."

A weight lifts off my chest. I considered telling Aurora, but I didn't want to burden her with more uncertainties. I also didn't want to hurt her, since I hadn't told her I was going. I hadn't told anyone.

"Shit." He adjusts his position. "Why? You putting a hit on Kyle?" There's a smile in his voice. He's cracking jokes to ease my tension.

"Don't say that out loud." I only want Jax and Aurora to be safe. I don't want to know the details of the rest, but I certainly wouldn't be sad if Kyle didn't wake one morning. "They put bugs in Aurora's apartment, you know?"

He blows out a long, throaty breath. "Motherfucking Ricky. I need to check mine then."

I drag my fingers through my hair, staring at his silhouette in the darkness. "Have you been careful?"

"Careful? With what I say? Are you really asking me that? I'm about as careful as you fucking an escort in the back of a limo with an expired condom while still married."

"Jesus Christ, get over it. She seduced me."

"Fuck you," he whispers, which, let me tell you, is far more terrifying than him yelling it. "She was on the rebound and sad. You got sad pussy."

My chest vibrates with silent laughter. "It was *definitely* not sad, dickhead. Quite needy, actually."

"I hate you."

I roll my eyes. "Shut up. You'd miss me if I weren't here."

"You and Ricky. He wants her, you know that, right?"

His speech is a tad rushed, and my next words might get me hit, but fuck it. "It's not a terrible idea."

"What? Putting a hit on Kyle? I got it handled."

"Stop saying that." Sometimes, it's hard to tell if he's joking or lacking a filter. Either way, I don't need him in prison. "No—having Ricky with us."

A sudden dip in the mattress suggests he's sitting up, possibly about to throw a punch. "In what universe is he a good idea?"

Our girl stirs at his raised tone, and I lower my voice, not wanting to wake her.

"The one where we both travel. Who'll care for her? Protect

her? The twins aren't going with us. Are we leaving her alone with the baby in LA? With your father?"

"Are you for real? You only like him because he does what *you* say."

"There's that," I joke.

But Jax's voice is anything but playful. "Whatever. I quit."

His stubborn anger triggers my own. "You're a brat, you know that? You're playing. You can give me a season or two for all the shit I've done for you." Even provoked, that was harsher than intended.

"Don't hold back. Tell me how you really feel, Coach. Are you gonna be in his bed next?"

"What?" A brat, one hundred percent. How did I end up with two brats? "Where the fuck did that come from?"

He doesn't respond. He lies down and faces away from me.

"All I'm saying is, Ricky knows her. He understands her anxiety. He can handle her panic attacks. He makes sure she eats. He goes all the way across the city for fucking pastries. He's aware of your father's history and mine, and he won't go running to the media. I trust he'll protect her *and* you."

"Whatever. You're the boss."

A heavy silence fills the space between us. I should've waited until the season started and we were strapped to discuss Ricky.

He sniffs, and I feel like shit.

"Jax—"

"I told you I'd figure out Kyle. I'll give you until the end of my contract. I want to see this baby, not spend half the year on the road. I respect your goals, but we have plenty of money, and you can win without me."

I close my eyes and let my frustrations go—for now. "I want the same as you." Then, a half-ass thought brings a smile to my face. "We could buy a team."

He scoffs. "We're wealthy, but we're not *that* wealthy. I'm not a billionaire."

I doubt he even knows his worth, considering all his grand-father's investments, properties, and businesses.

"We can buy that team in Alaska no one wants."

"Dude," he stretches out the word. "There's a reason no one wants that team, and I am *not* living in Alaska. What the fuck?"

I grin at his appalled tone. "We don't have to live there, not year-round."

"I'd rather live in New York."

"Perfect. I know an entire organization we can buy."

He gets it surprisingly fast. "Those are kids."

"You wanted a hockey team of kids."

"You're serious, aren't you?" He rolls toward me. "You wanna be with your family? Is that it?" There's no disdain or mockery in his voice, only understanding and consideration.

I now realize Jax wants one thing, something he's never had.

We aren't so different. Some divine intervention put us misfits together, all missing the same thing.

A family.

"Maybe. I don't know. I'll make a deal with the devil himself if it keeps you and Aurora safe. Besides, it wouldn't just be my family. It'd be *our* family."

55

AURORA

I LIE IN BED BETWEEN TWO MUSCLED SPACE HEATERS, BOTH LIGHT sleepers. I'll wake them if I try to climb out of bed, but when footsteps thud in the living area, my boredom gets the best of me.

Plus, the gait is familiar, and we need to talk.

Carefully, I free my legs from the blanket and crab crawl to the end of the bed. My boys must have been up late. Neither of them moves when I crack open the door.

Peeking my head out, I don't see anyone. Ricky is either in the kitchen or in his room. I haven't heard the clanking of the elevator, so he hasn't left.

I quietly close the door behind me and dash to the kitchen on my tip-toes. The smell of fresh coffee hits me, and my stomach growls. Maybe I can sneak in a cup before Ethan wakes.

Ricky's head turns as I enter the doorway, his gaze landing on my excited face before dropping to my bare legs. In my defense, Ethan's shirt is as long as a dress, ending at my mid-thigh.

Plus, Ricky has seen me in less.

"What are you doing, princess? Trying to get me killed?"

"I wanted to catch you before you left. Are you going out for breakfast? Can I go with you?"

He leans against the counter, coffee mug held to his lips. He's wearing his typical black cargo pants and black T-shirt. His blond hair is getting longer, curling around his baseball cap.

"You sure you want to? You haven't talked to me in weeks."

There's an unmistakable bite in his tone, and his heated stare roams my body with a different type of assessment. No longer am I his client and he my guard. He never was. He hasn't taken a penny from me, which makes sense if the government is paying him.

I cock my head and cross my arms over my chest. "Want to take me to breakfast or not?"

He sets the mug down and holds up a finger. "One: Ethan will have my nuts. Two: Your fiancé will hunt us down. I wouldn't be surprised if he had a tracker embedded in your neck. Three: The twins will have every mafia wannabe tailing us."

I roll my eyes and release a disappointed sigh. I'm ready to give up and return to my bedroom when he pushes off the counter and stands in front of me. I'm tall for a girl, but he's well over six feet, so I have to peer up at him.

He tucks a strand of hair behind my ear, and my stomach flip-flops, my lips parting at his dark look.

"Breakfast with a side of mayhem sounds fantastic. Go get dressed so I don't have to add murder."

I retrieve my clothes and phone from the bedroom, and then I dress in the hall bathroom.

I doubt my boys will be awake anytime soon, but I shoot them a text to prevent panic when they find me missing.

The cold New York air is exhilarating. Icy snowflakes stick to my eyelashes, and I tilt my face to the cloudy sky.

Ricky hovers next to me, although the streets aren't crowded. "Did you bring gloves or a hat?" He interlaces our fingers and squeezes my hand to get my attention.

"I'll be fine. I like the snow."

"You know I hate that word." He yanks my hood over my

head, ending my fun. "The last thing I need is you getting sick again, princess."

I furrow my brows. "Since when did you start calling me princess?"

"Since you started collecting a harem of men," he says matter-of-factly.

My jaw drops. "Who are you right now?"

He lets out a deep laugh, a sound I haven't heard in a while. It sends a shiver down my spine that has nothing to do with the cold. More and more, I'm finding I don't know the real Ricky. He's been quiet and distant, nothing like the giant teddy bear he pretended to be...if he was pretending at all.

We walk the few blocks to a café, only stopping once for Ricky to check on a homeless guy in an alleyway, mumbling something about his boots.

We take our seats at a table, remove our jackets, and order. The waitress delivers our food within minutes, and we remain awkwardly silent.

I pick at my Tiffany-blue painted nails before I cover my hands with my sleeves to stop the anxious habit, swallowing my nerves. "When you and I flew to New York, you took my phone from me."

The muscle in his jaw flicks. "You were getting flustered."

"Did you know Jax was in trouble?"

He shakes his head and averts his gaze. "I wasn't there."

"But you knew? You had someone watching him?"

"Not in the hotel room, no. It was impossible."

"They could've stopped him. You could've told me." Tears push at my eyelids. "I could've stopped him or Ethan."

He takes my hand and interlaces our fingers. "I couldn't. I'm sorry."

I rip my hand away. "You let him—"

"Following Jax that night allowed my team to identify two security guards who worked to scope out young girls and lead them not only to that penthouse, but to men associated with Kyle. Casinos are hotspots for human trafficking. Every asshole we apprehend means fewer girls become victims. I'm sorry, angel."

I hang my head, my mind a battlefield. He's right, and my soul aches.

He lifts my chin. "We ensured he got back to his room safely."

"Why not just arrest them? Kyle and these other men."

"It has to be done strategically. If we go after one, it will tip off the others." His knuckles brush along my cheekbone. "No more about the case. I'll work with Jax when the time is right."

"Why not go back to LA?" I don't mean for it to sound rude or dismissive. "Until Jax is ready," I clarify.

Something passes through his eyes. "You want me to leave?"

My slightly wind-burnt cheeks flush as I recall the days we spent together. How attentive he was. How comfortable we were together. "Am I why you're here?"

"Do you want me here?"

This is getting exasperating. "You lied to me."

A curt nod is all he gives me. "I did."

"You carried my bags," I say, appalled and a little disgusted with myself.

"I like carrying your bags."

"You made my food."

He shrugs. "I like feeding you. I still do."

"I'm engaged."

"I'm well aware." There's that jealous undertone again.

"You can't want this."

He settles into the red leather booth, arms crossed over his bulging chest, a smirk playing on his lips. "Want what?"

He's going to make me say it. Why? This isn't my confession to make. I'm giving him the opportunity to talk alone, and he's still dragging his feet, maybe teasing me. Either way, he can forget it.

I slide my artisan mocha closer, delighting in the heart-shaped foam. I almost don't want to ruin it. After a large sip that makes my soul dance with happiness and bravery, I stand from the table.

He grabs my wrist before I can walk away. "Where you going?"

"To get a bag and a to-go cup. If you're going to continue talking in circles, we might as well leave. Why would I risk getting into trouble with my guys if you can't even muster the balls to be honest with me?"

Shock washes over his face. "You want honesty?" He releases my wrist. "Sit. Eat."

56

RICKY

Aurora breaks off a piece of blueberry muffin and watches me with anticipation. I go to fiddle with my dog tags when I remember I left them behind purposefully.

She's young, seven years younger than me, gentle and innocent. The little things—cupcakes, snow falling, fancy coffee with hearts on top—light up her eyes. Her delicate demeanor makes her appear even younger, especially compared to my strict country upbringing and military background.

"I don't know what I want," I say earnestly. "I thought I did, but everything changed."

A frown appears on her pouty lips. "So why criticize Jax?"

My veins boil with irritation. "Is that what this is about? Your precious Jackson?"

She pushes her plate away, grabs her jacket, and stands from the booth. "You have no right to be mad or jealous of him. If you don't know what you want, you can keep your feelings to yourself."

She turns to leave, and I'm stunned stupid. I shouldn't be. She'll defend him to her last breath.

I'm not blaming her, but she has me twisted. I swear, she touched me, and I lost all ability to think straight. I'm terrible at flirting or dating or talking or whatever the hell this is, and she isn't like other women. She doesn't play games and has a heart of gold.

I've been in the military. I've never spent time with a woman, no more than one night. I have no clue what I'm doing. I was living with Aurora when I realized I was falling for her—more than a crush, like some life-altering phenomenon. It's not as if I could elude it.

The bell above the door rings, breaking me from my thoughts. I throw down two twenties and rush out, cursing myself for not feeding her more.

I catch up to her in a few strides. She doesn't have her jacket zipped. I fist the front of her hoodie and drag her into the alleyway next to the café. She stumbles and falls into me, her hand landing on my stomach, and I wrap my arm around her waist to steady her.

We're intertwined like a couple. It'd be so easy to grab her by the chin and kiss her, but I'm positive that'll get me strung up in a rat-infested basement and left for dead—and that's only after Jax, Ethan, and the twins kick the piss out of me.

I dip my head, her sweet vanilla scent flooding my senses. "If you were single, I'd know without a doubt what I wanted. If I weren't on a job focused on your fiancé, I'd know what I wanted." Just saying it out loud makes shit a whole lot clearer. Obvious. It's so obvious. "I want you," I growl. "Is that what you want to hear? There's nothing to do about it, princess."

Her chest heaves, her heart thundering. "Why didn't you tell me? Before?"

I clasp her neck and run my thumb over her skin, trying to soothe her anxiety. "Would it have made a difference? He would've come for you eventually, and same with Ethan."

Her only response is a shuddering breath.

"So you're right. I *am* mad. I'm mad he doesn't deserve you but gets to keep you. I'm mad you touched me. I'm mad I can't get you out of my head. I'm mad your smile makes the rest of my life seem bleak. I want you more than this job, but it's all I have. I've done everything right my entire life, played by the books. Then, fuck, you come along, and all I want is to break every hard-earned rule. All for you. Just to be close to you."

I attempt to withdraw, feeling vulnerable and foolish, but she refuses to let me go.

Her arms encircle my waist, and she peers up at me with glassy eyes. "I'm sorry. For what it's worth, I loved your company." Her voice breaks. "I needed you, and you were there for me." She swallows hard. "You deserve more than just being close to me."

I weave my fingers into her hair, cradling the back of her head. "What if this is enough for me?"

I've lost my damn mind. Despite my denial, it's obvious I want more.

"What? Being friends? Being my guard? Hugs? Holding hands? All the while being jealous of someone else? You can't want that. No one wants that."

Tell that to the idiot in my chest. Sex is great, but have you ever had your entire body light up from holding hands? That's a total mindfuck and I've been lost ever since.

"I want what we used to have. I want you hugging me, talking to me, letting me care for you." Jesus, I sound desperate. "Tell me you feel nothing for me."

She must have some interest in me. She lets me touch her and care for her. I've observed her around hockey players who she has known as long as Jackson. She doesn't show them the affection she does me. I was with her when she was barely pregnant, before she found out Ethan was Jackson's coach.

"No, I'm not saying that. I did..." She bites her lip, unwilling to betray them. "I thought we were close, but you lied to me. I want the friendship we had, but I'm afraid it was a figment of my imagination. I don't even know your real name."

"It's Reece. My name is Reece."

"Reece," she says softly, the word hanging in the air.

An icy chill erupts across my skin. Damn, I love how my name sounds on her lips.

"I like that better, but not as much as Viking. It suits you."

I'm not a Viking—I'm a straight-up Carolina country boy

who just lost some of his accent in the military. I initially disliked that she'd adopted Jackson's nickname for me, but...

"The Viking and the Princess. Perfect." My smirk is impossible to hold back.

"Stop that. No flirting." The snow continues to fall, and she draws her jacket tight around her. "You don't even know how long you'll be with us."

I grasp the front of her coat and zip her up. "Come on. Let me feed you for real this time."

"Can we walk instead?" she asks with those pleading eyes I can't refuse.

We walk to Bryant Park, where she's mesmerized by Winter Village and the half-frozen fountain, which continues to spray water, creating massive icicles. The park is not as pretty during the day, and I make a mental note to bring her at night, when it's lit with Christmas lights.

"I didn't know this was here." Her excited gaze bounces from one thing to the next. "You can eat in those igloos?"

She's dated a wealthy professional athlete and traveled the country over the last year, but she still hasn't lost that curious innocence. Everything is new, exciting, and fascinating to her.

Between deployment and undercover ops, I've been surrounded by the worst of humanity. Being with her is like taking that first breath after drowning.

Like being knocked on your ass by a brick wall of sunshine.

"You have to reserve them, but yeah. You want me to get a reservation?"

She gives me a pointed look. "For *all* of us?"

"Yes, princess, for your entire harem." I chuckle and dodge the smack she tries to land on my arm. "How many seats do you need? Are we including the twins?"

"Shut up." Her face flushes, but she grins along with me. "How do you know about harems anyhow?"

"Reverse harems, you mean?"

She stares at me in disbelief, her eyes widening as if she doesn't recognize me. It's comical.

"I'm not illiterate. I've had a lot of downtime. In the military,

I read anything I could get my hands on to stay sane. It's a nice escape."

She drops her gaze, a troubled expression on her face. It's not what I expected. Perhaps it was the reverse harem comment. She hides in her hood, and I realize people are trickling into the park, making her nervous.

"Let's sit. I'll find us a spot."

I lead us to a bench between two trees, hoping for privacy. The snow has stopped falling, the sun making a rare appearance. She removes her hood but scans the area with apprehension.

She's a bit of a distraction, but I've kept an eye out for anything suspicious or anyone giving her more attention than usual. "You're okay. I've been watching."

She checks her phone for the time. "We shouldn't stay long."

And the playful dynamic between us officially dies.

The atmosphere feels stiff. I've taken us out of the possible friend zone and into awkward territory. At least she's talking to me again and trusts me enough to be alone.

"I'm contracted per assignment," I blurt out, circling back to her previous statement. "You said I didn't know how long I'd be with you."

"And that means..." She picks at her nails and avoids eye contact.

I smile at her complete lack of nonchalance, and I say nothing until she peeks up at me through her lashes.

"Are you asking if I'll be around, princess? Will you miss me if I leave?"

"Maybe I want you to leave." She shoves at my shoulder. "I'm being serious. What happens next?"

"Nothing changes. I'm your guard. I go where you go."

She twirls the ring on her finger. Is she thinking of Jackson? The case? She could be playing me for all I know, but I doubt it.

I give in to my compulsion and take her hand. "I won't let anything happen...to anyone." *Even Jax.*

"And after?"

Her guess is as good as anyone's. There's a whole surveillance team on Kyle. They could pull something out of their ass and bring him in. There are rumors he might run for the Senate; we're all waiting for Kyle's next move—or Jackson's.

"Tell me what you want. What's your ideal future?"

I'm pleasantly shocked when she rests her head on my shoulder. "I don't mind if we travel with the team, but I want to settle down close to my grandmother. I miss her. I want a permanent place, you know? A home."

Her wistful words lead me to believe I'm part of her dreams. "I know exactly what you mean."

"Ethan has coaching, and although Jax will say otherwise, he also has hockey. It's good for him, and he's talented. They have each other, they're close. I want to find *my* place. I want to have *something* that's mine."

"Hey, look at me." Her gaze meets mine, our faces only inches apart. "Don't let their talent outshine yours. You're incredibly talented in everything you do. It's in your smile, your eyes, your heart... You captivate everyone. You're our home, that's for sure."

I kiss her nose and turn away before my lips drift any lower.

I WAKE UP IRRITABLE.

After our late-night bonding session, neither Ethan nor I could fall asleep, and when he's sleep-deprived, he snores once he finally knocks out. Fucker kept me up until dawn.

It's cold next to me. Our girl is not in bed. I listen for her in the bathroom—nothing.

I sit up and reach for my phone. "Motherfucker," I curse.

Now I know why I'm stabby.

Aurora is out with the Viking.

"Get up, asshole." I swing my arm out and punch Ethan in the shoulder. "Unless you want your baby to have a new stepdaddy."

His eyelids crack open, and he scans the room. "What the fuck are you whining about?"

I round the foot of the bed. "Your *baby girl* went to breakfast with Ricky forty-eight minutes ago and isn't back. I swear on my nuts, if he does something, I'll peel every one of his tattoos off, sew them into a sweater, and wear it to his funeral."

Ethan drops his head to the pillow and pinches the bridge of his nose. "It's too early for this shit."

Coach needs about three more days of sleep. He has a team to run, but he fell in love with Aurora and got me as a bonus— poor guy. I feel for him.

I throw on whatever clean clothes I have left in my bag. I need to buy more; I refuse to do laundry in the creepy-ass basement.

Legs in jeans, Ethan yanks a hoodie over his head, hobbles to slip his sneakers on, and rushes to follow me out of the room.

I pull on my boots and stab the elevator button at least ten times.

"That won't make it move any faster." He drags his fingers through his dark, wavy hair. "Are you manic? What's with you?"

Am I? My thoughts are *relatively* normal—for me—not racing at the speed of light, just...charmingly chaotic. I'm not hearing voices or paranoid.

It's our new dynamic and our discussion from last night.

I'm restless, my brain is *processing.*

I need to get to a gym or on the ice.

Or murder someone.

"No, I'm not manic. Thanks for your concern," I say, my tone sarcastic. "You're not pissed she's gone?"

He shrugs. "I'll deal with it. She should've woken one of us or taken the twins, but she probably wanted to talk to Ricky alone."

The elevator finally arrives, and we both step on.

I punch the button for the bottom floor. "That doesn't make me feel any better."

"You know how she is. She tries to fix things herself, especially for you."

Once the doors open, I hit the sidewalk. Buildings and people are all nothing but a blur. I check my phone several times—her location shows Bryant Park, and it doesn't take us long to get there.

Weaving through the crowd, I accidentally shoulder-check a guy and almost knock him into the water fountain. He shoots me a glare, and I don't even blame him.

"Shit. Sorry, man."

Ethan wraps his arm around my shoulders with a silent chuckle. "Calm down, stalker. It's not like he's kidnapping—"

Our feet come to an abrupt stop, and I see red before my mind fully makes sense of the sight in front of me.

Aurora and Ricky. *Snuggling.* Her head is on his shoulder, his arm around her.

I'm going to fucking kill him.

My fists clench, and my body vibrates with fury. I lunge forward.

Or at least I try to.

A forearm locks around my throat and knocks the wind out of me.

"You can't go over there in a raging blackout. Take a breath. You'll scare the shit out of Aurora, and it'll be all over the media."

I attempt to throw him off, but Ethan's a tough fucker. His arm is tight around my neck, his body a solid wall against my back.

"We're not losing her." He relaxes his grip but continues to hold me. "They're talking, and I'm sure it's about you, but she'd never leave us."

When I return to reality, Aurora is separating from Ricky, and the heartbeat whooshing in my ears quiets.

Ethan wraps his other arm around me in an embrace. "You can't get violent whenever you're pissed. Save that energy for the ice. You're going to need it. I won't let anything happen to her *or* you."

I nod and inhale a slow and deep breath, then another. I elbow him in the ribs playfully and pull away. We navigate past a group of moms with strollers and head toward the bench where they're seated.

Ricky leans in and kisses Aurora's nose. Honestly, I've seen enough of him touching her.

"Well, isn't this cute and fucking cozy?"

Aurora's gaze snaps to mine, and her face flushes as she glances between Ethan and me with an *oh shit* expression.

"What did I tell you?" Ricky says to her. "He's tracking you."

I scoff. "She shares her location with me, Einstein."

His phone buzzes. He removes it from his jacket pocket and scowls. "We need to pause this dick-measuring contest. It's Charlie, and he never calls." He places the phone to his ear and strides off.

Ethan juts his chin. "Get over here, brat."

She lowers her head and saunters over like a child about to be reprimanded. Her arms encircle his waist, and she peers up at him.

He clasps his hand over the back of her neck. "You and I will be talking later. You're supposed to be resting."

"When? When I'm not fucking one of you? Or both?"

I snort, and he levels a glare.

"Exactly." He recovers from her sass with a sly smile. "Perfect reason to rest. Now, next time you sneak off, even with Ricky—"

"It's Reece... His name. Not Ricky."

"Even with *Reece*, I'm taking you over my knee."

"Promises, promises," she says before those naughty eyes turn my way. "You look hot today."

I shake my head. "Don't suck up to me."

"I'm not! It's the backward hat and unlaced boots." She dares to give me a mischievous smile. "It gets me every time."

My chest swells, and the traitorous corners of my lips curl. "Shut up."

Ethan frowns. "What about me? Why am I never hot?"

She shrugs. "You are. It's your serious voice that does it for me. You get all growly and rough; makes me wanna behave."

"I'll make you behave, all right...with my hand on your ass."

Ricky—or *Reece*—approaches, his jaw rigid and his gaze on me. "We need to get home."

"Why? What's up?" I ask with a quirked brow.

"Your father is dead."

ABOUT THE AUTHOR

Jessica Lyn is a dark romance author who loves hockey, the mountains, and snow. She lives on the Oregon Coast with her family and a never-ending list of pets.

Her stories, initially chart-topping Kindle Vella serials, are influenced by a decade-long career in psych triage.

Outside of writing, she's into reading, traveling, crime docs, and a strong cup of tea.

Printed in Dunstable, United Kingdom